Since she'd kissed him, twice, it meant she had to want him too, somehow. He couldn't understand why she'd kissed him the second time, why she'd want him. She knew nothing about him other than that he was a carpenter and Mack's friend.

He groaned. Mack would beat him down hard if he knew what'd happened. Mack had asked him to watch out for Willow, to protect her. Not kiss her, and certainly not fantasize about going to bed with her.

An image of Willow's trim body draped over his formed in his mind. The erection he'd had since she'd first kissed him tightened painfully. Not even thinking about Mack's reaction could dampen the desire he felt for Willow. Desire that bordered on a need so deep, so profound, it shook his foundation.

He hadn't planned on this. He'd assumed he could pour his heart and soul into restoring the chapel and then leave, without a ripple in his wake. He'd thought he could hold himself apart from Willow, even while staying in her home, that he'd be able to keep his demons from resurrecting. While working on those defenses, he'd completely forgotten about protecting himself in other ways. He'd never expected her to kiss him, to want him. He'd never expected her to touch him, with a gentleness that spread like sunlight through him.

He'd called her a superwoman, but she was his kryptonite.

THROUGH THE FIRE

SERESSIA GLASS

Genesis Press, Inc.

Indigo Love Stories

An imprint of Genesis Press, Inc.
Publishing Company

Genesis Press, Inc.
P.O. Box 101
Columbus, MS 39703

ISBN: 0-7394-6636-4
ISBN13: 978-0-7394-6636-0

Manufactured in the United States of America

ACKNOWLEDGMENTS

To Betty, for sending me emails and keeping her promise to encourage me. Thanks so much! To Lynne the laptop goddess and LaDonna the ray of sunshine, who were both with me in the home-stretch. This book wouldn't have been completed without the three of you.

To my readers, thank you so much for waiting. I hope you find Brandt's story worth the wait.

AUTHOR'S NOTE

According to classical mythology, a phoenix was a bird of great beauty and the only one of its kind. Periodically it built its own funeral pyre and burned itself to death, only to rise from the ashes as a new phoenix.

CHAPTER ONE

Brandt Hughes sat in the shadows of his living room, searching for a reason not to die.

Photos lay scattered among the wood shavings of his carvings. Photos he didn't have to see to recall, snapshots of the life he'd once had. In the last four years memories had deteriorated into nightmares that haunted him and sapped at the innate instinct to survive.

Brady... He hung his head as his son's name echoed through the remnants of his heart. His son would have been eight years old tomorrow. Which meant Brandt would have to endure a day of phone calls and visits from his parents, brothers, and sisters. Maya would want to go with him to Brady's grave, his mother would concoct some home repair emergency to get him to visit, even though his father owned half of Brandt's construction business.

It had been bearable the year before, the year before that. But now the grief sat like a stone on his chest as it had those first few days, weeks, months after Brady, after Sarah. It weighed him down, threatening to sink him. Grief and anger. Always the anger.

He couldn't face his family tomorrow. Couldn't face his parents and siblings staring at him, pitying him, accusing him. No, he'd have to do something today.

The phone shrieked. He grabbed for it, clutching it like the lifeline it was. Probably Maya, probably worried. He had to convince her that she needed to look after her new family, not her sorry excuse for a brother. "Yeah?"

"It's Mack."

Brandt forced his muscles to relax as he heard his best friend's voice. "What's up?"

"I need a favor," Mack said in that same no-nonsense voice he'd used when leading their unit. Mackenzie "Mack" Zane had never been one for beating around bushes or tolerating fools. Why he still bothered with Brandt, the latter had no idea. "Can you come down to Serena Bay?"

Serena Bay. Brandt remembered that Mack had described it as a small lazy town on the east coast of Florida. He considered it for half a moment. Spending time in a small town during a Florida summer might do him some good. Anything would be better than where he was, what he was doing. "When?"

"As soon as you can," his friend answered, "but don't you want to know what the favor is?"

"Don't need to know." Brandt would do anything for Mack, especially since the commander had saved his ass on more than one occasion. Still, curiosity made him ask, "You out of deputies or something?"

He still couldn't believe that Mack had traded in his general issue uniform for small-town sheriff brown. Being brass in Miami, maybe, but Sheriff Andy? On the other hand, if Mack had gotten as tired of the bloodshed as he had, Miami wasn't the place to go for law enforcement.

"Nothing like that, though you know the offer will always be on the table," Mack replied. "An old Spanish mission on the coast is getting renovated, but no one's got the skills to restore the chapel. I think you could do it."

Brandt failed an attempt at a laugh. "Think they'll let me in the door?"

"I didn't get struck by lightning when I went inside," Mack informed him. "Besides, you didn't do anything I didn't order you to do."

"I've gotten more blood on my hands since then." Brady. Sarah.

"You know my opinion on that, so I won't waste my breath," his former commanding officer said evenly. "But I won't lie to you about the mission. The place would probably be better off if they razed it and started over. It's definitely a challenge. This building's just waiting for you to bring it back to life."

"A challenge, huh?" Why not? Getting away would probably do him some good. And maybe, just maybe, restoring the chapel would earn him some brownie points with the man upstairs.

"I've done work in St. Augustine, so I'm good to go. Give me two days to clear things here and I'll be there."

"Excellent. Let me give you the address and directions. Got something to write on?" Brandt retrieved pen and paper, and then Mack rattled off the information.

Afterward, Brandt disconnected, then sat back in his chair. Relief swept through him. It didn't matter if the construction help Mack needed consisted of building a birdhouse or an outhouse. It would give him something to do and somewhere to go, somewhere where memories wouldn't stalk his every waking moment and sleepless night. Somewhere where no one knew or cared about his past, his sins.

He didn't need two days to get things in order, either. He'd had everything in his life settled for years, no loose ends, just in case.

Leaning to the left, he placed the cordless phone on the table. He hesitated a moment, then grabbed his M9 Beretta and popped the clip out.

Today wasn't the day.

CHAPTER TWO

Willow sat back from her laptop, rubbing wearily at her eyes. With her creative flow blocked with the seeming permanency of Hoover Dam, her good nature had begun to erode. Actually, the writer's block was starting to piss her off. She had a month to get *Beyond the Phoenix Principle* to her editor, a task becoming more like *Mission: Impossible* every day. Add to that the never-ending construction of Phoenix Haven, her brother the sheriff worrying about empty threats made against her and the center, answering demands and pleas for help and speaking engagements, and it was no wonder she couldn't get a single page written.

She sighed. The last thing she wanted to think about was something negative. There would always be people who didn't like her work, what she was trying to achieve. As much as she wished the threats weren't directed at her personally, she knew there was nothing she could do about them except continue her work. For every negative letter she received, there were hundreds thanking her, and that made all the difference.

Rising to her feet, she left her writer's block and dark thoughts behind her, moving around her desk to the table that held her professional dream. The mock-up of Phoenix Haven sprawled gracefully across the wood surface. Retaining the charm and serenity of the old church it had been, Phoenix Haven would be a place of rest and rejuvenation, a place where she could help people manage their grief and guilt. A place that would be a haven for anyone who needed it.

Once it was completed, anyway.

Renovations on the old seaside mission were progressing at the rate of icebergs melting. She'd had no idea she'd need so many permits. Even having a brother as sheriff and an old high school friend as mayor of Serena Bay couldn't slice through all the red tape. Sometimes she believed she needed a permit just to breathe.

Enough. She quit her office, sweeping past her assistant. "I'm heading out into the gardens, Pattie," she announced. "I'm not here for anyone but my brother and Oprah. Okay, Isis too, but that's it."

"Writer's block again?" Pattie gave her a sympathetic smile as she looked up from a stack of correspondence.

Willow rolled her eyes. "Don't even get me started. Boscoe, are you going outside with me, or do you want to stay inside in the air conditioning?"

Her dog, part collie, part elephant, thumped his tail with an enthusiastic yes. "You should register him with the Defense Department," Pattie said, eyeing the white-and-chocolate spotted hound. "That tail alone could be considered a weapon of mass destruction."

"Very funny. There's absolutely nothing wrong with Boscoe or his tail. You're absolutely perfect, aren't you, boy?" Willow leaned over Pattie's desk. "What do you have there?"

"Oh no you don't." Pattie, who guarded her age better than the Coast Guard protected the coast, placed her well-manicured hands palms-down on the stack of letters. "If you're not writing, you don't get to read."

"Oh, come on," Willow wheedled. "Just one?"

"Nope." Pattie gathered the correspondence against her ample and, she was proud to say, natural bosom. "Not until after lunch. And only if you take your voice recorder into the garden with you."

Willow heaved a mock sigh of pique. She cherished Pattie for being an efficient assistant, taskmaster, and gatekeeper, and most of all, for treating her like a regular person.

"I've got my recorder with me in case I get struck by divine inspiration," she said, patting the bib pocket of her overalls. Which didn't stick out even half as far as Pattie's turquoise blouse, she observed with secret jealousy. "Though the only thing that's close to divine around here is what's left of the chapel. And even it's seen better days."

With Boscoe loping beside her, Willow left the office, passing through a side door that led to the living room that separated the business section of her house from the living quarters. Once the rectory for the old church next door, Willow had expanded it and made it her primary residence. Barring any construction delays, she and Pattie would be able to move into their new deluxe offices in the church at the end of next week.

After grabbing a bottle of water from her fridge, she cut through her Florida room and out the back door. A path of weathered stepping stones cut a stylized "V" through the thick Bermuda grass, the one straight ahead leading through a stand of palmettos and sea grapes to her small but private beach, the other to a thick wall of ficus trees and a tall wrought-iron fence that separated her quiet abode from the bustling renovations of Phoenix Haven.

For two seconds she hesitated, then resolutely chose the left path. If she couldn't write, she couldn't play, either. Besides, Pattie would know the instant she stepped onto the sand and would come hunt her down.

She didn't really envy Pattie her looks. Blonde and buxom wouldn't go with Willow's pecan-brown skin and five-seven frame unless she wanted to star in a rap video. What she actually envied was Pattie's ability to dress to the nines and be left alone. If she dressed up for any reason other than to attend some social function, she received catcalls and invitations to do things she didn't think were physically possible.

Shaking her head, Willow punched in the code that unlocked the gate between the properties. A new feature, thanks to her overly cautious brother. Ever since her good friend, former college roommate turned TV star Isis Montgomery, had interviewed her on her syndicated talk show, sales of *The Phoenix Principle* had skyrocketed. Willow was pragmatic enough to know that it had as much to do with being beautiful and articulate as it did with having a Ph.D. and a thought-provoking topic.

Being on Isis's show had transformed the reluctant Willow into a media darling, and working the talk show circuit had sent the hardcover version of her self-help guide into two reprints. Her second book, *Living the Phoenix Principle*, had been just as successful, especially after a hot Hollywood starlet swore by it after winning a Best Actress award. The money Willow had made allowed her to renovate the old mission its previous owner hadn't wanted to sell to a hotel chain or developers.

She was a success, and she hated every minute of it.

The master gardener, Carlos Rosa, was already at work. "*Hola*, Carlos," she greeted him, pulling a pair of work gloves out of the back pocket of her overalls.

"*Hola, Senorita* Willow," Carlos said with a wide smile. "The book, it's not going well?"

"Not you too," she groused, eyeing the assorted seedlings he'd stacked into a wheelbarrow. "I got enough from Pattie already. How are the landscapers doing?"

He shrugged. "Landscapers, you know how they are. Trying to mold the land into their image, instead of seeing the beauty in it. I thank the Holy Mother daily that you didn't let them touch the gardens."

Willow snorted. "Like you'd say no to the extra sales." Carlos owned his own tropical garden centers and made a healthy living off the landscapers. Willow had chosen him not only because he'd won awards for his custom gardens that enhanced the natural flora, but also because he was local and his enthusiasm for gardening matched her own. It explained why he was here in overalls instead of in his office in a suit.

"The gardens and arboretum fared better than the rest of this place," Willow said, picking through the plantings. "I'm hoping that the renovations will bring Phoenix Haven up to snuff, not to mention code. The chapel has me worried."

"Ah, the chapel. It is a special place," Carlos nodded in agreement. "You haven't found a carpenter yet?"

Seeing him wipe his dirty gloves onto the seat of his overalls caused Willow to wonder what Mrs. Rosa thought about him getting dirt in their Mercedes. Caridad Rosa would probably blame Willow.

"I've found plenty of carpenters, but no one feels right," Willow said, knowing Carlos would understand what she meant. In the two months that he'd been helping her right the gardens, they'd become fast friends, a fact that alternately pleased and irritated his wife. "Mack said he has a friend from Atlanta who's done some restoration work. Mack says he's good."

"It's an important job, restoring the chapel," Carlos said. "You want someone who's not just good, but can put their heart and soul into it. An artist."

"Yes. That hole in the roof did a lot of damage to the interior, and it's going to cost a lot of money to repair. So I want to make sure it's done right, more than right."

Carlos took a couple of deep purple seedlings from the wheelbarrow. "Caridad and I, we would be willing to make a donation to the chapel's repair."

"I know you would, but I won't hear of it," Willow said sternly. "The budget's there to cover the restoration. I'm just a worrywart. Besides, I know you're under-charging me for the garden as it is."

The master gardener smiled. "It's an honor to bring these gardens back to their former glory. It would be a sin against God to charge my regular fee. And you are letting the *Home and Garden* people photograph it when they interview me, remember?"

"Of course." How could she forget? Strangers tramping through the serenity garden, hoping to get a sneak peek of her and her home. Another event to be "on" for. But she didn't mind, as long as they gave Carlos top billing and stayed on their side of the gate. She could list on one hand the people she allowed into her house, and reporters certainly weren't among them. "When are they supposed to come by?"

"Two more weeks. They said it shouldn't take more than two days."

"Two days?" Her stomach knotted. Surely she could handle two days. If she couldn't do that, how would she be able to open Phoenix Haven to the public?

She grabbed some plantings off the wheelbarrow before Carlos could respond to her less-than-cheerful words. "Well, I'd better get busy, right? We want to knock their socks off when they see another Carlos Rosa masterpiece."

"My masterpiece, but your vision," Carlos said. "How is that night-blooming jasmine doing on your patio?"

They talked more about gardening before Carlos moved deeper into the garden to work on the troublesome water feature. Willow flopped to her hands and knees in the dirt, thinking of nothing more than what flowers, if any, should edge the stone path that wound through the serenity garden. The path was meant to be a meditation walk, with stations along the way to pause and reflect. Maybe putting a different-colored patch of flowers at each stop would work. No, maybe just a piece of limestone with a single word on it, like *Faith*, or *Dream*.

"Mack here?"

The deep, abrupt voice had Willow yelping as she scrambled to her feet, her heart in her throat. Instinct had her backing around the wheelbarrow, her calves coming up hard against a low stone bench. At once she realized two things: she'd trapped herself, and the stranger could take her out without breaking a sweat.

CHAPTER THREE

Willow found her breath and her voice as Boscoe charged across the grass. "Mack's not here—not right here, but he's around here somewhere, I'm sure." That was a lie, but she told it in self-defense. Besides, if the man knew her brother's name, he had to know Mack was sheriff.

The man didn't move, didn't acknowledge her words, just stared at her. Tall like her brother, standing well over six feet, he had toffee skin and a natural tilt to his storm-gray eyes that had nothing to do with laughter or the hot Florida sun. Muscles crouched beneath the smooth skin on his arms and the gray t-shirt on his back, like a pack of lions waiting for a zebra to stray too close before springing into action.

Oh my.

Boscoe must have caught the tremble that moved through her. He growled. The man looked at him—simply looked—and her seventy-pound tower of terror dropped to his haunches with a whine.

Willow managed an inaudible swallow, and wrapped her fingers around Boscoe's collar. Maybe Mack was right. Maybe it was time to hire security. She'd been so deep into her thoughts about the landscaping that she hadn't heard the man approach. Mack would hit the roof when he heard about this. If he heard about this.

"Sir?" Her voice quavered, and she hated it.

The man finally blinked, and something less empty seeped into his expression. "Brandt Hughes. I'm here about the chapel."

Relief almost unhinged her knees. "Oh, you're Mack's friend. He told me that you're an excellent carpenter," she said, brushing her hands off on the seat of her overalls as she forced herself to relax. If her brother claimed this guy as a friend, he couldn't be all that bad. "Why don't I show you around? Mack might show up around lunchtime."

He stood his ground, tan work boots planted solidly in the gravel, and she had a feeling that if he wanted he could stand there all day in the worn jeans that clung to his muscular legs, and there would be nothing she could do about it. Except maybe climb into a mini-dozer.

"Not interrupting, am I?" he asked in a tone that said he didn't care one way or the other. Just like he didn't seem to care that he'd scared the crap out of her. His eyes held dark secrets, yet they didn't sweep her from head to toe like so many men seemed to have a need to do.

Point for him.

"I don't mind taking a break," she said cheerily, slipping into her PR persona. "And walking the property is good exercise."

He didn't say anything, just fell in beside her as she started down a worn path. "The church has been here since Spain owned most of Florida," she explained, trying not to babble as they headed along the western path to the main entrance. The man beside her moved silently and easily, and she wondered if Mack had met him in Special Forces. Her brother didn't talk much about what he'd done, but considering some of the places he'd been sent to, she knew it hadn't been all sunshine and roses. How did one go from the military to carpentry?

She pulled open one of the ornate doors that she'd spent hours polishing, leading him inside the relative coolness of the grand entry. Despite the small size of the mission, sounds of construction were muted, though the smell of plaster and paint pervaded everything.

"There's a wing off each side of the mission, added on about fifty years ago," she explained, automatically lowering her voice as she pointed to their right. "This wing holds meeting rooms and the administrative offices, and the northern wing is being converted to dormitory rooms, a kitchen and dining hall. The part we need your help with is the chapel."

Though he remained silent, Willow was all too aware of him standing behind her, claiming space and most of the air. Her hand shook a little as she reached for the tarnished brass handle on the dark paneled door that led into the chapel. *He's not going to hurt you,* she chastised herself, but she didn't breathe again until she stood back to allow him to precede her into the chapel.

He moved into the center of the room, taking in everything. She bit back an apology for the state of the sanctuary she'd loved since childhood. The chapel had seen better days. Dust motes danced in streams of sunlight coming through a clear pane of glass at odds with the remaining stained glass windows. The pews were in varying condition; some just needed cleaning and polishing, while others were destined to become firewood. The floor faced the same fate, and she didn't dare tell him about the condition of the rooms behind the pulpit.

He ran his hand over one of the better-preserved pews. It had taken her days to scrub years of neglect off it. Once she'd gotten it clean, blistering her hands in the process, she'd made the decision to hire professional help.

"The salt air and time have done a number on most of the wood," she said quietly, appreciative of the peace that still lingered in the room. "But if you're hired, I hope you can save most of the pews and the floor. I know the pulpit will have to be rebuilt, and the ceiling and roof are a mess. There's a large room behind the pulpit that you can use as a workroom."

She watched him step carefully around the chapel, gauging the work to be done. She couldn't shake the feeling that he seemed some sort of predator, her mind likening him to all sorts of animals. Lions and panthers and wolves.

He turned back to her and she actually felt the weight of his stare. Oh my.

"Is there anything else?" he asked.

"Not much," she said, resisting a nervous shuffling of her feet. "Behind the church is a natural arboretum of seagrapes and palms that leads down to the ocean. The path we met on, that's the meditation garden and it joins the walkway down to the sea. Beyond the wall of ficus and the fence is the garden of the rectory, which has already been reclaimed. If you come with me to my office, and I can show you the mock-up of the completed project and we can talk more about what the job entails. Then you can show me references and pictures of your work."

He walked back up the center aisle. "I should talk to Mack first."

Oh really? "You can if you want to," she said easily, "but since this is my project, you'll be working for me, not Mack. Do you have an issue with that?"

He looked her over, measuring her capability and not her physical features. "Unless you're a master carpenter, this restoration will be my project. I don't need an architect or a GC breathing down my neck while I'm working."

"Are you that good, that you don't need a general contractor over you?" She tilted her head, curious about his answer.

"Yes." He said it simply, as if she'd asked him if the sky was blue. "There's a reason the chapel's been kept separate from the other construction. This place deserves special care to bring it back to life, and I'm the one to do that. I've done a GC's job, in Atlanta and St. Augustine. Don't need another one getting in my way."

Wow. Four whole sentences in a row. Or was that five? "I'm not the contractor or the architect. Do you have a problem working for a woman?"

That flat look returned to his eyes. "No."

He actually sounded as if she'd insulted him by asking the question. She breathed deeply, determined not to let this rock of a man be a stumbling block to her positive outlook or her plans. "My brother told me that you're an excellent carver and that you run a carpentry and woodworking business in Atlanta, specializing in restoration. He says you're good, and I trust his word. I want Phoenix Haven to be a place where anyone can come for help and healing. I want it to be a place of rest and rejuvenation. And I want people who are excellent at their jobs to help me make that a reality. But I will not have someone coming in here and tinkering with my vision, master carpenter or not."

"Wait." If possible, he became even more still. "By brother, you mean Mack?"

She nodded. Disbelief raised his eyebrows, the first hint of emotion she'd seen in the man so far.

"So your last name's Zane. Willow Zane? As in, *Doctor* Willow Zane?"

"Yes. And you're standing in what's going to be the heart of Phoenix Haven. I guess Mack didn't bother to give you any details about my project?"

Something ran over his face, and the psychologist in Willow went on full alert. Surprise, pain, fear, hope—she saw it all in a split-second slideshow of unguarded emotion. She was about to ask him if he was all right when her cell phone chirped.

She patted herself down, looking for the tiny device, finally finding it in her back pocket. Pattie just had to pick up the tiniest phone on the market. She glanced at the readout and barely suppressed a groan. Her agent, probably wondering if she'd completed the outline for the companion book.

She looked up in apology. Brandt Hughes looked frozen on the spot, the proverbial pillar of salt. "I'm sorry, I have to take this, shouldn't be more than a moment." She headed for the door.

Brandt watched her walk away for a second before turning back to the pulpit. He hadn't been caught off guard in a long time, but this, this was unbelievable.

Mack's sister was Willow Zane. Dr. Willow Zane, self-help guru, author of several books explaining why bad things happened to people, helping them understand the need to keep on going. He had a dog-eared copy of her first book, *The Phoenix Principle*, by his bed. He'd kept it because his sister Maya had given it to him. He'd opened it one sleepless, nightmare-ridden night, expecting to laugh out loud at ridiculous homilies. Instead he'd read the damn book through several times.

She didn't look a thing like her book photo. 'Course, while he didn't expect Willow Zane to be walking around a construction site in heels and a business suit, he certainly didn't expect workboots and over-sized overalls that looked like a third-hand shop had rejected them. Her pecan skin hadn't possessed a trace of makeup, not even on her dark doe-eyes. A washed-out blue bandana held her thin, shoulder-length braids away from her face, and her t-shirt looked like something Mack had crawled through enemy fire in, then tossed into the rag bin.

How many times had he thumbed through her book, imagining meeting her face to face, demanding that she explain why losing his son had to happen? How many times had he imagined that she wouldn't have any answers, that she'd be a quack just like all the others, getting rich off other people's pain?

Dr. Willow Zane. Mack's sister. About to become his boss. It was a coincidence of divine proportions.

He would have found it funny, if he still knew how to laugh.

He glanced up at the sky. "You've got a sick sense of humor."

CHAPTER FOUR

"You didn't tell me your sister is Willow Zane."

Brandt fixed his gaze on a bulldozer several yards away, trying not to let his aggravation show. Getting away for a couple of months' hard labor had seemed like a good idea at the time. But working for the woman many people thought of as the second Oprah wasn't what he'd had in mind.

His mood didn't improve when Mack leaned against his patrol car, folded his arms across his chest, and smiled. "I didn't think it was important. Besides, to me she's just my sister, not some hotshot psychologist."

"Calling her a hotshot psychologist is like saying Bill Gates works with computers."

"If you say so. Would you have come down if you'd known?"

"No. Yes." Brandt shook his head. "Hell, I don't know. I needed a getaway, and I owe you good."

"That's why I figured you'd come," Mack said. He gave Brandt a hard look. "You all right?"

Brandt knew what Mack meant. "I came down here to work, not get psychoanalyzed. I just don't appreciate getting jumped like that."

"I know that. But if you've seen the inside of the chapel, you know it needs your help."

"True enough. I've got my work cut out for me."

"So you're staying?"

"I already gave my word."

"So you did." Mack settled his sunglasses into place. "I just need one more favor. Means I'll owe you."

"Say it."

"I need you to stay onsite. In Willow's house."

"What?"

"I need you to—"

"I heard what you said. I'm just not sure why you said it."

Mack pushed off the patrol car, his mouth set in a firm line. "My sister doesn't know how to say no. Stray dogs, stray people—she'd take them all in if she could. She'd listen to the devil himself if she thought she could help him."

He tossed a casual glance around the grounds, then leaned back against the cruiser. "There have been some threats."

"Against your sister?"

Mack nodded. "Her, and the place she's developing. Someone here in Serena Bay isn't thrilled with her and what she's doing."

Brandt called up Willow's image. Despite the sorry excuses for clothes she wore, he'd been able to tell she was trim, taller than average. She had an open, eager expression beaming from her dark eyes and smooth, mocha face, which was completely unlined and required no makeup. Willow had that kind of quiet beauty that started within and suffused her features, her voice, her expressions.

She was also naïve as hell.

"Does she know about the threats?"

Mack nodded. "Yeah, she knows. It still took major brother points just to get her to put in security cameras and the automatic gate for the rectory."

"That explains why she jumped ten feet when I walked up on her," Brandt said thoughtfully. He knew he'd scared her, but had just chalked it up to his less-than-friendly nature. Now he knew better.

"Scared her, huh? Maybe she'll take my advice and let some security patrol the place." Mack pushed off the patrol car, heading for the relative shade and privacy on the south side of the building. Brandt fell into step beside him.

"Like I said, she was initially against putting the fence around the house next door, until people started ringing her doorbell all day everyday. She likes her privacy, so the house's pretty much off limits to everyone except me, her assistant, and a couple of friends. She's pretty safe there although some determined idiot on a jet ski could come up on her beach. It's the mission that has me worried. Any and everybody can just walk right in, and she's planning to move her office there next week."

"Basically becoming a sitting duck for whomever's threatening her." Brandt could understand Mack's concern. Hell, he'd do whatever he could if someone threatened one of his sisters. "Got any ideas who you're looking for?"

"No." The disgust in Mack's voice was palpable. "No ex, no stalker. No one with a grudge she knows about. And if any of her patients followed her here from Los Angeles, she's not telling me."

"So I'm supposed to be your secret deputy?"

"Exactly."

Brandt folded his arms. He could handle working for Willow, as long she stayed away from the mission while he worked. But being close to her, interacting with her? Staying in the same house with her? "You don't know what you're asking, Mack."

He remembered how she'd looked at him after he'd realized who she was. She'd read him, seen his surprise and probably his fear before he could control it. Fear that she'd crawl under his skin, see the ugliness of his sins that he gave everything to keep buried.

"I know what I'm asking Brandt," Mack said, his voice low. "You know I wouldn't ask if it wasn't important. You don't have to be her shadow, just keep an eye on her without letting her know that you're keeping an eye on her."

Brandt hunched his shoulders. "Does she know?"

Mack shook his head. "I didn't find out for six months, remember, after I sent Bra—after I sent the birthday present. If you didn't want me to know, I certainly wasn't going to tell anyone else."

Heat burned Brandt's ears. It wasn't that he hadn't wanted Mack to know. But you didn't just call your best friend up and casually announce that your life had just crashed and burned. He hadn't wanted to tell anyone, hadn't wanted to say the words that would tell the world that he'd failed his son. His next-door neighbors had been the ones to call his parents and paramedics while he'd sprawled at the edge of the pool, clutching Brady's still form and screaming.

"Brandt?"

He pulled himself back from the edge of the abyss. "Your sister's a smart woman. What if she doesn't go along with your plan?"

"She will," Mack said confidently. "I'll suggest that you bunk down in the rooms behind the pulpit so you can be onsite. She'll immediately volunteer space in her house."

Brandt grunted. "As long as you realize I'm here for the chapel first, and watchdog second. But the moment she tries her psychobabble on me, I'm out."

"Duly noted. Whatever Willow finds out about you won't be from me."

"Good." He'd make damn sure Dr. Zane found out nothing, nothing at all.

Willow replaced the phone receiver in its cradle. Brandt Hughes' references were as impeccable as the photos and letters of recommendation in his portfolio. It wasn't mistrust of her brother's word that had made her place the call to a random client. Something about Brandt Hughes' expression in those few unguarded seconds had struck her hard, some overwhelming emotion in his eyes that made her want to instinctively reach out to him.

Now she knew why.

He'd lost his son four years ago in a swimming accident, his wife shortly after. Now Willow understood the emptiness she'd seen in Brandt's eyes, the stillness in which he held himself. Grief stretched Brandt Hughes like a taut string, and he was near his breaking point.

She wanted to help him. The psychologist in her demanded that she do something. She had the feeling Brandt hadn't sought therapy four years ago. If not then, he certainly wouldn't seek it now. She could tell by the way he'd reacted to who she was.

He'd probably try to stay as far away from her as he could, which meant she'd have to do something to keep him nearby, to create the opportunity to talk to him. He was Mack's friend, he was restoring her chapel. And he was hurting. She *had* to help him.

He could stay here.

Her heart gave a nervous jump at the thought. Even her brother had never stayed overnight. Could she handle his tall, dark, handsome, and brooding friend?

She had to. He needed her help, whether he knew it or not. She could convince him that staying was a good idea. He didn't know anyone in Serena Bay besides Mack, and he certainly couldn't stay in Mack's about-to-be condemned bungalow. Staying in the rectory, he'd be close to the chapel, could set whatever hours he chose without having to drive around an unfamiliar town in the dark on top of being tired.

They could talk about the chapel and once they built a rapport, she could offer her expertise.

Of course, she'd probably have to convince him that he'd come up with the idea. Or she could get Mack to suggest it. All she needed to do was mention to her over-protective brother that having Brandt around would be a deterrent to whatever threat of the week Mack had concerns about. Lord knew, Brandt was scary enough when he was trying to be polite. He could scare paint off the walls if he had a mind to.

Pattie stuck her head in the door. "Your brother's here, along with some guy who looks like he came from the same mold, except he doesn't smile. That your carpenter?"

"I hope so," Willow said, climbing to her feet. "He's got glowing references."

"Hire him," Pattie urged. "Please tell me you're going to hire him."

Recognizing the predatory tone, Willow frowned at her assistant. "Pattie."

"Did you take a good look at him?" Pattie demanded. "Just imagine what he's going to look like when he takes his shirt off!"

"Pattie!" An image immediately came to mind, shocking her, as she pushed past her assistant. She didn't want Brandt Hughes that way, but she didn't want him at Pattie's mercy either. The poor man simply wouldn't be the same afterwards. "If Brandt Hughes takes the job, he's off limits. I mean it." Not that she intended to follow her own advice, but she had her reasons for that.

She went into the hallway and headed for the part of her house that Mack always hit first: her kitchen.

He was there, leaning against the terra cotta island, helping himself to her homemade lemonade. He nodded at a large bowl, the plastic wrap peeled back. "Thai noodle salad. Writer's block again?"

"Thanks for noticing." Despite the latest gadgets and a kitchen to die for, she only cooked when Mack came over for Sunday dinner or she had writer's block and couldn't work in the garden. Last night had been one of those times. "Where's your friend?"

"He went for another walk around the chapel." He poured lemonade into a glass, handed it to her. "What do you think?"

"He's done some awesome work, and a lady in St. Augustine raves about the restoration he did to her inn." She paused, wondering if Mack knew what had happened to his friend. She couldn't recall him mentioning Brandt before, or taking any sudden trips to Atlanta. Still, they were friends. They had to talk occasionally. Mack probably knew but since he hadn't mentioned it when he recommended Brandt, he probably wouldn't bring it up now.

"He's a good man, isn't he?"

Mack swallowed lemonade. "A good man and good at what he does. He was forever carving things when we had down time. What the man can do with a piece of wood is nothing less than a miracle."

"So I heard." She scooted around the island to the golden oak cabinets, her boots thumping on the green-tiled floor.

"Are you going to bring him on?"

"I think so," she answered, opening a cabinet door to retrieve several bowls. "Any more delays would put me too far behind schedule. Of course, now I'm wondering if I can afford him."

"Room and board."

Willow almost dropped her stoneware at the sound of Brandt's heavy voice. He stood in the open area that led into the casual dining room and family room, taking all the air again. How did someone that large move so quietly?

"Did you just say you'll restore my chapel for room and board?" She carefully set the bowls on the counter. "Just room and board, as in food and a place to stay?"

He nodded. "It would be a crime to charge my usual rate for the chapel. She's got great bones and she's still beautiful. Once I get the roof repaired and gut the pulpit, the work will go smoothly. I'm looking forward to the work."

Willow blinked. Brandt Hughes seemed like a different person when he talked shop. Vibrancy filled his words, and she recognized the fire of a true artist eager to start a project.

"I like to work long hours, odd hours," he continued. "It looks like your closest neighbors are far enough away, but I'll stop the power tools at a decent hour and do hand carving. I'll muck out the rooms behind the pulpit for my workshop and living quarters."

He really wanted to stay onsite. Willow wasn't about to let the opportunity pass. "I don't have a problem with you having a workshop out there, but you can't stay there. I don't have clearance yet for living quarters. So you'll just have to stay here."

He actually looked at Mack before turning back to her. "I don't want to be an imposition."

"I don't need my brother's permission for houseguests, Mr. Hughes, even if you think you do."

"You're his blood, I'm just his friend," he replied, his voice returning to that flat, emotionless tone. "I'd expect the same if it were one of my sisters."

"A fact that must thrill your sisters to no end," she muttered, spooning noodles into bowls with unnecessary force. "And then they do what they want anyway."

"A fact that thrills me to no end," Mack said.

Willow resisted, barely, delivering an elbow to his stomach. Somebody had to act like a professional here. "You won't be an imposition, Mr. Hughes."

"Brandt."

Back to grunts again, she noted. "Brandt. I'm not a nine to fiver either, so your schedule won't bother me. My assistant Pattie arrives between eight and nine, but we'll be moving our offices to the administrative wing after the inspection next week. The kitchen stays stocked, so feel free to fend for yourself."

"All right."

It was almost too easy. So easy that she felt a stab of guilt. "You know, I have to insist on some sort of nominal fee. There's a lot of work to do on the chapel. Even I realize that."

She watched him plant his feet. "I can do it."

"I don't doubt it. But I'm not about to take advantage of your friendship with my brother, even if both of you need to be dragged into the new millennium."

"Fine. We'll work something out."

Mack rubbed his hands together before taking a bowl from her. "So it's a deal, right?"

"Sure it is," Willow said. She stuck out her hand. "Welcome to Phoenix Haven, Brandt."

He hesitated a moment, then stepped forward. Almost in slow motion he stretched out his hand, his fingers grazing her skin before their palms connected.

Willow looked down at their hands, feeling the calluses and strength in his fingers. Heat raced up her arm and punched her solidly in the gut. Startled, she darted a look at his face, saw the same surprise and fear from before. This time, however, she felt it too. What had she just agreed to?

She was about to jerk her hand out of his when he eased his grip. Only when he backed away did she realize she'd been holding her breath.

Somehow she plastered a smile on her face. "Now that that's settled, how about I show you around? There are three extra bedrooms here, including a full suite right above this room, but I also have a small guest house near the front of the property. It still needs some work, but would be good for a workshop if you have tools that need to be secured."

"That'll do." Brandt took another step back. "Are you wireless, or on DSL? I'd like to get started planning a few things."

Willow didn't blame him for his hesitation. She felt like retreating to her office herself. "Wireless. I'll get the information for you. While I do, why don't you take a moment to settle in, grab a bite to eat? You've been on the road for what—eight hours? Besides, I'm sure you and Mack have some catching up to do."

He nodded, looking relieved. Obviously he didn't want to spend any more time with her than he had to. At that moment, she had to agree.

CHAPTER FIVE

A short time later, Mack entered her office, shutting the door behind him. "Are you okay with this?"

Willow looked up from her laptop, arching an eyebrow at her brother. "Perhaps I should ask you the same thing, since apparently you don't think your sister has enough brain cells to think for herself."

At least he had the grace to look sheepish, though he spoiled it by saying, "I'd do the same thing in his place, just like he said. It's only right."

"Two peas in a pod, except you're Mr. Sunshine and he's Mr. Grumpy. I suppose I should be glad you two have some sort of honor code."

Actually she was more than glad. She'd spent the last few minutes regretting her hastily made decision to let Brandt stay in the house. But Mack wouldn't have gone along with it if he thought his friend would cause her trouble. She had to trust that her instincts for people were better than they used to be.

"Your friend's something else," she said then. "I take it that he's been through some things?"

Her brother sat in one of the navy club chairs across from her desk. "Yeah. Stuff I'm not going to talk to you about."

"I hope not." Mack wouldn't be Mack if he ratted out friends and family easily. Besides, she already knew what caused the pain she'd seen in Brandt's eyes. Pain he fought hard to keep buried. She knew the signs.

So, apparently, did her brother. "Don't even think about it."

"Think about what?" She fluttered her eyes, innocent.

Mack rolled his eyes. "And don't try that either. Brandt's a private person. He won't appreciate you trying to psychoanalyze him."

"I'm not going to." Not psychoanalyze, just help, and hopefully heal. It was splitting hairs, but Mack didn't need to know that.

"Willow." Warning ringed his voice.

"He's hurting, Mack!" she exclaimed, rising to her feet. "He's doing a good job of hiding it, but I can see it. I can feel it."

"I figured that." He climbed to his feet, looking impressive in his tan uniform. "That's why I'm here, to warn you off. Brandt's a good man, and he'll do a good job with the chapel. You won't have to worry with him being here. But if you push him, he'll push back. I don't want you to get your feelings hurt."

"You think this is about feelings?" She folded her arms. "I'm a big girl now, Mack. I don't need you to protect me."

His eyes emptied. "No, I don't suppose you do."

His words came easily enough, but she could hear the hurt in them, the self-condemnation. She remembered the dark place she'd been crawling herself out of when Mack had finally tracked her down in California during her last year of undergrad study.

Six years had passed since she'd gotten his last letter, four years since she'd left Serena Bay. By then, she'd resigned herself to the fact that he'd turned his back on her as their father had done. She'd been wrong, but it had taken time to believe it.

Another problem she had to thank her father for.

"You know," she said carefully, "one of these days you're going to have to stop blaming yourself for what happened after you left. I never did."

He lifted one massive shoulder. "Yeah? Well, today's not the day. And you're a better person than I am."

Her fingers curled with the need to go hug him, but she didn't move. That simple gesture was beyond her, even with her brother.

She tried to lighten the mood. "You know what you need? You need a girlfriend."

Mack groaned. "Not this again."

"Hey, at least I didn't say the 'm' word."

"Thank God for small miracles." He shuddered. "There's no way in hell I'm getting married."

"Never say never, brother dear," she chided. "You know Serena Bay's Ladies' Auxiliary won't rest until you and Tony are married."

"The sheriff and the mayor, Serena Bay's most eligible bachelors. I'm sure Salazar's just as thrilled about that as I am." He shook his head in disgust.

Willow laughed. "You can say that again. I saw Tony running down Federal Highway the other day, then realized he was being chased."

"At least I can shoot anybody coming after me."

"Mack!"

"Not saying I would, but the threat's there," he said, resting his hand on the butt of his gun. Then he glanced at his watch. "Speaking of duty, I've got to run. I gave Brandt my set of keys and the codes for the front and back gates and the security system. Hope you don't mind."

"Of course not. I'll send Pattie out to make a new set for you tomorrow."

"Good. I'll stop in before the week's out and make sure you and Brandt are still getting along. Anything I need to bring for Sunday dinner?"

"Other than a date?"

"For the love of God, stop." He opened her office door. "Besides, I've got my heart set on Pattie making an honest man out of me."

Her assistant grinned as Willow followed her brother out. "The only thing lawful about you is that badge," Pattie said in her sugar cane voice. "Come give us some sugar."

Mack dutifully let himself be mauled by the only woman who could get away with it. Willow felt wistfulness creep into her smile. She admired the easy camaraderie they had, even as she felt a flash of jealousy.

She waved at them, then retreated to her office. The serenity fountain gurgled at her as she sat in front of her computer again. The cursor winked at her, not in welcome, but in mockery.

Her fingers trembled as her hands paused over the keyboard. Her train of thought had left the station, but forgotten to take her along for the ride. She looked over at her notepad, but her vision blurred, making her scrawls difficult to read. A single word crawled through her mind.

Hypocrite.

Her hands fisted, and she forced herself to take a deep, preparatory breath. She knew this fight well. Every time she thought she'd beaten her opponent, the game would change. It had been like this since her first psychology course in college. Actually, since her first night away from her father's house. And the first time she'd tried to forge her frantic journals into a manuscript.

Physician, heal thyself.

The critic in her head always took her father's voice to mock her. Calling her a hypocrite. It didn't matter that she knew intellectually what her problem was. Emotionally it was her personal Mount Everest, and she was trying to scale it with straws instead of ice picks.

Yet she had to keep going. She had to write the words. Too much depended on getting the book done: Phoenix Haven, her livelihood, as well as that of her assistant and others who depended on her. In a way, even Serena Bay depended on her. She had to write because if she didn't, she'd be beaten, and everyone would know she was a fraud. And she couldn't allow that.

More than that, she had to write for herself. She wrote to understand why her life had gone the way it had, to understand why people behaved the way they did. She wrote because more than anything else, she had to find answers for herself.

Her fingers dropped to the letters, began to type. *Moving beyond the Phoenix Principle is not only about finding answers, but also about taking those answers…*

It was after ten when Brandt returned to the house. It wasn't that he was avoiding being alone with the doctor. Organizing his workspace and clearing the last of the debris had eaten up the hours. Then walking the perimeter of Phoenix Haven and securing it for the night had taken longer than he'd intended, simply because it wasn't secure.

Mack hadn't been lying when he'd said anyone could walk right through. Willow didn't even have locks installed on the main doors of the mission. Once she moved her offices out there, it would be open season on the good doctor.

The house was quiet when he entered the door off the sun room. Shaking his head, he locked the door, setting the alarm before heading for the kitchen.

A bark greeted him, followed immediately by a shriek. Willow whirled to face him, a butcher's knife fisted in her right hand. Her shoulders slumped when she saw him.

"God, you scared me. How in the world do you move so quietly? I thought you'd retired for the night!"

He advanced slowly into the room, pausing when the cocoa-colored mutt bounded over, then bumped his hand in entreaty for a pat. He complied, though he never took his eyes off Willow. "If you thought I'd gone to bed, why did you leave the door unlocked?"

That brought her up short. "Did I?" She shrugged. "I'm still working, and someone would have to be pretty desperate to climb that fence or swim over from the neighbor's. Besides, Boscoe and I go down to the beach sometimes."

"At night?" Alone?

She gave him that slanted-eyed look of a black woman about to get attitude. "At night, first thing in the morning, sometimes at high noon," she answered, putting the knife down with exaggerated movements. "I know you and Mack are a lot alike, but I really don't need another jailer, all right?"

Brandt bit back a retort, refraining from reminding her of how she'd just jumped three feet when he'd walked in on her. He wasn't supposed to know about the threats against her. He sure wasn't supposed to be concerned.

He shrugged, turning back the way he'd come. "Your house, your business."

A heavy sigh sounded behind him. "I'm sorry, Brandt. This—I swear I'm not usually like this. Just because I'm stressed out doesn't mean I should be rude."

Turning back, he simply nodded, surprised that she'd even apologize to him.

She blew out another breath, picked up a spoon. "Are you getting settled okay? I have a cleaning lady who comes by a couple of times a week, but I usually do my own laundry for the most part. Just toss my things into a hamper if I leave them in the dryer and you need to use it. I also have a set grocery list that's delivered each week, but I sometimes like to pick up my own fruits and vegetables. So if there's anything else you need, feel free to add it to the list on the fridge, or just let me or Pattie know. Speaking of, you shouldn't worry about Pattie. I promise, she's harmless."

His brain hurt from trying to follow her rapid-fire train of thought. "Why would I worry about your assistant?"

She flashed a smile. "I love Pattie to death, but she's a force of nature. I'm not sure I believe her about being a former exotic dancer and Playboy bunny, but the stories are definitely entertaining."

Pattie, a Playboy bunny? He recalled the older woman with the wild outfit and healthy curves. Where in the world had Willow found her—and how? "I'm not worried about stories."

"It's not the stories, but how she tells them," Willow said. "And she likes to collect WIPs."

He took a step back. "As in leather?

Willow laughed. "No, works-in-progress, as in single men. She'll either try to mother you or smother you. Just ask Mack. It's harmless flirting, though, because she's been happily married for thirty years to a man she allegedly met at the Playboy mansion. He doesn't dispute it, so sometimes I wonder."

He took another step back. Oh, he'd be asking Mack some questions all right. Like what exactly had he gotten himself into? Maybe the whole town was crazy and Mack and Willow were the wardens.

"There I go, running off at the mouth." She stirred the pot, then looked up at him with another one of those wicked-warm smiles. The kind that said, *I'm going crazy, you should come along for the ride.*

"You must be hungry if you're just coming in from the mission. When writer's block hits me, I cook. The more elaborate the recipe, the better. There's more than enough for two. Besides, I did agree to board as well as room."

Brandt hesitated, aware of his empty stomach. He'd been rude enough in the few hours that he'd known her. It wouldn't kill him to be nice. But he didn't think he could sit at a table with her and make casual conversation, even if she did most of the talking. Talk could easily turn to personal issues, and he couldn't go there, even to be polite. Especially with her.

Her smile became brittle. "Sorry again. You're probably more tired than hungry, and I bet you want a hot shower more than you want to be a guinea pig for my culinary tests. I'll just leave a plate in the fridge so you can get it later if you want."

She turned her attention back to the simmering pot. Brandt nearly breathed a sigh of relief, but felt a pang of guilt instead. Willow was trying to be nice, and he was showing his ass. His mother would take a spoon to him if she knew.

But he couldn't spend time with Willow Zane yet. It was too soon after his last crash, when Mack had called and unknowingly stopped him. Everything in him, all the grief and guilt and rage, still boiled just beneath the surface. He wasn't all that sure he could keep it hidden from Willow, and that was reason enough to keep his distance.

Still, it wouldn't kill him to remember his manners. "Thank you, Doctor. I appreciate that."

When she looked up at him with that soft, understanding smile, something inside him shifted. "Please, if I'm calling you Brandt, you have to call me Willow," she said, her voice pleased and gentle. "And you're quite welcome."

He nodded. It was as much as he could do. Without another word, he turned and left. Sometimes strategic retreats were necessary.

CHAPTER SIX

"So I hear you've finally found a carpenter to tackle the mission."

Willow paused, the cup of tea hovering before her lips. "Not even a week. News sure travels fast."

Monica just smiled at her. "Serena Bay's a small town. You have to work hard to keep secrets around here."

Willow took a sip of tea, grimaced at the over-herbal taste, then put her cup down to reach for sweetener. "He's hardly a secret, Zee. His name is Brandt Hughes, and he's a master carpenter from Atlanta. He's a friend of Mack's."

Sunlight glinted off her dramatic ebony bob as Monica leaned forward. "So tell me, is he sexy and single, or does he suffer from permanent carpenter's crack?"

"Zee!" Willow smothered a shocked laugh, feeling her cheeks heat. Zee's irreverent words called up an image Willow had been fighting for days, an image of Brandt with sleeves rolled up and tool belt slung low, looking strong and solid and capable.

"So, I gather it's door number one, huh?" Zee teased. "Well, well, well."

"Zee, you're too much!" She'd known Monica Zanteras only peripherally in high school, and had been more than happy to begin a friendship with her class's most popular girl after returning home. As much as she valued their friendship, sometimes she just didn't understand Zee. Like now.

"Hey, I can't help but be curious." A sly expression crossed Zee's sultry features. "So what do you know about him?"

"That he's a hard worker and his clients rave about him," she answered, concentrating on stirring sweetener into the concoction Zee called tea. She had no intention of sharing Brandt's history with her friend. It was one thing to delve into someone's personal life; it was quite another to share it with someone else.

"You're letting a virtual stranger stay at your house?"

"You know about that too?" Willow couldn't believe it. Not that she'd wanted to keep Brandt's living arrangements secret or anything, but she liked the idea that what happened behind her gate, stayed behind her gate.

Zee shook her head, incredulous. "You're a big time celebrity here in Serena Bay, don't you realize that? That's why we have lunch here at my palatial estate instead of on the sidewalk on Beach Avenue, so every broke or broken resident of our fair town won't accost you. If you wanted to be anonymous, you should have stayed in L.A."

Willow hunched her shoulders, stung by Zee's rebuke. "This is my hometown. I don't want to be a celebrity here."

"Then you shouldn't have gotten famous."

It was a familiar refrain between them. Zee had handled her own variety of stardom with equanimity. After going into modeling straight out of high school, she'd earned fortune and fame before walking away at the top of her game to marry into Serena Bay's oldest, richest, and most powerful family.

Ricardo Salazar, Tony's older brother and the apple of the family's eye, had died tragically, leaving Monica with forty-five percent of the extensive Salazar business. More than one Serena Bay resident had said that widowhood more than agreed with Monica.

"You know very well that it was luck and timing more than anything else that made *The Phoenix Principle* a household name," Willow said evenly. "I'm writing to help people. And if dolling up and hitting the talk show circuit will help me help more people and make Phoenix Haven a reality, I'll keep on doing it."

"And I'm not saying you shouldn't." Zee patted her hand briefly before refilling Willow's teacup. "I just don't see how you can fulfill your plans here in Serena Bay."

Willow suppressed a sigh then reached for sweetener again, wondering how Zee could drink the God-awful tea with a straight face.

Still, she didn't want to hurt her friend's feelings, even though pickle juice would taste better. Besides, Zee's banana nut bread more than made up for the tea.

"You always said you didn't feel like you belonged in this town," Zee said then. "I'd think New York or L.A. would work better for you and your plans. Maybe even Atlanta."

"I said that nearly twenty years ago, Zee," Willow said evenly, taking another sliver of banana bread to counteract the tea. "I did my stint in Los Angeles. I talked the talk in New York. And I'll do it again when the new book comes out. But this is home. This is where I want to be."

"All right, all right. You don't need to convince me." Zee lifted her teacup, settled back in her rattan chair. "Just don't be surprised when people stay all up in your business."

Somehow Willow managed to wrestle the conversation back to safer topics, like the upcoming community fundraiser at which she'd be delivering the keynote address.

With the banana bread gone and the tea spreading in her stomach like an oil slick, Willow decided to head back home. Relief filled her as she turned onto the A1A highway. She had several reasons to be thankful for her success, but one of the many was being able to afford an ocean view. Even if it meant being behind a ten-foot-high fence.

Even though she'd been less than gracious at losing the argument with Mack, she appreciated the physical barrier that separated her personal and professional lives. And the fence really wasn't as bad as she'd first envisioned. Since the house actually sat a little distance back from the road and behind a stand of trees, the fence had been recessed into the property, blending unobtrusively into the lush landscape. If you weren't looking for the unmarked driveway, it was easily missed.

The only true landmark for Willow's home was the north side of the property. There the vegetation dipped toward the sea, and there Spanish nuns had decided to erect a mission. Willow eased into the right turn lane to pull into the parking lot of what was soon to be Phoenix Haven. Just the sight gave her the lift to the spirit that she needed.

She remembered the letter she'd received from Sister Astencia three years ago, just after the first book became a national bestseller. *If you've thought about coming home,* the letter had read, *now is the time. The mission is in its final days unless you are willing to continue its work and yours, with God's grace.*

Willow had immediately called the sister, then taken a flight home shortly after. Sister Astencia had been there for Willow at her lowest point; the mission had truly been a refuge for her. That she was able to save it as it had saved her was truly a miracle.

She parked her SUV import close to the property line to her house. She intended to head back out to the garden center, but she wanted to change clothes first. Before that though, she wanted to check on Brandt's progress and make a peace offering.

His monster of a truck, as intimidating as its owner, sat in front of the doors to the mission.

He'd only been onsite for five full days, in Florida for six. In that time Willow had learned little about her brother's best friend, but the little she knew impressed her deeply.

He had proved dedicated to his craft, spending long hours working in the chapel. She knew for a fact that he'd worked nearly twelve hours straight the previous day before taking a quick break and then working another three hours.

She understood because she pushed herself at the same breakneck pace. That morning she'd reviewed files on current and former clients and made phone calls, getting ready for the painters to begin next week. Her office suite waited for her, needing nothing more than electronic equipment and a final cleaning before she moved in this weekend. Then she could really get to work.

She sighed, pushing her sunglasses up into her hair. Pattie would say she was pushing herself too hard. Pattie was probably right, but Willow thrived on the pace and the load, for reasons she hadn't shared with her assistant. She had a feeling that Brandt's work ethic had as much to do with what he'd lost as who he was. Not that she didn't appreciate reaping the benefits, but she didn't want a renovated chapel at the cost of Brandt's psyche.

The whine of a table saw took her around the chapel to the small open space that served as a break between the building and the ocean.

What a view.

Brandt was hard at work, just as she expected. He had his shirt off. That she hadn't expected, or her reaction to the sight.

She'd never seen anything so perfect in her life.

The afternoon sunlight caught the sheen of sweat on his beautiful arms, causing his bronze skin to glisten. Muscles rippled along his arms and shoulders as he pushed a plank of dark wood through the saw. He had a scar on his right arm, a deep furrow that did nothing to detract from the grace and power of body, bone, and blood.

Lord have mercy.

She was a writer, but she had no words to describe how beautifully powerful and fluid he seemed, engrossed in the art of turning wood into wonder. Maybe she did have a word, *dancing.* She'd never thought of carpentry as a dance before, but watching Brandt, staring at the graceful, coordinated movement of his body and his hands, she thought she heard music in her head.

She closed her eyes, suddenly wondering what it would feel like to dance with Brandt, to have her hands on his powerful shoulders as he guided her through an intricate rhythm.

"You want something?"

That hard voice jerked her eyes open. "Nice."

He powered down the saw. "Excuse me?"

Focus, girl, focus. She lifted one of the plastic bags she held. "Ice. Iced tea. You said you couldn't find a place here that made decent southern-style tea, so I bought stuff to make you some."

He lifted the safety glasses. She suddenly wished that he'd put them back on—for her safety. Glancing away from those storm cloud eyes caused her to focus on his chest. Averting her eyes again had her looking at his arms. She felt as if she were watching a fast-paced tennis match. She didn't want to ogle him, but it was hard. Real hard.

"Real sugar?"

"What?" She blinked, focused on his face, and tried not to feel stupid.

"Did you get real sugar, not that artificial stuff?"

She nodded, then tried to smile. "Yes, and a bunch of lemons, to make lemonade."

"I suppose it's time for a break." His features lightened. Nowhere near a smile of course, but not a frown either. "Thank you, Willow. I'll be around in a moment."

She managed to close her mouth. He was making an effort to be nice and she was making eyes at him. "All right, see you in a bit."

She turned and headed back for the split in the path that led to her house. She felt downright light-headed. Even during her years in Los Angeles, she hadn't gone gaga over the sight of a nice-looking man. But Brandt was more than nice-looking. He was in a whole other category.

And he was staying in her house.

Something fluttered in her chest, something precariously balanced between apprehension and giddiness. She didn't want to think of Brandt Hughes as a man with bronze skin and gorgeous arms that could pick her up and toss her over his shoulder without a thought. She didn't want to think of him in the shower, rinsing off the dust and work of the day.

She didn't want to think about him like that, because she had no idea how to deal with someone like that living in her house.

"Dr. Zane?"

Willow looked up to see one of the construction workers standing by the gate entrance to the house. She hadn't even noticed him. "Hello. Jesse, isn't it?"

"Yes, ma'am." He gave a pleased smile as he stepped closer. "Let me help you with that."

He reached for the sack she carried in her left arm, close to her chest. She stepped back, wrapping both arms around the bag, clutching it to her chest. The weight of the bag of lemons hanging from her right wrist dug into her skin, but she didn't dare lower her arms.

"No, thanks. I've got it under control." She tried to move around him, but he stepped closer. Her lungs seized up as he invaded her personal space. It was an effort to ask, "Isn't your boss looking for you?"

"You shouldn't have to carry that by yourself," the young man said. "Shouldn't be up in that big, old house by yourself either. I can help with that too."

Willow backed up, suddenly realizing she couldn't reach her pepper spray without dropping her bags. She did, however, have a five pound bag of sugar and two pounds of lemons pressed against her chest. He hadn't really given her an excuse to use either in self-defense, but it didn't hurt to be prepared.

"I really think you should get back to work," she said, dropping the vaguely polite tone she used with most of the construction workers. "If you have something you need my professional opinion for, you can call my office for an appointment."

He blocked her way again. "Come on, Doc, I know you're by yourself. I'm told I'm real handy to have around, know what I mean?"

She did, and it made her stomach roil. Before she could begin a sharp retort, he touched her arm.

Her lungs shut tight as she jerked backwards, ready to see how much damage a bag of lemons could inflict. One moment the man had his hand on her forearm, the next he was on his knees, his arm twisted behind him.

Surprised, Willow looked up into Brandt's face. He'd moved so silently, so quickly, she hadn't even heard him approach. She wanted to say thank you, but his expression stopped her. The man on his knees wasn't nearly as threatening as the man who held him there.

"Man, what're you doing?" Jesse demanded.

"Apologize to the lady." Brandt's voice was even, almost pleasant, but you had to be a fool not to hear the threat in it.

"We were just talking!" Apparently Jesse was deaf. "That hurts!"

"No, this hurts." Brandt shifted, and the worker howled in pain. "Apologize to Dr. Zane."

"I'm sorry, Miss Z—ow!—Dr. Zane! I didn't mean it, I was just playing!"

The situation moved from panic to embarrassment. Willow looked away from Jesse, met Brandt's gaze. "Please stop."

The gray eyes flared with anger, then shuttered as he released Jesse. It took the man moments to realize he was free. He scrambled away a short distance before springing to his feet. "I'm gonna sue!"

Just great. Willow stepped forward, but Brandt stepped in front of her, blocking her view. "You assault the sheriff's sister on her own property and you want to sue? You are stupid. And here I thought you were just disturbed. You got two choices. One leave the property on your own, and you'll be paid out the week."

"And what's number two?"

"You leave in a wheelbarrow. Then I tell the sheriff."

He meant it. Willow felt the danger in the air, saw it in the absolute readiness with which Brandt held himself. Jesse was one wisecrack away from a wheelbarrow.

Apparently he came to the same conclusion, because he took off, taking the path that led to the mission parking lot.

A shudder went through Willow's shoulders as her lungs eased, allowing her to breathe. "I would have stopped him."

"I'm sure you would have."

His tone was neither condescending nor angry, but it pricked Willow nonetheless. "I would have. I was trying to figure out how to get him to back off without creating an incident. You heard how he threatened to sue me. If I'd bopped him on the head with the bag of lemons like I wanted to, he'd still be on the ground screaming bloody murder. I am not about to let some idiot hack away at my ability to help people."

Something flickered across his face. "You were going to bop him?"

"With the lemons. Or the sugar. Or my knee."

He reached around her to punch in the gate code. "Would have been a shame to waste a perfectly good bag of lemons."

She looked up at him, trying to gauge his mood. Was he trying to make her feel better? Why was he trying to make her feel better? "That's what I thought."

He pushed open the gate. "If you're still up to it, I'd appreciate that tea."

She nodded, not breathing until she'd passed through the opening. Now that the adrenaline had evaporated, she felt shaky. Despite what she'd told Brandt, she didn't know if she could have really stopped Jesse, a thought that frightened and infuriated her. She was suddenly grateful for the fence that separated the properties, grateful to be on the private side of it. If it weren't for the fence, if it weren't for Brandt—

She lifted her head, pushing her emotions away, even though she knew it was just a temporary reprieve. "Are you coming in?"

He pulled the gate closed. "Got a little cleaning up to do."

"All right." She hurried up the path to the back entrance. Boscoe greeted her at the patio door, and she let him out. By the time she put her groceries in the kitchen, she was shaking uncontrollably, her good mood shattered. Luckily Pattie had already gone for the day, as she usually did when Willow visited with Zee. Good. She didn't think she'd be able to keep it together for her assistant's benefit, to explain.

She couldn't even explain it to herself. How did you explain being haunted by ghosts of memories you'd long thought buried?

She quickly stripped off the turquoise sheath dress, a dress that had been her favorite. Now she wanted nothing more than to burn it. Instead, she hurriedly crumpled the silk into a ball, then stuffed it into the under cabinet trash bin before dashing upstairs for a long, long shower.

CHAPTER SEVEN

Two hours passed before Brandt made it back to the house. Besides packing away the rest of his equipment, he'd needed to walk off some of his anger before going to see the construction boss. At least the man had the sense to know who buttered his bread. Jesse wouldn't be working on any other projects for Willow, which suited Brandt just fine.

He couldn't explain why he'd reacted so badly to seeing Willow grabbed like that, or how he'd known it wasn't just a friendly conversation. But something in the way she'd jerked back, the stiffness of her expression, had told him that things weren't okay. He'd taken one look and just reacted, wanting nothing more than to break the idiot's fingers.

He entered the kitchen, spotting two plastic grocery bags on the counter, apparently where Willow had left them. He began to empty them, dimly aware of a low hissing rumble that suggested Willow was still upstairs taking a shower. The woman took the longest showers in history.

An instant image filled his mind, an image of her toned dark body covered in lather and a sheen of water. He immediately pushed the image away, angry with himself and his immediate reaction. The last thing Willow needed was someone else pawing at her. The last thing he needed was lusting after a woman, especially one as complicated as Willow.

Grabbing the empty bags, he turned to the cabinets that hid the trash and recycling bins. He tossed the bags into the recycling and was about to close the door when a spot of color caught his attention. He reached into the trash bin, his fingers closing over cloth.

Willow's dress. He held it up. Except for the wrinkles from being crumpled in the trash, there was nothing wrong with it. Why in the world would she throw away a silk dress? She didn't seem like the wear-it-once type of society woman.

Shaking his head, Brandt returned the dress to its hiding place. Definitely complicated, he thought as he washed his hands. Yet another reason to stay clear of Willow.

He grabbed a knife, sliced open the netting holding the lemons, then took out a few to roll on the counter.

Oh yeah, he could easily see it in the deep molasses of her eyes, see the thoughts and plans spinning in her mind. Not calculating, but considering. As if the outside world were only a fraction of the bustling place inside her head. A woman perfectly content to be alone with her thoughts.

He'd always had a thing for complicated women.

One of the lemons squished open beneath his hand. Biting back a snarl of self-defense, he opened a cabinet and extracted a blue ceramic pitcher and a hand juicer. His photographic memory made it easy to remember where everything was in her house, but the familiarity suddenly grated on him, made him feel as if he'd gotten too close, too comfortable. Especially since the blue of the pitcher reminded him of the color of Willow's dress, the curve of the glass, how she'd looked in it.

He'd been stunned to see her in something other than those clown-sized overalls. The sleeveless dress had just skimmed her knees, showing a nice length of leg and trim ankles above silver heeled sandals. She'd even had on makeup, though she didn't need it. He'd felt like an idiot staring at her as she'd smiled and offered to make iced tea for him, all sweetness and light. All he'd thought of was that she had the prettiest smile he'd ever seen.

He sliced the lemons in half. Ignoring the juicer, he squeezed the juice into the pitcher, venting his frustration. The last thing he needed, he repeated to himself, was to feel attracted to his best friend's sister, the complicated Willow Zane. Make that the complicated Dr. Willow Zane. He certainly didn't need those dark eyes trained on him, her brain focused in his direction.

He picked up the knife and another lemon. She was probably dating the damn mayor anyway.

"Oh!"

Willow's gasp—and maybe his conscience—made him careless. He sliced into the lemon and his thumb. His colorful curse as lemon juice hit the cut had Willow scurrying closer. "Is it bad?" She reached for his hand. "Let me see."

He snatched his hand away from her questing fingers. "I'll live." It just hurt like a bitch.

"I said, let me see." The surprising steel in her voice had him holding his hand out to her. She wrapped a towel around his thumb, guiding him to the breakfast nook, pausing long enough to grab a first aid kit from beneath the sink. With surprising efficiency she soon had him sitting in front of her as she examined the cut.

He noticed she'd changed into a long-sleeved, shapeless bag of a dress in some muddy gray color that skimmed the floor in a blatant crime against cotton. Discomfited by the fact but not knowing why, he decided to study her hands instead. The slender, tapered fingers were roughened at the tips, probably from her time in the garden.

Her light, gentle touch had him relaxing his guard. "I thought you were a head doctor."

"And I thought you were good with your hands." Mischief danced in her eyes before she bent her head, the thin braids falling around her face to obscure her features. "I took a few courses in basic first aid and emergency care. With a sheriff for a brother, I figured it wouldn't hurt."

"I don't suppose it would," he agreed, trying not to wince as antiseptic hit his skin.

She cupped his hand between hers. "It doesn't look deep enough for stitches, but if you want a second opinion, it wouldn't hurt my feelings."

Dark eyes glanced up at him, just a brief locking of gazes that made something inside him lurch. He had to lick his lips before he could speak. "Don't need a second opinion."

She nodded, a movement of braids as she reached for the antibiotic salve. "I want to apologize to you."

"It's just a scratch."

"Not for this," she said, short-circuiting his brain as she rubbed ointment into his skin with a soft, circular stroke. "I'm sorry you had to see that, what happened earlier."

"The guy was an idiot," he snapped. "Don't apologize for his stupidity."

She dipped her head lower, leaving his hand resting palm-up on her knee as she opened a packet of gauze. "I know. I would have handled it better, but I was distracted by—well, never mind."

He tapped her knee with the back of his hand. "Why did you throw your dress away, Willow?"

A tremble went through her fingers, so faint anyone else might have missed it. "It was dirty."

Brandt knew the dress didn't have a mark on it. Maybe the encounter with the construction worker had affected her more than he'd thought. The idea that Dr. Zane had a hang up of her own made her seem more human, easing some of his tension. That didn't mean he enjoyed the vulnerable sound in her voice.

Without thinking about it, he touched his free hand to her chin, lifting it. "Hey, it was a nice dress for a ninety-degree-day lunch date. No one in their right mind would expect you to wear those overalls when you're not working the property, and that thing you're wearing now is definitely not fit for public display. You shouldn't let a little stain like that ruin a dress you like. If you want, I'll go beat up said little stain for you."

He wasn't talking about a mark on the dress. She apparently realized it, because she laughed just as he'd intended. Her whole face lit up, delivering a sucker-punch to his gut. Not what he intended. Luckily she bent her head back to the task of taping gauze to his hand. "Thanks, Brandt."

"Don't thank me," he said gruffly. "Mack would have done the same thing."

"Oh, that would have made it even better." She tightened the tape around his hand. He'd have to loosen it later or risk cutting off the blood flow. She tossed him a baleful glance. "The sheriff assaults a man for talking to his sister. The *Serena Bay Herald* would have a field day with that one."

"You get headlines a lot?" He hadn't thought about that.

"Not so much anymore, thank goodness," she answered. "For a while there, I thought the society section was called 'What's Willow Doing Now?' Everyday they talked about me, me and Mack, me and the mayor. Now it's mostly Tony that they hound."

"Tony?"

"Antonio Salazar, the mayor. I think I disappointed the local news outlets by not being more Hollywood. Now the only coverage I get is when Tony and I go shoot pool."

"You shoot pool with the mayor?" Figures.

"Almost every Thursday." She flashed him another smile as she loosened the wrap on his hand and began again. "Tony's been my best friend since high school. We went out west to college together, but he came home a few years before I did."

"That's a lot of history." Enough history to threaten Willow with? Politicians involved in scandals were as old as the political process. Was the mayor tired of his old friend stealing the spotlight? Did he want more from Serena Bay's celebrity resident than she wanted to give?

"Yeah, a lot of history," she agreed. Her hands stilled on his. "It amazes me sometimes that we're still friends."

She patted his hand, then got to her feet. "There you go, good as new. Now you just have to make sure you have a good story together when the reporter comes by."

His blood ran cold. "Reporter? You really think this is newsworthy?"

"Me? No. But I've recently been reminded that Serena Bay's a small town." She gathered the first aid supplies. "Apparently the town already knows we're shacking up."

"Shacking up?" An image unfolded in his mind, an image of Willow lying in tangled sheets, her braids sliding over her bare shoulders as she reached for him. He hurriedly stamped down the vision, but couldn't do a damn thing about his body's reaction except remain in the chair and wait for the sudden ache to ease.

"Yeah. My friend Monica asked me about you at lunch today."

"I haven't even been here a week."

"That's what I said." She bent to replace the first aid supplies, and he took the opportunity to get up, return to the lemonade. "I certainly didn't go telling her, but if she knows you're here, so does the rest of the town."

"Does that bother you?" It bothered him. He didn't like the idea of people being curious about him, delving into his business. His past.

Willow filled a kettle with filtered water. "It bothers me that having guests in my home is a newsworthy event." She set the kettle on the stainless steel stovetop, a high-tech contraption with a flat surface and buttons instead of knobs. "What happened today won't help."

"So what are you going to tell the press if they come calling?"

"The truth. That you're a friend of the family, staying here to rebuild the chapel. That's all anyone needs to know as far as I'm concerned."

Brandt stared at her, his pulse ramping into high gear. Did she know? If she'd done an extensive background check on him, it wouldn't take a week to uncover his past. Would she fire him, send him away, once she knew?

"Does your hand hurt?"

He looked down at his hand, surprised to find it shaking. "No."

"Liar." She reached into one of the cabinets, pulled out a large white bottle. "Take two of these and the rest of the day off. Doctor's orders."

He reached for the bottle and for calm. "Sure you're not an M.D. in disguise?"

"I know pain when I see it." When he paused, hand extended, she shook the bottle. "Migraines. My head aches constantly, some days worse than others, and my doctor can't find a cause. Says I need to be less stressed. Like that's going to happen anytime soon." She palmed the lid, then tipped two tablets out.

"Seems like you have a lot on your plate," he said as she handed him the pills. It was more than curiosity, he told himself. He couldn't report anything to Mack if he didn't fish for information. Willow obviously felt talkative now, and it wouldn't hurt to listen, gather what information he could.

"You could say my plate's full." She turned on the spout for filtered water (he'd quickly learned that Florida tap water was undrinkable), then filled a glass with water before offering it to him. After he took it, she got two tablets and a glass of water for herself. She tossed down the pills and a sip of water with the economical motions of someone who'd done the act many times.

"Sometimes I think there's no way that I'm going to make my deadlines, with the book or the center. It would be too easy to panic, so I don't. Still, it was a miracle that you showed up and agreed to take the chapel on."

Brandt didn't know what to say to that, so he kept his mouth shut. The only thing miraculous about him was that God hadn't struck him dead yet. There were days when he wondered what the old guy was waiting for.

Willow smiled at him as he stirred sugar into the lemonade. "Grunt all you want, Brandt Hughes, but I know a miracle when I see one. I'm grateful that you're here. Even if you're spying for my brother."

CHAPTER EIGHT

The man of few expressions could actually look surprised. She had a feeling that few people could catch Brandt Hughes off guard.

He recovered quickly. "What makes you say that?"

"Oh, come on. I may be stressed, but I'm not stupid." She took the lemonade from him, opening the top half of the fridge and sliding the pitcher inside. "You seem like a man who likes his space, so for you to barter room and board is a big deal. That means my dear brother put you up to it. And the only reason he'd do that is because he wants you to spy on me."

He grunted. He was good at that, she noted.

"No wonder you're a doctor."

"That's right." She shut the fridge, turned to face him. "Are you doing it?"

"Excuse me?"

She'd gotten him again. After the day she'd had, it gave her a certain, tiny pleasure to know that she had some sort of control, however miniscule, over him. "Spying. Are you spying on me for my brother?"

He took his time answering her, turning off the kettle, getting a plastic pitcher out of the cabinet. It amazed her how he'd made himself at home so easily. It should have made her nervous, or at least edgy, to have such a large, brooding male in her home. Instead, knowing Brandt was there gave her a measure of comfort she hadn't known she needed. It also gave her something to think about besides her own issues and shortcomings.

"I'm not spying on you, Willow," he said, pouring water from the kettle into the pitcher. Steam curled around his still features, always so serious. "I'm merely passing on information."

At least he didn't deny it. She gave him a point for that, and another for whatever it was that had caused him to agree to her brother's idea. Loyalty, honor, or the payment of a debt, it said something about Brandt Hughes that he was there when he clearly didn't want to be.

She lowered her head, suddenly feeling very tired. "You're going to tell him, aren't you?"

He turned towards her. "As the sheriff, he needs to know. As your brother, he'd want to know."

"Why?" She didn't want to tell Mack about the incident with Jesse. All the men and women who worked the site were recovering from one thing or another. They just needed a break, and someone to give it to them.

"Why?" he repeated. "What if this guy decides to come back in the middle of the night, wanting to get back at you?"

"Why in the world would he do that? It's not like I'm going to try to keep him from getting a job somewhere else."

"You're unbelievable, you know that?" His voice showed the first real trace of emotion she'd heard from him. "That creep manhandled you, and you're concerned about his job? Obviously he wasn't concerned about his paycheck when he grabbed you."

She shifted away from him, and away from the memory. "He won't come back. He knows he made a mistake. You shouldn't have to pay for every stupid mistake you make in your life."

Brandt just shook his head. "You're too nice."

"I'm what?"

"Too nice. For your own good. You're a nice person, so you expect everyone else to be just as nice."

He made it sound like an epithet. "What's wrong with being nice?"

"The world isn't nice." He said it starkly, a simple statement of fact from someone who called it as he saw it, and he'd seen a lot. "The world is mean, and insensitive to the point of being cruel. People are the same way."

"I don't believe that."

"It's the truth, plain and ugly. People will take what they want from you, and then they'll turn on you. Especially if it suits their own needs and lets them get ahead. It's human nature."

"It's a sad way to look at the world."

"Yeah, well, I never said I was nice. I'm a realist. It's much better to prepare for the worse and get the best than it is to hope for the best and be blindsided by the worst."

She knew then that he was speaking from personal experience. She'd promised not to psychoanalyze him, but she couldn't help responding to the anger that thrummed through him, anger that covered a deep and permanent anguish.

"I know people are fallible. But I also know that people are capable of goodness, if they're given the opportunity."

"Bull. If you give that guy another opportunity, you could be hurt—or worse."

He couldn't have picked a more hurtful, or more accurate, thing to say to her. "But that's why you're here, isn't it?" Her voice softened as she moved past anger, past pain. "You're Mack's eyes and ears while he's not here. Looking out for poor, helpless Willow who's obviously too weak, too gullible, or too stupid to protect herself."

She pressed a palm to her forehead, feeling the beginnings of a headache creeping in, despite the extra-strength painkillers she'd taken a few minutes ago. Without another word, she turned away from him, heading for the den.

"Willow." He followed after her. "Come on, Willow, I don't think of you like that. And I bet Mack just wants to protect his baby sister. It's what big brothers do."

"Including calling in favors from old combat buddies." She sat on her couch, rubbing at her temples. "What kind of debt do you owe him?"

"He saved my life. More than once."

She nodded. "Of course. What else would make you stay here?"

"That's the reason I came down, but it's not the reason I stayed."

Surprised, she stopped rubbing her forehead to stare at him. "W-why did you stay?"

"The mission. The chapel was crying out for help. I have to bring her back. If I can do it, if I can repair her—"

He caught himself, as if afraid he'd said too much, revealed too much. She finished the thought for him. "Your reputation would be set, wouldn't it?"

"Yeah." But he shoved his hands in his pockets, and she realized that hadn't been his thought.

She drew a deep breath. "Then I suppose I should be grateful that you're ambitious as well as talented. The chapel's in good hands."

"Thank you." He swallowed hard, as if pushing down his emotions, then pulled his hands out of his pockets. Her gaze immediately dropped to them. Why was she so fixated on his hands?

Maybe it was because she'd never been creative, not in a physical sort of way. Art had never been her thing; she could appreciate it, but not create it. She certainly appreciated what Brandt was doing for her, transforming the chapel. He had an artist's hands, a craftsman's hands. But those hands had also gotten Jesse away from her, quickly and easily, proving that the carpenter was also a warrior.

She remembered how it had felt to hold his hand between hers, to stroke her fingers across his skin. His hand dwarfed her own, making hers seem almost childlike in comparison. Long thick fingers roughened by years of sanding and polishing, a palm more like a bear's paw, drove home the knowledge that Brandt Hughes was a large man.

It should have made her uncomfortable, after Jesse, knowing that this virtual stranger now lived with her. Instead, she felt safe, more at ease than she could remember. Not that she intended to need his help for anything other than repairing the chapel, but she felt better, knowing he was there.

She settled back into the chair. "Do you, uhm, do you think you could teach me basic self-defense?"

"Sure," he said easily, studying her. "Did something else happen, besides today?"

"No, but it's something every woman should know, don't you think?"

"Absolutely."

"I took a self-defense class at the Y during college," she said hastily, not wanting him to get the idea that she was completely clueless. "Mack offered to teach me a few things, but we could never work it into our schedules."

Actually, taking the self-defense course had been traumatic, even in the anonymity of Los Angeles. She'd learned then that try as she might to put the past behind her, and bury it, it would always be a part of her, flaring up in the form of panic attacks. She wouldn't expose Mack to one of her episodes, especially since he blamed himself for so much already.

"Speaking of schedules," he said, breaking into her thoughts, "when would be a good time to work this in?"

"I'm usually up at sunrise, doing yoga on the beach," she answered. "It helps me start my day off focused. If that's too early for you..."

"It's not. I'm an early riser." He looked at his bandaged hand, then at her. "I hope you're planning to wear something besides those sack dresses or overalls."

"Oh." She normally wore yoga pants or bike shorts paired with a swimsuit out to the beach. If he hadn't said anything, she would have followed her normal routine of dressing for yoga and a swim before starting her day.

He must have sensed her hesitation. "You're going to need your arms and legs free, and I'll have to make sure you're holding yourself properly," he explained. "If I can teach my sisters and mother, I can certainly teach you."

Did he think of her as one of his sisters? She supposed it made sense, as he was her big brother's best friend. The thought put her at ease. He really was nice, whether he wanted to admit it or not.

"All right then, shall we start tomorrow?"

"Sounds good to me."

CHAPTER NINE

"So how's your houseguest settling in?"

Willow chalked her pool cue, searching the forest green felt for her next shot. She should have known Tony would bring Brandt up sooner or later. At least he'd waited until after the break.

"Fine. You should see the redesign he created for the chapel. It repurposes the space, but still stays true to the mission's intent. And it's going to reduce the budget by more than ten percent." Given the cost of hardwoods for the project, she was still dancing for joy over that.

"That should give you enough money to put him up in one of Serena Bay's fine hotels," Tony said. "Our fair town would appreciate the business. Oh, bad shot," he added as she missed.

"Your sincerity underwhelms me," she retorted as she straightened, letting him at the table. She leaned on her pool cue and stared at Antonio Ramos Salazar, mayor of Serena Bay, richest man in town, and most eligible bachelor.

She could count on one hand the people she called friend: talk show host Isis Montgomery, Zee, Pattie, the late Sister Astencia, and Tony. He was the only guy on the list, and he'd been her best friend since their first day of high school, fifteen years ago. Tony had been dubbed "the spare" back then, a geeky afterthought to his all-American older brother Ricardo, just as Willow had willingly lived in Mack's shadow. They'd bonded over drama and debate and French, always together until Willow had turned down his request to take her to the senior prom. She'd gone with wrestling co-captain Porter Garrick instead, an act she'd regretted every day since.

"I have to say I'm surprised you didn't show up last week, you know, to officially welcome Brandt to Serena Bay," she said as he missed his next shot. Shooting pool and the breeze at Zeke's Billiards and Beer had been their Thursday night ritual for the last three years. Willow enjoyed the good-natured ribbing almost as much as Zeke's ribs and plantain chips platter.

"I thought about dropping by," Tony admitted, giving the trademark Salazar smile that caused a dimple to appear in his right cheek and more than one female voter to swoon. "I settled for a background check."

"Tony!" Willow missed the cue ball, scrubbing the felt and causing a few observers to groan. Gambling wasn't officially allowed in Serena Bay beyond playing the lottery, but Willow knew more than a few locals had a vested interest in the best-of-three games between her and Tony. She put her hands on her hips. "Tell me you did not investigate my master carpenter."

Tony delayed answering by lining up his next shot, cleanly sinking the three. Some people said summer in Serena Bay began with the Memorial Day boat parade; others claimed summer season began when the mayor traded his suits for khakis and colorful dress shirts. Willow had to say the sea-green shirt complemented his dark hair and golden skin perfectly.

Personally, Willow had wanted nothing more than to wear one of her long knit dresses out. However, since she and Tony had turned their Thursday night outings into casual town hall meetings, she had to dress the part. Her concession to that fact consisted of pale yellow linen trousers and a short-sleeved moss green blouse. Pulling her braids back into a ponytail and wearing pearl earrings completed her professional but personable look.

Tony sank two more balls in quick succession. "If I tell you I didn't investigate him, would you believe me?"

"Not even for a second." Tony, computer geek extraordinaire, had single-handedly brought Serena Bay into the twenty-first century, making it the most wired town of its size in South Florida. If there was an electronic record hidden somewhere, Tony could find it.

Tony missed the next ball. "Do you want to know what I found out?"

"No. Eight ball, corner pocket." She executed a perfect shot, to a round of applause. For some reason, the men cheered for her while the women cheered for Tony.

"Looks like dinner is on me," Tony said, placing his cue on the table while Willow racked hers. He waited until she joined him before asking, "Aren't you curious about the carpenter with the kung-fu grip?"

Willow almost missed a step as they headed for the main dining area. "How many people know about that?"

"A few," he admitted, seating her in the booth before taking his seat. Teresa, their regular waitress, brought over their drinks, a beer for Tony and a bright blue concoction for Willow that Zeke's bartender called Serena Sea, as well as a basket of plantain chips and *mojo* sauce for dipping. "Are y'all having your usuals today, or do you want something different?"

They looked at each other, nodded. "The usual," they said in unison. Teresa left, and Willow leaned forward. "How many is a few?"

"Just people who need to know. Jesse Thompson's having to drive all the way to Miami for work now."

"Poor guy."

"Poor guy?" Tony's dark brows lifted. "How about stupid guy? He's lucky Mack didn't find out until after he'd left town."

"Mack knows?" She groaned. Of course Mack would know. Brandt hadn't promised that he wouldn't tell her brother, just that he'd stop spying on her for him. Then again, if Tony knew, Mack had to know.

She wondered why Mack hadn't confronted her about it, then realized that Brandt had done the job for him. She couldn't decide if that irritated her or not, so she decided to let it go. For the moment anyway.

"We're just looking out for you, Willow," Tony said. "We're all glad you decided to come back home. No one wants you to leave."

That wasn't necessarily true, but she couldn't tell Tony that. Another printed letter had arrived in her mailbox Monday, the same day as the incident with Jesse, but she hadn't opened it until Tuesday. Like the others, it didn't have a postmark. All that meant was that someone within two days' drive had delivered the letter warning her to leave Serena Bay. As far as she was concerned, it was tame compared to some of the email she'd received.

"I appreciate your concern, Tony, you know I do," she said, dipping a plantain chip into the citrus sauce that she loved to pour onto everything. "But I'm not stupid. I checked Brandt's references before I agreed to take him on. Besides, do you really think Mack would have recommended someone he didn't trust?"

Tony grunted. Willow looked at him in surprise. Black eyes bored into hers. "Mack's judgment isn't always impeccable."

She took a deep breath. "You sure can hold a grudge, especially one that isn't yours to hold. You've got to let that go. Mack doesn't know what happened after he left, and he did look for me as soon as he was able. I'm glad I've got him as a brother."

Tony took a swallow of his beer, grimacing. "I suppose yours did turn out all right."

"Ah, Tony, I'm sorry." Ricardo, darling of Serena Bay and the apple of his parents' eyes, had driven his car into the bay five years ago. Tony had returned home for the funeral, and hadn't left. It had taken years for him to repair all the damage his brother had done to the Salazar business, family name, and the town.

"It's all right," Tony said then. "Besides, we were discussing your carpenter, not me."

Luckily, Teresa brought their food: mojo-marinated ribs with thick wedges of plantains for him, and for Willow, *lechón asada*, slow-roasted pork so tender she always used her fingers when she was alone. Two steaming bowls of black beans and white rice accompanied the entrees. After setting down a basket of warm sliced sourdough, Teresa put down two empty plates, knowing that they always split their food, then left.

"There's nothing to discuss about my carpenter," Willow said. "So how about we drop it and concentrate on dinner? You know they're only going to give us about forty-five minutes before they open the floor."

"Okay, we'll drop it," Tony said in that easy tone that told Willow the topic was far from dropped. "But you can't blame me for being jealous. I never got invited to stay over."

"When your oceanfront view is better than mine? Please." The Salazar home was large enough to be called a compound. The family had been among the first to settle Serena Bay, and Tony used to joke that their success lay in the family motto of "I connive to survive."

No one could joke about the fact that Serena Bay existed because of the Salazars. The town was lucky that the good son had returned to save it.

"You know that you have an open invitation to my oceanfront view," Tony said, signaling for another beer. "Not that you'll accept it."

"For anything other than a fundraiser or party for two hundred of your closest friends? No thanks, I don't need to give the town anything else to talk about." People wondered enough about their friendship that they worked hard to avoid any semblance of impropriety. Sometimes Willow thought she worked a little harder at it than Tony did.

"Hey, I just want you to be careful, that's all," Tony said, wrapping long, elegant fingers around his second beer. "I mean, all you know about this guy is that he's a friend of Mack's and a carpenter."

"He's Mack's best friend, and a damn fine carpenter," Willow clarified. "You should see the work he did on an inn up in St. Augustine. Which is older than the mission by a hundred years. Phoenix Haven's in good hands, Tony. I know what I'm doing."

"Famous last words." Tony saluted her with his beer. "I just hope you don't live to regret them."

"Your sister and the mayor seem to get along well."

Mack lifted his beer. "Why do you care? I thought you weren't spying for me anymore?"

Brandt grunted. He'd accepted Mack's invitation to beer and pool readily, needing to get away from Willow and the perfect serenity of her home. But the last thing he wanted was to see her smiling and relaxing with the mayor while the citizens of Serena Bay paid them homage. Not that it was any of his business what Willow did with the mayor.

"I said I wouldn't overtly spy," he pointed out. "That doesn't mean I'm not going to look out for her like you asked. Do you trust the guy?"

"Mayor Salazar is a man of integrity, and Serena Bay's lucky to have him," Mack replied.

"That's the sheriff talking. How does the brother feel?" Brandt nodded towards the rear of the main dining area, where Willow and the overly charming mayor held court. He didn't know what else it could be called, the way everyone gathered around the town's most illustrious residents. Recalling that Willow claimed Salazar as a long-time friend, he couldn't help wondering if that meant "friends with benefits."

Mack leaned forward. "Willow and Antonio have been friends since they started high school together. He had her back while I was gone."

Mack's voice held an edge Brandt could easily hear. He knew there was bad blood between Mack and Salazar, stemming from when Mack received a letter from his father stating that Willow had run away from home, with Antonio.

They'd been deep in combat, but Mack had been able to compartmentalize his worry and anger and still lead their team safely. It was only during down time and only in front of Brandt that Mack had allowed his concern and frustration to show, especially since his father had refused to talk about Willow's disappearance. Mack had written letter after letter to his father and to the Salazars, only to be stonewalled. His only option had been to pour his pay into hiring private investigators, sight unseen. It wasn't until their tour was up that Mack was able to return home to Serena Bay and track her and Antonio down at a college in California, a full six years after she'd disappeared.

"So if he looked out for her, why don't you trust him?" Brandt didn't trust the man either, but he couldn't put his finger on why. He was curious to know Mack's reasons.

Mack turned in his chair, looking towards his sister and her friend. "Have you known any straight man who wanted to just be friends with a woman?"

Brandt followed his gaze. Salazar and Willow had their heads close together, discussing something vitally important, judging by their expressions. Something more filtered across Salazar's face, something intimate and possessive.

"There's no such thing as friendship between men and women," he finally answered. "A man calls a woman friend, it just means he hasn't made his move yet."

"And I guess you're speaking from experience?"

Brandt swung around, meeting Mack's assessing stare. "No. I'm not pretending to be your sister's friend. You've got nothing to worry about."

"If I was worried, I wouldn't have had you set up shop in my sister's place." Mack reached for his beer again. "Willow could use a friend, though."

"What, you don't trust Salazar?"

"It's not that I don't trust Salazar. He's a good man and I don't think he'd ever deliberately hurt Willow."

"But?"

"But." Mack sighed. "I suspect his feelings are a little blind where my sister is concerned, and I'm not sure I can comfortably say that what he thinks are her best interests actually are."

"You think he's the one sending threatening letters to Willow?"

"My gut says no, but I can't rule him out."

Brandt stared at the mayor again, his dislike ratcheting up a notch, and he hadn't even met the man yet. "If he has feelings for Willow, why would he send threatening letters demanding that she leave?"

"Maybe, instead of getting her to leave, he wants her to come to him for help." Mack shrugged, picking up a gigantic onion ring. "It wouldn't be the first time he's played the hero for her. Besides, I know for a fact that although he was all for her coming home to Serena Bay, he was against her renovating the mission."

"Really?" Brandt tried to focus on his meal, but his thoughts kept straying to Willow. He'd only known her for two weeks, but knew she only saw the good in people. If she wouldn't think badly of some jerk pawing at her, she certainly wouldn't think badly of her high school friend.

"Why would Salazar not want Willow to renovate the mission?"

"To be fair, I was against it at the start, too," Mack said, nodding at a lady who'd paused to smile at him. "Willow's throwing almost all of her income at that place, and then some. I did find out, though, that one of the Salazar family companies was interested in the mission. Apparently, they'd wanted a big time developer to turn the place into a resort, and they'd been wooing the former owner to sell it to them. Sister Astencia chose Willow to inherit it."

Brandt nearly choked on a swallow of soda. "Your sister inherited that church?"

Mack nodded. "That mission's been here as long as the town's been here, which is saying something. It started as the church for the Salazars and others who settled the town, with a daughter of one of the founders running it. It was always passed down like that, run by a small group of nuns. Sister Astencia was the last one. She had Willow promise to keep and renovate the chapel, then transferred the property to her."

Brandt gave a low whistle. Beachfront property wasn't cheap, no matter where it was. The mission sat on some pretty prime real estate, and Willow's spread could very well be called an estate. He didn't even want to think what the hurricane insurance premiums were on it. "I'm betting that didn't make the Salazars happy."

"Not even a little," Mack said with a grim smile. "Old man Salazar supposedly dropped dead when he got the news. He was hoping the deal would redeem the family name in the town's eyes."

"What do you mean?" Brandt leaned forward, telling himself it was all part of the investigation, and not the need to discover that pretty-boy Tony had some flaws.

Mack scanned the bar before answering. "Like I said, the Salazars were one of the first families in Serena Bay. They still own a large part of it. Juan-Carlos Salazar, the mayor's old man, took it to the extreme, thinking that he could do whatever he wanted. He pretty much passed that along to Ricardo, Tony's older brother. That attitude nearly drove the town into bankruptcy."

"How in the world could something like that happen?" Brandt wondered. He had no idea how small town life worked, but it had to be pretty damn difficult to bankrupt a town.

"I wasn't here for most of it," Mack replied. "Basically, Ricardo didn't amount to much after high school, besides marrying the prettiest girl in town. Juan-Carlos was mayor at the time, and letting Ricardo run the family business. Ricardo knew crap about business, dear old dad tried to bail him out, and one thing led to another. Ricardo drove his car off Bay Bridge one night, which a lot of people will say, off the record, was the best thing he did for the town."

Mack sat back in his chair. "Anyway, Antonio came back from California for the funeral. When he heard what Ricardo had done, he flipped. He and his father had never gotten along—people used to call him 'the spare.' But he decided he had to do right by the town. Antonio reportedly made a lot of money with Internet companies and computer services before the big dot-com bust, so he bailed the town out. You could say that he owns the town now."

Brandt was unimpressed. "Is that why he's mayor now?"

Mack smiled. "Actually, he told the town he'd do the job for free, if they'd have him. The gamble paid off, but he's done more for this town than his father and brother combined. Like I said, Serena Bay's lucky to have him."

Brandt revised his opinion of Antonio Salazar. Not by much, but enough. Just because the man was capable of pulling an heroic act didn't mean he could keep it up all the time.

He wondered if Willow knew how bad the mayor had it for her. She had to. That beautiful face hid a mind like a bear trap, quick and sharp. She had to know, she was just ignoring it. Which made him wonder if she knew about him, about the blood on his hands.

A flare of anger heated inside him as he realized he was watching her again. He was about to turn away when he noticed her frown, then rub her forehead before briefly closing her eyes. Her fingers shook as she fisted her hand, dropped it to the tablecloth. It was a quick gesture, and the woman talking to her didn't seem to notice, but he did.

He turned back to Mack. "Rain check on the rest of the conversation, all right?" He stood, pulling his wallet from his back pocket.

"I've got this," Mack said, turning towards the back of the room. "Something going on?" The casualness of his words and posture didn't fool Brandt for a moment. He knew Mack was more than ready to handle any trouble Serena Bay could dish up.

"No, I think Willow's ready to go." He didn't know if Willow had told Mack about the intensity of her migraines, but he figured it wasn't his place. "I'll go see if I can give her an out."

CHAPTER TEN

"Mrs. Donaldson, I'm sure your son will be fine," Willow said, struggling not to rub her forehead again. "What he's going through is perfectly natural."

"Are you sure?" The older woman's round face quivered with anxiety. "I don't know."

"Willow, may I speak with you a moment?"

Brandt. She almost shook in relief at the interruption, but found it impossible to lift her head enough to meet his eyes. "Mrs. Donaldson, I'm sorry, but I need to go. Please, feel free to call my office on Monday and schedule some time to talk."

The chair groaned as the other woman hoisted herself to her feet and the sound reverberated in Willow's head like a jackhammer. She knuckled the tablecloth and managed what she hoped was a smile until the woman turned away. "Brandt, I'm—"

"Ready to leave, I know." He reached out his hand to her. She had to blink again, slower, seeing the spots swirling at the edges of her vision, before she could separate the shape of his hand from the shadows in the bar.

When she couldn't make her hands release the tablecloth, he reached down for her elbow. "Did you bring your medicine with you?"

"No." His voice was a distant rumble, blending with the low ebb and flow of pain that stirred just behind her eyes. She felt it like a fast-approaching thunderstorm, violent and destructive and completely indefensible.

"H-how did you know?"

"I happened to glance in your direction, saw you rubbing at your forehead," he explained, lifting her to her feet. Just the change in height caused her eyes to water. "You looked like you wanted to be anywhere but here, and I remembered you saying something about migraines."

She shut her eyes, clutching at his forearms. "Thank you."

Heat enveloped her as he stepped close. "It's going to get bad, isn't it?"

"Yeah." She had to swallow as a wave of dizziness swirled over her. "How do you want to do this?"

"As unobtrusively as possible," she replied, glad that he'd asked. "Is it okay if I just lean against your arm and keep my head down? I'm pretty sure I can make it out to the car without throwing up."

"Sure, but it might cause you some talk."

A shudder went through her. "As long as you don't throw me over your shoulder, I don't think I care."

"I can handle it," he said, "as long as you don't mind it looking like we're…close."

She sucked in a deep breath to steady her shifting insides. "That's the least of my worries."

"Okay."

She heard the jangle of keys, then he put her purse over her shoulder. Without another word he pulled her close, one large arm wrapping around her shoulders. She realized the top of her head barely reached his chin. She automatically froze up.

He paused. "Are you all right?"

"Yeah." She took another deep breath, forcing herself to relax. This was Brandt. Her brother's best friend. He was trying to help, not hurt her. Besides, tensing up only intensified her headache.

"I'm all right," she said, carefully putting her arm around his waist. She let her head drop, wishing she had her sunglasses. Even the dim lighting in Zeke's was enough to make her eyes water. "Let's go."

They hadn't gone three steps before Tony approached them. "Willow, what's going on?"

Brandt turned slightly, blocking her view. "We haven't met yet," he said, his voice a deep rumble along her side. "I'm Brandt Hughes, Mack's friend. Willow's ready to go home, and I'm taking her."

"Hughes." Willow could clearly hear ice in Tony's tone. "Antonio Salazar. I'd like to speak to Willow for a moment, if you don't mind."

She felt Brandt tense, and spoke before he could say or do something she'd regret. "I'm a little worn out, Tony."

"Evening, Mayor, Wil." Mack took that moment to join them, causing Willow to close her eyes on a groan of frustration and pain. "Brandt, thanks for driving my sister home. I appreciate it."

"No problem." Brandt relaxed, though not by much. Obviously he was taking his role as protector quite seriously, and Mack was clearly letting him. Like she needed protection against Tony.

Still, Willow decided to put a little distance between her and Brandt, though she still held onto his arm. She turned towards Tony's general direction. "I'll talk to you sometime tomorrow, okay?"

"Count on it." Mistrust colored his voice. Whatever he disliked about Brandt, Willow was glad he chose not to make a scene about it. Just thinking about all the testosterone flying was enough to ramp up the thunder in her head.

"We're almost at the door," Brandt said quietly. If she weren't in pain she'd marvel at his perceptiveness. Only when the moist heat of the night air hit her face did she try to open her eyes. The answering stab of pain made her cry out, clutch her head.

Brandt loosened his grip. "Mack, stay with her. I'll go get the car."

"Get the car?" Concern tightened Mack's voice. "Maybe we should call the hospital instead."

"No, I'll be fine, soon as I get home." She'd never told him how bad the migraines got, and she still didn't want him to know. "Stop worrying."

"Yeah. As soon as the tide stops rolling in." He wrapped an arm around her shoulders, supporting her. When he spoke again, his voice was little more than a breath. "Stop trying to keep everything from me. I'm your brother, and I'm going to have your back until I die, no matter who's in your life. Got it?"

"Got it." Her throat tightened against the threat of tears. The migraines always made her more emotional, but Mack's words threatened to do her in.

"You can trust him, you know," he said quietly. "Whatever faults he may have, Brandt is fanatical about protecting those he considers part of his family. You can trust him."

"Mack." The soft purr of an engine stopped her words. Mack guided her forward, opening the door and helping her into the passenger seat. Not wanting to be completely helpless, Willow fumbled with the seat belt.

"Go straight home and take care of yourself," Mack warned as he reclined her seat slightly. "I'd hate to have to arrest you for reckless endangerment." He shut the door, and then they were off.

Willow covered her face with her hands, wishing the pain would go away, wishing she could talk to her brother. Wishing her private life was as successful as her professional one, that she could just be herself with the people in her life. She sighed, and it made her head throb. Obviously the migraine was making her more maudlin than normal.

"Will air help?"

She let her hands fall away. Brandt drove the way he did everything else, with quiet competence that bordered on grace. Staring at his hands, she was suddenly overwhelmed with gratitude that he was there.

"Air would be nice," she whispered thickly. "Thank you."

He turned the air conditioner to its coldest setting, then looked at her before making a slow right turn. "Maybe a doctor should check you out."

"No." Blindly, she felt for the vent, adjusting the air flow to hit her face. Luckily she lived just a handful of miles south of the center of town; in a matter of minutes they'd reach the turn into her driveway. She could hold out that long without groaning. Or worse yet, throwing up. "I just have to ride this out. I wasn't expecting an attack today. Things were going pretty good before this."

It had been a good day. Her morning workouts with Brandt had settled into a comfortable routine. She'd been tense the first day, but his no-nonsense manner had quickly put her at ease. Now she almost jumped out of bed each morning, looking forward to their sparring. Just that morning she'd managed to throw him to the ground. Even if he'd let it happen, it had given her a sense of power that she'd carried straight into her office, tackling a difficult chapter and a phone call from a frantic client with complete assurance.

Two short weeks, and Brandt Hughes was already exerting a large influence on her life. If only she could return the favor and ease some of the darkness in his eyes. He hid it well, but there were times when she'd catch him staring into space. His features never changed, but the bleakness in his eyes in those unguarded moments hurt her to her soul. She'd do just about anything to see him truly smile.

Moments later, she had him pull over as her nausea got the better of her. He stood by her, calmly and quietly supporting her as she left her dinner in the pink oleander and bougainvilleas lining the road.

Mortification hit her full on. "I'm so sorry," she whispered, wiping at her mouth with a tissue he'd dug out of the glove box.

"You're sick, there's nothing to apologize about." He opened the rear passenger door. "Maybe you'll feel better if you stretch out."

"Good idea," she agreed. Then she could cry in private. The aura that heralded the imminent arrival of her migraine had been so bad that everything had been reduced to flickering lights and throbbing shadows. She stretched out on the back seat, closed her eyes, and concentrated on breathing. If she didn't get home soon, she'd claw the leather seats apart.

Luckily, Brandt seemed to realize that. The SUV moved smoothly and swiftly. In moments she felt the big vehicle slow, turn, then stop momentarily. She assumed that they were in front of her gate, the vehicle's sensor triggering the tall wrought-iron panels to open. Again, movement, then Brandt stopped, shifted the car into park, and killed the engine.

"Stay here," he said, getting out before she could answer. She'd barely dragged herself into an upright position when he returned.

"Can you make it?" His voice was doubtful. It made her want to try, if only to keep from embarrassing herself in front of him again.

"I'll certainly try," she sniffled, sliding off the seat and to her feet on the cobbled drive. Barely able to see, she stretched her hands out, depending on memory to get her up the four granite steps that led to the grand columned entrance.

Brandt dogged her steps, and again she was grateful for his presence. She usually had plenty of warning before one of her migraines struck, in the form of increasingly rough headaches for a handful of days beforehand, and always made sure her calendar was clear in case. That the mother of all migraines had pounced on her unawares filled her with apprehension.

She had to pause at the door as another wave of nausea struck her. Carlos Rosa would have a fit about her deposit in the potted topiary beside her door, but better there than on the sand-colored tile of her entryway.

Brandt handed her another tissue. She took it without looking at him, ashamed at being so weak. She'd always made sure she had no witnesses to her debilitating attacks; not even Pattie knew how horrendous they truly were. This one, though, felt as if it would be a personal best. She had ten, maybe fifteen minutes before the real pain began.

Brandt shut and locked the door after they entered. "I'll take you up to your room."

She stretched out a hand. "No, you've already done enough. The couch in the family room will be fine. All I need is the prescription stuff in my bathroom upstairs."

Her skin tingled as he stepped close. "I wasn't asking if it was all right. I just wanted to warn you." He scooped her up, as easily as if lifting a toddler.

She sucked in a surprised and fearful gasp. Everything in her wanted to protest but she couldn't muster the strength. Brandt had more than demonstrated his gentlemanly ways. He could have just gone up to his room after locking the door, his duty done. Instead, he was looking after her in such a kind, nurturing way that Willow knew it was more than duty, it was part of his nature.

She could trust him. She'd known that even before Mack had told her she should. More important, she felt safe with him. Even if she felt foolish for being carried up the stairs, sniffling and weeping like a baby, she felt protected. Only two people made her feel that way, her brother and Pattie, and she didn't think she could be this vulnerable with them. She didn't want to consider what she'd have done if the rogue migraine had ambushed her while she was alone.

"I'm really sorry about this," she said, even as she relaxed and rested her throbbing head against his shoulder.

"Shut up," he answered, his voice pleasant. He reached the top of the stairs, turning unerringly for the wing that housed the master suite. It didn't surprise her that he knew the way, any more than it had surprised her that he knew the most direct route home. He'd probably already scouted her house his first night in town, looking for weaknesses in her defenses. Brandt Hughes was definitely a planner and a strategist, studying all contingencies before acting.

Still, once they reached the door to her suite, she tensed. The only men who'd been inside her master bedroom were the men who'd delivered the rosewood platform bed and matching furniture, and Pattie had supervised that.

The world tilted as Brandt placed her on her bed, high among the mountain of pillows. "I'm going to slip off your shoes for you," he informed her, "then you can tell me where your medicine is."

She hugged a couple of pillows tight, not breathing as he pulled her shoes off. "It's fine now. Really. You've done enough already."

He ignored her words. "Where's your medicine?"

"Bathroom cabinet," she whispered, grateful for the pillows framing her, the darkness that shielded her.

"Close your eyes," he warned her before moving away. She complied, hearing a snap as he turned on a light, probably looking for her bathroom. Another click, then footsteps retreating, heading for her bathroom.

She heard the low sound of him rummaging around, but felt too much pain to feel embarrassed at the thought of him sorting through her medicine cabinet.

Soon enough he returned. "I'm going to get you a glass of water and let Boscoe out of his crate. Anything else you need?"

She opened her eyes to half-mast. "Sledgehammer?" She half-meant it. The low rumble had elevated to a mean rumbling.

His lips quirked. Had he almost smiled? "Good thing I locked those up before we left." A click, the sound of the bedside lamp being switched off. "I'll be right back."

Willow waited a beat, then opened her eyes all the way. He was gone. She eased upright, breathing hard to combat the dizziness. Climbing to her feet, she navigated the rapidly expanding distance to her bathroom by the light of a small automatic nightlight. By the time she reached the vanity area and flipped the switch for the walk in closet, she was sweating, her brain throbbing.

Rinsing her mouth and splashing her face with cool water eased the thunder crashing through her brain back to a dull roar. Brandt had brought her prescription to her, but she knew only time would truly end the agony. Time, and half a bottle of rum for encouragement.

With alcohol out of the question, she settled for changing into her nightgown. She unzipped the linen pants, letting them slip to the floor. Unfortunately she ran out of steam trying to pull the blouse over her head.

Suddenly, everything overwhelmed her. She leaned against the wall, trapped in her stupid blouse, and burst into tears.

A soft whine and thudding footsteps announced the arrival of Brandt and Boscoe. Her dog pressed against her legs protectively as a pair of hands gently turned her, reached for the keyhole button at the back of her neck that kept her prisoner in her blouse. She stiffened as he helped her pull the fabric over her head, afraid to move or say anything.

He immediately turned away, a large shadow outlined by the glow filtering from the nightlight beside the louvered doors of her walk-in closet. His hand reached out, fumbling for her nightgown pooled on the counter. He thrust it behind him in her general direction. "Here."

Taking a deep breath, Willow pulled her gown out of his hand and over her head. She hurt too much to be apprehensive about his attention or intention, but she felt as close to dying of embarrassment as she could get. "Thank you."

He didn't turn around, as immovable as an Easter Island statue. "Should I call Pattie for you, someone to help?" Someone female, he meant. He sounded as uncomfortable as she felt, and that reassured her.

"No." She sagged against the counter, wiping at her leaking eyes before cupping her forehead in her hands. "I'd rather not have anymore witnesses to this. I'll be fine once I lie down."

"Do you promise to stay down this time?" He caught her up again, not even a grunt at her weight, and stalked out of the bathroom and to her bed with sure strides. She didn't bother protesting.

"Yes," she said meekly as he set her down beside the bed. She sank onto the mattress as he opened her prescription and shook a tablet out. "I'm so tired."

He handed her the pill and the glass of water. "Then you need to relax, try to get some sleep. Even you can't be Superwoman all the time."

Was that the way he saw her? She certainly didn't feel super-capable these days. If anything, she felt as if she'd eaten some high-grade kryptonite.

"I don't want to be a superwoman," she whispered, lethargy overcoming her as she slipped beneath the covers. "I just want to be me, whomever that is."

Boscoe nosed her once in entreaty. Brandt made a sharp gesture with his right hand, and her border collie heeled. "It's all right," she whispered, her eyes sliding shut as she patted the side of the bed. "I can use the company."

Boscoe carefully leapt onto the bed, nosed her once, then curled into a ball beside her. She dug her fingers into his fur, comforted by his presence.

She heard Brandt clear his throat. "I'm just going to leave your door open a crack. If you need anything, just give me a call. I'll come back and check on you every once in a while."

"Brandt." She paused, gathering the effort to say what she needed to say. The process of forming words, of thinking, increased the pounding in her skull. She had just minutes before the full force of the migraine hit, and she didn't want him to witness it. "Don't put yourself out. Just because you promised Mack—"

"I'm doing this for you, not for Mack."

The anger in his voice jerked her eyes open. She'd insulted him. "I'm sorry."

"Stop apologizing." Heat left his voice. "Just try to get some sleep."

Still, she had to let him know, "You've done more than a lot of people would have. Thank you for that."

"Good night, Willow," she heard him say, and then felt him leave. She curled against her dog and the pillows, the tears streaming down her face from more than the migraine.

CHAPTER ELEVEN

"Willow. Wake up, Willow."

She jerked her eyes open, running away from fragments of dark dreams. Brandt's face wavered in her vision. Brandt?

Gasping, Willow pulled the sheet high around her neck. What the hell was Brandt doing in her bedroom? She struggled to sit up. Her head and stomach immediately offered simultaneous protests. She slumped back against the pillows as she remembered the previous night.

"You were moaning in your sleep," Brandt offered as explanation, looking towards her instead of at her. She appreciated the nicety, especially since she probably looked like a zombie.

She brushed at her eyes and her braids, pushing sleep away. Daylight filtered through the bamboo blind that covered the balcony door. She usually slept with it partially open, preferring to be lulled to sleep by the ocean instead of medication. Although her migraine was marginally better, she was glad sunrise hadn't awakened her. It would have been like Dracula caught outside at dawn.

"Good morning?" She tested the phrase, hoping it was still morning.

"Morning," he confirmed, watching her carefully. He was already dressed for work in his trademark faded jeans and a dark green t-shirt that put moody shadows in his eyes. The tan leather toolbelt circled his waist like a gunslinger's belt and drew attention to his chest and arms. He took more care of that belt and the specialty tools it held than most people did their cars. Despite wearing the belt, he didn't look like he'd started his day yet.

Actually he looked tired, and she wondered how often he'd gotten up and checked on her during the night. As she studied him, a neutral expression shaded his features. "How do you feel?"

"Better?" She heard the question in her own voice and wondered if he'd caught it. The frown he gave indicated yes.

"Better being a relative term," he observed, snagging the amber pill bottle off her nightstand to hand to her. "Here. I'll bring you a fresh glass of water."

She shook her head, handing the bottle back to him. "No, but thanks. I'll just use the over-the-counter stuff today."

He frowned again. "This is maintenance medication. You're supposed to take it every day."

"I know that." She paused, staring up at him. "How do you know that?"

His eyes shifted away from her. "I read the label, and did some research on the Web." He stiffened to defense mode. "I said I'd watch out for you."

He meant what he said and did what he meant. Brandt Hughes kept his promises. If she'd learned anything about him in the past few days, she'd learned that he had a code of honor that defined him, just like her brother did.

She sighed. "I guess I needed watching over last night, right?" It galled her to admit it, though, to admit to being vulnerable. Embarrassment at needing him to help her undress swept up her throat to burn her ears. "Now you know more about me than you probably wanted. You could sell the story and make a quick buck: 'Celebrity Shrink's Mysterious Illness' or something dramatic like that."

"Not interested." His gaze focused on her again. "Are you going to take your medicine?"

He was like Boscoe playing tug-of-war with his favorite chew toy. Completely immovable. "No. It turns me into a zombie. I can't afford to be zoned out like that."

"Is that a technical diagnosis, Doctor?"

Willow just stared up at him. Had Brandt Hughes just made a joke? "Did you just make a joke? Because shock therapy isn't going to work either."

"Fine, no medicine." When she struggled to get up, he held out his hand. "That means you should take it easy today. I'll bring you some coffee or tea to help your head. I'll even bring up your legal pad and voice recorder."

"My laptop would be more efficient."

"Yeah, getting a crook in your neck staring at the screen will do wonders for a migraine," he said dryly. "Not gonna happen."

She opened her mouth to protest. He frowned at her, and she chose silence instead. She'd become adept at interpreting his frowns. This one was a blend of "you're being irresponsible," and "I'm getting my way and you'll thank me later."

He'd used that combination the first time she'd balked when he'd ordered her to hip-toss him to the sand. He'd made her feel like a ten-year-old, and it had ticked her off enough that she'd tossed him, exactly as he'd asked. And she'd felt so good about being able to do the move that she had thanked him for it.

He didn't have to teach her self-defense. He certainly didn't have to help her out last night. He didn't have to hold her upright while she lost her dinner, or haul her up the stairs. He didn't have to rescue her from her own blouse, or turn his back while she changed, then make sure she made it to bed. He didn't have to watch over her while she slept, or check up on her this morning.

He didn't have to do any of it, but he had anyway.

Brandt Hughes was amazing. And she had to admit, if only to herself, that she was thrilled that he was there.

Fully prepared for an argument, Brandt was caught by surprise when Willow smiled at him. Her eyes were still hazy from sleep or the migraine or both, but that smile told him the worst was over. That smile made him feel ridiculously pleased. If he had a tail, he'd be wagging it.

He scowled instead. "What?"

If anything, her smile grew. He tried not to feel panic, or fear, or anything else. Especially not the unfamiliar warmth that spread through his chest like indigestion.

"I just wanted to thank you," she said, her voice shy behind the smile.

Discomfort settled hard on his shoulders. He tried to shake it off. "You thanked me yesterday."

She tilted her head to the left, something she seemed to do when thinking. No, not thinking—analyzing. The movement made her frown, and she reached up to rub her forehead. Maybe the worst wasn't over. It worried him that she still hurt. And it bothered him that he was worried.

"I thanked you," she said slowly, "but that was before I realized how much it meant. You didn't have to help me, you probably didn't want to help me, but you did."

"I couldn't leave you like that," he said brusquely, growing more uncomfortable by the second. She didn't need to keep thanking him. He'd done what needed to be done, that was all. "I wouldn't leave anyone like that."

"I know." She said it softly, gently, and it made him wonder exactly what she knew. "Still, most people wouldn't have done what you did."

"I'm not most people." Why didn't she just drop it?

"I know that too." She slouched back down into the pillows. "I'm glad you're not. I hope that means you're not just Mack's friend, but my friend too."

How in the hell was he supposed to be her friend? Every friend he'd had outside of business and family had faded into the woodwork four years ago. Only Mack remained, and only because he didn't live in Atlanta. Brandt had no clue how to be anybody's friend anymore.

He remembered what he'd told Mack the previous night. *There's no such thing as friendship between men and women. A man calls a woman friend, it just means he hasn't made his move yet.*

"I-I'll go get your coffee, or tea, or something," he said, backing away from her. She continued to smile at him, and it was all he could do to whistle for Boscoe instead of turning and running.

He didn't try to breathe until he reached the hall. He turned, then froze. *Oh, hell.*

Pattie stood in the hall at the head of the stairs, one hand still on the rail. Dressed rather conservatively in a lemon yellow sundress, she looked as surprised as he felt.

He snatched his hand away from the doorknob. "It's not what you think."

Pattie looked past him to the closed door. "Too bad."

"Excuse me?"

Pattie's strawberry-red mouth widened in a grin. "I personally think it's a great idea."

He didn't have to ask what she meant. He'd quickly learned that Greyhound buses were subtler than Pattie DuPri. Brandt stalked past her, suddenly needing fresh air. "I'm not having this conversation with you."

"Why not?" Pattie shadowed him down the stairs, waiting while he let Boscoe out into the side yard. "You're here, she's here. She needs someone like you."

A half-laugh seeped from him. "Willow definitely doesn't need someone like me." He wouldn't wish himself on anyone, certainly not someone as tenderhearted as Willow.

He entered the kitchen, Pattie following him. The smell of high-octane hazelnut coffee filtered through the room. Idly, he wondered if it was too early to add a shot of Bailey's to it.

Willow with him. It was too impossible to even contemplate. "Willow doesn't need me," he said again, wondering who he was trying to convince. "Besides, she can take care of herself." At least, when she wasn't suffering from migraines.

Pattie nodded. "Herself and half the town, and never break a sweat. She doesn't need someone to take care of her. I'm not talking about that kind of need. I mean the kind of need that wakes you in the middle of the night, the kind of need that makes her sit out on the beach and stare into the ocean for hours, just her and the sea and the sand."

She opened a cabinet, removing a large coffee mug. "I'm talking about companionship, pure and simple."

"Isn't that why she's got a dog?"

Pattie just looked at him. "Human companionship. Being curled up with another person, it's the best thing in the world. I have a feeling you could use a little of that too."

Brandt stared at the woman, wondering if she'd lost her mind. Or maybe he was the one who'd entered an alternate universe. "You've barely said two words to me since I got here, and now you're offering your boss up on a silver platter?"

She looked offended. "If that's what you think I'm doing, then I've misjudged you. Worse, you've misjudged Willow. I've been with her for a long time, since she started her practice in Los Angeles. My husband and I followed her here because I'm loyal to her and love her like a daughter. So understand, I will always have her best interests at heart."

Her movements were quick, angry, as she prepared a tray. "I'm not asking you to fall in love with her, or try to make her fall in love with you. She'd see through that in a heartbeat. But you're a healthy single man, and she's a healthy single woman. And you're both lonely. Seems only right to think that you'd be less lonely together."

"I don't think about Willow like that!"

The older woman laughed. She actually laughed. "Sugar, you can lie to yourself all you want, but you can't lie to me."

"She's my best friend's sister!"

"All the more reason, if you ask me." She poured coffee into the mug. "Means you'll be more inclined to be honest."

She set the mug on a tray, added cream and sugar servers before retrieving a bowl of cut melons from the fridge. "Once you're honest with yourself, that is." She lifted the tray, smiled at him. "Now, I'd better get this coffee upstairs before it gets cold."

He shook his head and poured a cup of coffee as Pattie left. The women in Serena Bay were crazy. He had no other explanation for it.

Willow took kindness to a fault, when she, of all people in this town, needed to be cautious. Pattie suddenly playing matchmaker, or madam, out of nowhere.

Like he needed help in that area. When he'd wanted to find willing women, he'd found them. Even after he'd made sure they understood that he wasn't a long-term man. It had amazed him to find women who were the same, more than a few globe-crossing, professional women who didn't have time for anything other than their careers, and were satisfied with their choices. No promises, no regrets.

While Willow definitely fit into the globe-trotting, professional category, he had a feeling she didn't do casual relationships. Nothing about Dr. Willow Zane was casual or simple. Those dark eyes held a world of secrets that lured him like a siren calling ships to their doom.

He remembered how she'd felt cradled in his arms the night before, all warm and trusting even while in pain. Her height might be average, but her figure wasn't, as he'd learned when he'd freed her from her blouse. Even by the thin light from her closet he'd seen the lushness of her figure, a figure only hinted at during their early morning workouts.

She was a mixture of tone and curves, round in all the right places. Seeing a woman in her underwear was different from seeing her in a swimsuit or bike shorts. A lot different. He couldn't deny the rush of heat that had blindsided him while he'd attempted to be a gentleman.

That was his problem. He'd been trying with a desperate single-mindedness to keep things strictly impersonal with Willow while keeping his promise to Mack to look after her. Every protective instinct his parents had bred into him had swung into action last night when he'd realized Willow wasn't feeling well. He'd told her the truth when he'd said he couldn't leave anyone like that. Truth was, though, he definitely couldn't leave her hurting like that.

Maybe it had been the look on her face when he'd dealt with the construction worker. Maybe it had to do with the fact that to see her as anything other than so damned composed seemed unnatural. All he knew was that taking care of her was something he'd had to do, including getting up every hour to check on her, despite her not wanting him to.

It had been the same way with Sarah, this instinctive need to protect. She'd needed him, and he'd needed to be needed. Taking care of women and kids was the way the men in his family were built. Even though he knew Willow and his late wife were nothing alike, he felt the same driving desire to look out for her.

Desire crawled through him, and he realized that protecting her wasn't the only thing he wanted to do for Willow. He couldn't immediately remember the last woman he'd been with, or when. A montage of new memories swept through his mind: Willow in her turquoise dress, smiling at him as she offered to make sweet tea. Soft fingers caressing his hand, soothing the sting away. He could still recall the brilliant smile she'd given him a little while ago. He wanted more of that.

He wanted more of her.

"Damn it," he muttered, rinsing out his coffee cup before putting it in the dishwasher. He didn't need to think about Willow as anything other than his best friend's sister. Anything else would only lead to trouble, and he'd had enough of that to last a lifetime.

He headed for the door, wanting to leave before Pattie returned and he did something really stupid, like ask her what Willow thought of him.

CHAPTER TWELVE

"That Mr. Brandt is something, isn't he?"

Hearing the speculative tone in Pattie's voice, Willow set aside her notepad. Her migraine had mostly abated. With another half hour of recuperation she'd be ready to shower, dress, and head down to her office in the mission. The damn book wouldn't write itself, and she definitely needed to get ahead before Pattie left on vacation.

"Brandt is nice," she said carefully, trying to guess at Pattie's intent. Her assistant had arrived with coffee and smiles, big, bright smiles that made Willow wonder if Pattie had caught Brandt leaving the bedroom. Not that she intended to ask. What Pattie didn't know wouldn't come back to haunt Willow later.

Pattie flitted around the room like a human-sized canary, rolling up the shades on the balcony door and the windows, tossing the discarded clothing in the closet hamper. Willow tried not to wince. With Pattie in nurturing mode, Willow knew she was headed for trouble.

"*Nice*, she says," Pattie muttered. "All that hard work on the chapel, mostly by himself, hardly ever taking a break. And all those muscles!" She became glassy-eyed. "Why, if I wasn't married, I would be all over that!"

"But you are married," Willow pointed out, almost against her will.

Pattie opened the balcony door, letting in the late June heat tempered by the omnipresent ocean breeze. "Yes, I am married," she said, taking a deep breath. Her expression grew sly. "But you're not."

Ah-hah. Willow narrow her eyes, part-defense against streaming sunlight, part warning. "Pattie."

"Oh, don't look at me like that. A body'd have to be dead not to notice how fine that man is, like toffee and Belgian chocolate. I may be old, but I sure ain't dead." She speared Willow with a meaningful look. "And neither are you, if you don't mind me saying so."

Willow did mind. Quite a bit. "He's my brother's best friend, and a guest in my house," she reminded her assistant. "And I'm his client. Remember, he's the guy fixing the chapel?"

"That old church ain't the only thing needing an expert touch."

Willow felt her ears heat. "Pattie, that's enough!"

"No, it's not." Pattie settled her fists on her curvy hips, a sure sign that she'd ramped up to mothering and lecturing mode.

"You haven't been on a date since we came here. Don't try to tell me that it's because there aren't any single men in Serena Bay, because that's a lie. Besides, you hardly even dated in L.A."

"I had a full schedule in L.A.," Willow pointed out. "Things haven't slowed down just because I'm on the East Coast. You know what my schedule's like."

"Of course I know, I'm the one who makes it," Pattie retorted. "Which is why I know that if you actually wanted to date, you'd find time to date."

"Fine. I don't want to date." Willow swung her legs over the side of the bed. "What's wrong with that?"

"What wrong? You inherited the mission from a nun. She didn't say you had to become one."

That hurt. Willow reached for her robe as she climbed to her feet, pulling the edges together with jerky motions. "I am not becoming a nun."

"Really?" Pattie folded her arms under her ample chest. "All you do is work. The books, your clients, charity. Even your vacations are work-related since you combine them with different conferences and speaking engagements. You're thirty-two and at the top of your field. Don't you think it's time to play, at least a little? Take time for yourself?"

God. Willow felt like a teen being lectured about not going to college. Pattie was the closest thing she had to a mother, and it killed her to hear the disappointment in Pattie's voice.

"That's why I moved back here, you know that. To try to slow down, be near Mack. And I do take time for myself."

"You turn dinner with the mayor into pro bono sessions for the entire town. You have lunch with Miss Zanteras like it's a business appointment. You don't take time for yourself, Willow. You don't."

Willow clenched her hands into fists. "Did Mack put you up to this?" She'd kill him.

"No. This is my own bright idea." Pattie crossed the room to stand next to her. "I just—I just want you to be happy, Willow. You deserve to have fun."

"I am happy." If her own assistant didn't believe she had a full life, what did other people think? A garden-variety headache made its presence known at the back of her skull. "I have a full life, a dream career, and wonderful friends."

"What about family?"

The soft question struck like an open slap, hard and stinging. The idea of having a family, of being a mother, frightened her. Her own mother had walked away when Willow was six, leaving her and Mack with a father as cold as he was strict. By the time Mack left, that coldness had hardened to cruelty. While she knew behaviors were learned, not inherited, Willow felt terror that she might do to her children what her parents had done to her.

"Not every woman wants or needs to reproduce," she said, staring out at the ocean. "If it's good enough for Oprah, why can't it be good enough for me?"

"It's not a question of what's good enough," Pattie said. "I'd also like to remind you that even Oprah has a steady. Even if you don't think about the future, you should think about right now, enjoying life to the fullest right now."

"You mean think about Brandt."

"Why not?" Pattie wondered. "You're both single, right? You're both fine-looking people. And you're both here. What's the harm in having a simple little fling?"

Because it wouldn't be simple, for either of them. Brandt obviously still had issues with losing his wife and son. Willow herself had issues with intimacy that the word frigid didn't even begin to cover.

"There's a lot wrong with it, beginning with the fact that it wouldn't be right," Willow said, turning away from the view to face her assistant. "The only reason Brandt came down here is because Mack asked him to spy on me. The only reason he's staying is because of the mission. I'm sure Brandt views me as a little sister, nothing more."

"Sure he does." Sarcasm filled Pattie's voice. "Just like you view him as a carpenter, nothing more. You keep thinking like that. You might even start to believe it."

With that, Pattie left the bedroom. Willow stared after her for a full minute before shaking her head, causing her head to pound in protest. Brandt wasn't interested in her. Even if he was, playing nursemaid to her last night had surely killed whatever interest he'd had. Something about holding her hair while she puked in the shrubbery told her that Brandt Hughes wouldn't be kissing her anytime soon.

Did she want him to? She thought about it as she started her shower. Brandt Hughes was fine. She couldn't deny that. The way he shaped a piece of wood made her nerve endings stand at attention and salute.

She could almost imagine a different outcome to the previous night: Being carried up to her bedroom in his capable arms. Seeing the need on his face as he placed her on the bed, his fingers reaching for her blouse. Hearing the fabric rip even as she begged…

She jerked her eyes open with a ragged gasp. Memories nearly two decades old swamped her, causing goosebumps to stand out on her arms. She'd tried forgetting, she'd tried fighting, and she'd tried psychoanalyzing. Nothing had eradicated the memories. Not even time. The images, the sounds, all of the sensations were as sharp and biting as if she'd been assaulted yesterday.

Shivering, she stepped into the steaming shower. The temperature reddened her skin but did nothing to ease the chill in her bones. Her fingers curled into her palms as she wrestled with age-old fears and emotions. Pattie could attempt to convince Willow of the joys of relationships as long as she wanted, but it wouldn't change anything. No matter how much Willow longed for a relationship, a family, her body would make sure she never got the chance.

CHAPTER THIRTEEN

"Hughes, I want a word with you."

Brandt looked up from the box of flooring he held. Antonio Salazar stood in the doorway of the chapel, dressed for business in khakis and a red button-down shirt.

Great. He had a good idea what the words were that the honorable Mayor Salazar wanted, and he wasn't in the mood to hear them.

He placed the box of floorboards onto the log-cabin shaped stack he'd already begun. "Can it wait? I need to let these floorboards acclimate for a couple of days before the installation. If you have questions about the chapel, or anything else for that matter, you should probably discuss them with Dr. Zane."

"Actually, the questions I have concern you," Salazar said, moving into the chapel so that the door swung shut behind him.

"Something you need my professional opinion on?" It was an effort to keep his tone disinterested when he really wanted the mayor to make his point and get it over with.

"Something like that." The mayor stopped, surveyed the progress.

"Hope you don't mind if I keep working." Brandt moved past him, not caring if the mayor minded or not. "This floor's not going to install itself, and I still have to bring in the medallion centerpiece."

"How are you enjoying our fair city?"

"Well enough, I suppose." He reached the foyer and propped the door open again, then headed for the pallet of boxed floorboards. "Haven't seen that much of it."

"I highly recommend taking a tour," Salazar said easily, shadowing him. "There's a lot of history here."

"So I hear." Brandt balanced three boxes on his shoulder, then turned, narrowly missing the mayor. Too bad.

"I know several of our local hotels offer tours as part of their packages," Salazar said easily, following him back into the chapel. "You should think about checking into one."

"Why?"

"Why?" the other man echoed, as if surprised that Brandt would have the nerve to question him. "Because supposedly the only reason you're here is to work on this chapel. There's no reason for you to stay here. I think you're taking advantage of Willow's kind-hearted nature, Mr. Master Carpenter."

Brandt put down his load, then stripped off his work gloves. "My arrangement with my client is none of your business."

"Considering she's one of my constituents, I'd say it's very much my business," Salazar said. "The needs of Serena Bay's citizens will always be my primary concern."

Brandt ran his forearm across his brow, wicking away sweat. He couldn't believe the man had actually made the statement straight-faced. "I'm onsite at my client's request, and the sheriff's," Brandt finally said. "If you've got a problem, maybe you should take it up with them."

"Does she know about you?"

Brandt froze. "Know what about me?"

The pleasant, humble civil servant demeanor slipped off the other man as if he'd shed a raincoat. "Don't play stupid with me. You know very well what I'm talking about."

"That's enough."

Willow's voice, harsher than he'd ever heard it, cut between them. Brandt turned towards her, ready to apologize without knowing why. The sight of her standing in the doorway, dark sunglasses over her eyes and with her hands firmly planted on her hips had him shutting up. He knew that stance boded ill for anyone ignorant or stupid enough to push the woman holding it.

Salazar apparently had no idea what the pose meant. "Willow, give me a moment—"

Oh no, he didn't.

"Excuse me, Mayor Salazar." Willow's chin lifted. "As pleased as I am to have you stop by Phoenix Haven, it would help us if your office called ahead so that we could make suitable arrangements for you. For instance, the chapel is off limits to non-essential personnel. Even I don't step in here without a hard hat and workboots, and I own the place."

Her smile reminded Brandt more of a lawyer going in for the kill than a compassionate psychologist. "I'm sure you can understand my desire to adhere to safety regulations?"

The mayor straightened. "Of course, I was just—"

"Checking on the progress of the center?" Willow half-turned, gesturing back into the hallway. "If you'll follow me to my office, I'll be happy to give you a quick report. That way, we can all get back to our busy schedules."

Salazar looked pissed, which pleased Brandt. He made sure none of his pleasure showed on his face as the other man stalked across the concrete subfloor to join Willow.

Willow resisted the urge to fold her arms across her chest and concentrated on reining in her anger instead. "Brandt, we'll let you get back to work."

He looked at her, something unreadable in his eyes. "Thank you, Doctor."

She simply nodded, turning as Tony came abreast of her. "As you can see, the chapel still needs a lot of work, but the roof is completely sound again. The floors will start first thing Monday, including carpeting the remaining offices and tiling the main dining room. Let me show you my offices."

Keeping up a stream of detached information, Willow led Tony down the hall to her suite of offices on the ocean side of the building. The hallway belled into a waiting alcove painted a pale green. All it lacked were the chairs and greenery that would transform it into a reception area.

The door just north of the alcove stood open. Willow entered to find Pattie at their new favorite toy, an espresso wet bar that fronted the ocean view. Both their offices were done in soothing sea blues and greens, the wood in the furniture the blond color of golden sand.

"Give me just a few shakes of a sheep's tail, and I'll have a caramel latte ready to go for you," Pattie said. She turned, surprise crossing her face. "Oh, Mr. Mayor, I didn't know you were coming here today."

"Don't worry about it, Pattie," Willow said, crossing to the connecting door to her office. "It's just an unofficial visit. Mayor?" She stood aside so that he could enter the office.

"You've got a lot of nerve, Tony," she fumed once the door closed behind them. "Do I come down to City Hall and grill your employees?"

"None of my employees are sleeping down the hall from me," he retorted. "If he is still down the hall."

Willow pulled her sunglasses off as her anger spiked. "That's a low blow, Mayor. I don't care how long we've been friends, you've got no right to tell me who I can invite into my home."

"I'm not going to apologize," Tony said. "Something about that guy rubs me wrong. What do you know about him?"

"I know enough," she said, pulling open a desk drawer to retrieve a bottle of aspirin. She was only a couple of hours into the backside of the migraine, but dealing with this was sure to trigger a minor episode.

"You know enough." Tony stared at her in exasperation. "You're letting the guy stay in your house, and all you can say is that you know enough?"

"For the last time, I know everything about Brandt Hughes that I need to know." She dry-swallowed the aspirin, putting the bottle back and shutting the drawer with more force than necessary. "I told you that last night. You have no right to come onto my property and talk to him behind my back."

"Someone needs to do something. Your brother obviously doesn't care how this looks for you."

"I'm not running for office, so I don't really care how this looks to anybody." She narrowed her eyes. "But you should be relieved. At least this will kill the rumors that you and I are having an affair."

"Dammit, Willow!" He dug a hand through his hair. "I don't care what people say about that."

"Well, you need to make up your mind, because you can't have it both ways. You either care what people say or you don't. Either way, you need to stop acting like a jealous boyfriend!"

She stopped as a guilty flush stole through his olive skin. "Ah, hell, Tony."

Awkwardness fell between them, heavy and dead. Willow silently cursed herself. She'd been careful to keep her revived relationship with Tony completely platonic, to leave the failed attempt at romance in the past where it belonged. Obviously, hoping that Tony could do the same had been a mistake.

She and Tony were close, as close as two unrelated people could be. He'd been the one person who had always been there for her, and she'd always been there for him, since freshman year of high school. That they'd been able to salvage their friendship meant everything to her. Had she led him on in some way, made him believe they could be more than friends again?

"Willow. *Mierda*." He swore softly in a fluid string of Spanish, a sure sign of being upset. He turned to her, settling his hands on her shoulders. "I got my hopes up when you came back here, and that's not your fault. Just like it's not your fault that I'm too stupid to let go of a teenage dream. You haven't done anything other than be my friend, and I'm grateful you gave me a second chance at that."

He rested his forehead against hers, and she had to lock her muscles to keep from stepping away from him. "I'm coming to grips with that, I swear. Just give me time to figure out what I'm supposed to be with you, okay?"

She wiped a surreptitious hand across her eyes, then took a deep breath, gently pulling away. "Okay."

"I still think you should be careful around this guy." He held up his hands as she started to protest. "Last time I'll say it, I swear. Just keep your guard up, okay?"

He stepped back from her, then pasted a smile on his face. "So tell me, are you making this place wireless or what?"

She welcomed the blatant change of subject. "I'm trying, but it looks like we're having issues with the hub."

He unbuttoned his cuffs, then began to roll up his sleeves. "I've got an hour or so until they need me back at the office. Let me see what you've got. Tell Pattie I'll give her email if she'll give me a toffee nut latte."

CHAPTER FOURTEEN

"What are you drawing?"

Brandt flipped the pad over as Willow entered the sunroom carrying two glasses of red wine, Boscoe at her heels. She'd changed from work clothes into a long black dress that looked like a potato sack. Her braids swung freely about her freshly-scrubbed face as she handed him a glass, then curled into the loveseat opposite him, tucking her bare feet under her.

"Thanks. I'm sketching my nieces," he said easily, though he tensed inside. She'd been subdued throughout dinner, even with Mack stopping by to check up on her. She'd blamed it on a headache, but Brandt wasn't so sure. The extra glass of wine proved it. She usually had half a glass at dinner, and that was it. Obviously her talk with Salazar hadn't gone well, and he wondered if the time had finally come for him to come clean with her.

She took a sip from her glass, leaning back to dim the setting on the lamp beside her. "Will you tell me about them?"

"There's nothing much to tell," he said, not wanting to reveal himself to her, yet not wanting to drive her away. "Leila and Tamera are nine and ten and belong to my oldest sister, Nadine, and Taylor's nine and stepdaughter to my middle sister, Maya. The littlest princess is two-year-old Gianna, who belongs to my middle brother, Dwayne."

"No nephews?"

"Two," he answered. "Jaremy is four and Zachary is almost a year and a half."

She drew her legs up and rested her chin on her knees, if the stiffness of her back could be called resting. "It sounds like you have a large family. How many brothers and sisters are there?"

"Three brothers and three sisters," he said, putting down his glass before turning the sketchpad back over. He wondered if he could capture Willow as she was now, caught between the glow of the lamp and the shadows in the corner, between wanting to stay and preparing to go. She was nothing but a study of contrasts, two different people in public and private, making him wonder if she ever revealed her true self to anyone. "Once my youngest sister left the house, Mom and Dad decided to become foster parents. Ten foster kids and their entire neighborhood call them Ma and Pa Hughes."

"They sound like good-hearted people."

"They are." He stopped drawing. "Everything I know about loyalty and doing what's right I learned from them. They'll be celebrating their fiftieth anniversary in a couple of years, and all the kids are getting together to send them on a trip around the world."

"Wow. That must be nice, having that kind of family," she said, a wistful smile playing at her lips. "You're very lucky, you know."

"Yeah." He did know. He hadn't really thought about it before, not in terms of being lucky. He did know that the only reason he was still around was because of his family, particularly Maya. Whenever he felt the darkness threatening to swallow him whole, Maya or Taylor would call, unknowingly bringing him back from the edge.

He cleared his throat. "I guess it was completely different for you, with it being just you and Mack."

"Yeah." Her voice changed, as if she'd strayed onto a topic she'd rather not discuss. She hugged her knees, rocking slightly. "Mom gave me this ridiculous name, then left when I was six. I don't remember anything about her, though, and our father didn't keep any photos or anything. Then Mack left for the service and it was just me and our father until I left right after high school."

He remained silent. If she didn't want him to know she'd run away, he wouldn't call her on it. He had his own secret to keep.

"I don't think it's ridiculous."

She lifted her head, focused on him. It was like being touched. "What?"

"Your name. It suits you."

A frown crossed her features. "What, I'm a spindly, weak thing that bends in the slightest breeze?"

"Shows what you know. Sure, a Willow is delicate and graceful, but it's more than just a pretty tree. People use Willow for paper, charcoal, and making baskets. They've been using Willow bark for centuries for its medicinal value. It's where aspirin comes from. Willow grows quickly; you can cut it down to nothing and it'll spring back in a season. That's why different cultures associate it with vitality and even immortality. It's pretty and helps people. So yeah, I think the name suits you fine."

She blinked at him. Then she straightened, staring at him in wide-eyed wonder. "You…thank you. That was poetry. I got teased so much in school that I hated my name by the time I got to college. I think I love my name now."

He started sketching again, uncomfortable. "Yeah, well, I'm a carpenter. I know wood. I could go on for days about oak, or even mahogany."

A smile lit her face, the first he'd seen in a while. He'd missed it. "Maybe some other time."

She lifted a hardcover off the African-style kettle drum that doubled as a coffee table. It was an epic fantasy novel, which probably shouldn't have surprised him, but did. Somehow he hadn't thought she'd be into commercial fiction.

"I'm sorry about that thing with Tony," she said into the quiet. "He's usually very nice."

"Don't worry about it," he said, knowing that she would. "I'd have a problem too, if a strange man moved in with my lady."

"I'm not his lady."

The vehemence in her voice came through loud and clear. He believed her. "You might want to tell him that." At her sharp glance, he added, "His Honor didn't say you were seeing each other, but that's the impression that I got."

She sighed, looking away. He busied himself with trying to capture her mobile features, waiting. Just as he did, Willow talked about herself only when she was good and ready.

Finally she stirred. "I told you that Tony and I have been friends for years. What I didn't tell you was that we were engaged once."

His pencil lead broke.

She didn't seem to notice. "It was during college, before Mack found me. I said yes for all the wrong reasons. I was lonely, I felt comfortable with Tony, and I did love him, just not the way he loved me."

It took him a moment to speak into the silence. "What happened?"

An imaginary piece of lint on the couch's arm captured her attention. "I ruined it."

"What makes you think you ruined it?" He could just bet that Salazar had been an ass about something, causing Willow to end the engagement.

"I know I ruined it, because I suck at sex."

His sketchpad slid to the floor. "What?"

"Sex," she repeated, her voice blunt. "I'm awful at it. The first time, I thought it was nerves, because I didn't know what to do. Then we tried again, and it was worse."

She took a deep breath. "I was worse. I froze, then I panicked, then I started crying. Tony tried to comfort me, which only made me freak out more. I gave him the ring back that night and couldn't face him for a week."

The wounded tone of her voice cut through him, made him angry—with Salazar. "Salazar didn't try to help?"

"Of course he did," she answered, sounding exhausted. "He swore he'd help me through it, that he'd marry me anyway. But I couldn't do that to him. It was bad enough that I wasn't in love with him, and he knew it. I couldn't let him burden himself with me like that."

The tears and self-condemnation in her voice called to his protective streak. "You couldn't be a burden, Willow," he told her. "Any man would consider himself lucky to have you."

"Tony said something to that effect, and swore that he'd always be there for me if I changed my mind. He's been there for me more times than I can count, despite how badly I hurt him. I don't understand it, but we've somehow remained friends."

Except there was a possibility that Salazar wasn't her friend. Maybe Mack didn't think the mayor could threaten Willow, but Brandt wasn't so sure. It was obvious to him that Salazar still had feelings for his former fiancée. Had those feelings warped over the years, festering into jealousy?

Jealous men could be as vindictive as jealous women, and a lot more brutal. With his resources, there was no telling what lengths Salazar would go to if he thought something threatened his place in Willow's life.

"I can't believe I told you this," Willow said, wiping at her eyes. "I haven't even told Mack."

He rose, crossing the carpet to sit beside her. Understanding her reaction to the construction worker, he made sure he kept a respectable distance between them. "You've obviously kept it inside for a long time. You needed to tell someone."

"Yeah," she sniffed. "I really wanted to confess that I'm less of a woman."

He kept his hands on his knees, fighting the urge to comfort her. After what he'd just learned, touching Willow was the last thing he should do.

Instead, he chose words, something not nearly as easy for him. "I'm going to tell you something, but you have to promise to keep it a secret. Maya would kill me if she found out I told you."

"Your sister Maya? What would she kill you for?"

"A few years ago, Maya went through a nasty divorce because she couldn't have children," Brandt explained. "It devastated her, not only because she really wanted kids, but because her rat-bastard of an ex made her feel like half a woman. The family tried to convince her it wasn't true, but you know, sometimes you can't hear what family tells you. Then she read your book."

Willow lifted her tear-streaked face, staring at him with those dark, wide eyes. "She did?"

He nodded. "She said it changed her life. I saw it for myself. She'd started the adoption process before she met and fell in love with Taylor, the little girl who lived next door, and Taylor's father."

"That's wonderful." Her hand reached out, wrapped around his.

"That's not the best part." Casually, he turned his hand palm up, entwining their fingers.

"What happened?" When he didn't answer immediately, she bumped her shoulder into his. "Come on, don't leave me hanging like that. What happened?"

"Nick and Maya have been married two years, Taylor and Maya are virtually inseparable, and they now have a little boy. It turns out that Maya wasn't the infertile one."

"Oh, my God," she breathed, squeezing his hand as fresh tears sparkled on her lashes. "I'm so glad that things worked out for her."

"Yeah, she's doing great, and she's as confident and happy as I've ever seen her. But it all started when she read your book. So I have to thank you for helping her find happiness."

"No, thank you. Thank you for telling me this. The books, the philosophy of dealing and overcoming, all started from my own need to understand and come to grips with my own problems. I feel blessed, knowing that my search for answers helps other people."

"It does." Her book had helped him manage his grief, even if he had yet to deal with it or overcome it. He found himself waiting for the inevitable question, the question of whether he'd read any of her books himself. It was a question he waited for every day, and debated answering truthfully every day.

She didn't ask. Instead, she squeezed his hand again. "You're a good man, Brandt Hughes. Beneath that tough exterior beats the heart of a teddy bear."

Surprised, he turned to face her. Her lips, probably intending to smack him on the cheek, brushed across his mouth instead.

He expected her to pull away. She didn't. Instead, her eyes slid shut, and her lips softened against his. She had an incredible mouth, he thought, taking in the kiss while holding everything he was still. Years of discipline almost cracked when her fingers reached up to lightly caress his cheek, a feathery touch that burned all the way to his soul.

Desire, instant and potent, roared to life inside him. It was all he could do to not take over the kiss, to not drag her closer and taste her fully. Given what she'd just confessed, he knew he couldn't, not without scaring her off. Still, he couldn't resist the need to angle his head slightly so that her lips met his completely.

All too soon she pulled away. "I didn't mean to do that."

The huskiness of her voice fired his blood. "I know."

She gave him a soft smile. "I'm glad I did, though."

He sucked in a breath, found his voice. "I'm glad you did too."

"Really?" Desire sparked in her eyes, amazing him. "If I kiss you again, will you kiss me back?"

He wanted to tell her no. It just wasn't a good idea, pushing his control. Not with her. He'd barely hung on the first time. "Sure."

She leaned into him, lifting her face to his. This time he took the lead, cradling her cheek in his palm before lowering his mouth to hers. That electric sensation pulsed through him again, stoking the fire that burned deep. He heard her moan, just a soft whimper, that made his blood pound as he realized she'd felt the same current. Again her fingers came up to touch his cheek, to hold him close as he deepened the kiss by degrees.

He shook with the need to drag her into his lap, to really kiss her. As it was, she curled into him like a branch of the tree she was named after, yielding without breaking.

Reluctantly he drew back from her. It was enough that she trusted him this much. It would kill him if he caused her to panic by losing control. It would definitely kill him if she kissed him again. Hell, it would probably incinerate him on the spot if she looked at him again with that heavy-lidded, sexy gaze.

He said the first thing that came to mind. "Let's go for ice cream."

She blinked at him, surprised. "Do what?"

"Let's grab Boscoe and take a drive down the A1A. I think I remember seeing an all-hours diner a few miles south. They had a sign claiming they made the best sundaes in South Florida. Let's get a couple."

Willow stared at him, head cocked to one side as she analyzed his words for hidden meaning. He kept his face composed.

"Okay," she finally said. "Give me a moment to change?"

"Of course," he said easily, more easily than he felt. "You go ahead and change while I go online for directions."

"Sure." She got to her feet in a series of staccato movements, then headed for the hallway and the stairs. Just as he began to rise, she turned, and he immediately sat back down.

"Are you sure?" Hesitancy filled her voice. "About the ice cream?"

Those were words with hidden meaning, but he chose not to read anything into them. "No doubt. I'm even buying. But you've got five minutes before Boscoe and I hop into the truck and take off without you."

"I'll hurry then." She left.

He waited until he heard the distant sound of her bedroom door closing. He didn't harbor any doubts that things had changed between them, had veered into territory more complicated than keeping his tragedy from her.

He wanted her. Badly. Kissing her had made him feel good, better than he had in years. He felt damn-near intoxicated, and that kiss had been tame compared to some he'd had. What would happen if she really kissed him and he kissed her back with all the pent-up need currently throbbing through him?

She'd run for the hills, that's what.

Maybe she wouldn't. Since she'd kissed him, twice, it meant she had to want him too, somehow. He couldn't understand why she'd kissed him the second time, why she'd want him. She knew nothing about him other than that he was a carpenter and Mack's friend.

He groaned. Mack would beat him down hard if he knew what'd happened. Mack had asked him to watch out for Willow, to protect her. Not kiss her, and certainly not fantasize about going to bed with her.

An image of Willow's trim body draped over his formed in his mind. The erection he'd had since she'd first kissed him tightened painfully. Not even thinking about Mack's reaction could dampen the desire he felt for Willow. Desire that bordered on a need so deep, so profound, it shook his foundation.

He hadn't planned on this. He'd assumed he could pour his heart and soul into restoring the chapel and then leave, without a ripple in his wake. He'd thought he could hold himself apart from Willow, even while staying in her home, that he'd be able to keep his demons from resurrecting. While working on those defenses, he'd completely forgotten about protecting himself in other ways. He'd never expected her to kiss him, to want him. He'd never expected her to touch him, with a gentleness that spread like sunlight through him.

He'd called her a superwoman, but she was his kryptonite.

CHAPTER FIFTEEN

She didn't know what to make of him, and she hated it.

On the surface, the ice cream excursion was wonderful. A sliver of moonlight had risen over the ocean as they drove down the A1A in Brandt's oversized truck, Boscoe happily strapped into the back seat. The oppressive heat and afternoon clouds had lessened with sunset, revealing brilliant stars.

People were out in droves, enjoying the Friday night and the ice cream stand that delivered on milkshakes as good as promised. Despite the crowd, they'd managed to find a bench oceanside. With Boscoe devouring a small portion of peanut butter ice cream, she and Brandt had had a chance to talk about things.

Except that they didn't.

They hadn't sat in silence. They'd talked about the flooring that would be installed on Monday, the first set of pews that would be delivered ten days later. They'd discussed the cruise she planned to surprise Pattie with to celebrate her anniversary, even the status of a tropical depression swirling about six hundred miles southeast.

They just didn't talk about the kiss. Either kiss. Maybe he didn't think it was as big a deal as she did. Maybe he thought she'd lied to him about her panic attacks, though the last thing she'd lie about was sexual disfunction. Maybe the truth was that he just wasn't into her. The most fantastic, mind-blowing kiss of her life hadn't even fazed him.

Or it could be that the kiss had fazed him too much. She knew he still mourned his wife and son, still had issues with their deaths. Sure, it had been four years, but what was time to a broken heart? She knew better than anyone that time could only dull the pain, not heal it.

Shifting on the leather, she tried to refocus her thoughts. It had been years since she'd felt interested in someone. After the debacle with Tony, she'd gone on a string of casual dates. She'd been close to only one other person, and that relationship had ended like a train wreck after he'd groped her. Since then, nothing had tempted her to put herself or anyone else through that potential embarrassment.

Brandt was the first person she'd been upfront with about her problems. She hadn't felt any of the frightening tension as she'd kissed him. In fact, tension of a wholly different sort had teased through her when he'd kissed her in return. All she could think about was how wonderful his lips had felt, how the way he'd cupped her cheek both soothed and excited her.

Longing, pure and sweet, had pulsed through her. She wanted to feel that again. She wanted him. If they tried and she freaked out, though, she'd die. She couldn't do that to him, or herself, then try to face him every day.

"Headache?"

The sound of his voice in the silence of the truck startled her. She turned to his profile, his features indistinct in the light from the dashboard. "No, no headache."

"Thinking?"

Back to an economy of words. Her fault for pushing him, even though he'd said he didn't mind. Apparently, he was just being nice. "Yes."

"Stop."

Anxiety simmered into irritation. Two could play the one-word game. "No."

"Why?"

She folded her arms. "Because."

He made a sound that could have been a laugh, except that he never laughed. "Not good enough."

Three words. She could come up with a three-word retort.

"So sue me."

The growl of the engine lowered as he slowed his speed. "What are you thinking about, Willow? I'd really like to know."

Damn. She had no defenses against his niceness. "I made you uncomfortable. That makes me uncomfortable."

"What makes you think I'm uncomfortable?"

"Aren't you? As soon as we stopped kissing, you suggested we go out for ice cream. We've talked about everything but what happened, and you haven't said a word since we got back in the truck. If I sucked that badly, you should just say so."

He jammed on the brakes and pulled over, sending them all straining against their seat belts. Willow instinctively braced her arms on the dashboard, swallowing a yelp of fear.

"Dammit," he swore softly, then shifted into park. "Are you all right?"

She swallowed, nodded. He sighed, then turned to the backseat to pat Boscoe's head. "Sorry about that, boy," he said, his voice rough. "Didn't mean to scare you."

Boscoe licked his hand. Brandt straightened, then turned, placing both hands on the steering wheel. "You didn't suck. I felt that kiss down in my gut, and it was all I could do to hold back."

He had? "Why?"

He tilted his head as if in thought, then shifted into drive again. Tires crunched as he pulled back into the driving lane. "You called me a teddy bear. I'm anything but. I don't know how to be gentle, just controlled. If we'd kissed for much longer, I would have done something stupid like try to pull you closer, or haul you into my lap so I could really kiss you. Given what you've told me about your past experiences, I figured it wouldn't be a good idea. So I stopped and suggested the ice cream to get us out of the house."

His concern surprised and warmed her. At least one of them had been thinking. "Thank you."

"You're welcome." He increased speed.

Willow looked out her window, staring at the lush, dark vegetation that separated them from sand and sea. She often drove this coastal road, usually heading north, taking in the view of the ocean by sun or moonlight as it peeked through the trees. Driving the A1A helped her clear her head, focus, and think.

She focused on the man beside her. "Are you seeing someone back in Atlanta?"

He grunted, apparently surprised by her question. "No. You?"

"No. Defying all principles of my profession, it's easier to avoid my issue and the potential embarrassment by not being involved."

"You didn't seem to have any issues kissing me," he pointed out.

"No, I didn't." Because she felt comfortable with him. More than that, she trusted him. He'd held back so he wouldn't scare her. That told her more than anything that she'd be safe with him. The thought of being with him intimately made her heart pound, but not in apprehension.

Could she be intimate with him? She'd all but resigned herself to the fact that her life would be a string of casual dates, that all her relationships would end once her partner wanted more than she could comfortably give. As Pattie had said, she was dangerously close to becoming a nun.

Maybe not. Her gaze slid back to Brandt. Maybe he could help her. He'd understood her needs without explanation. Maybe she wouldn't have to confess every dark and dirty secret. She was tired of being afraid, tired of being incapable. Maybe the best form of therapy for her issues was the man sitting beside her.

"Brandt."

"Hhm?"

She curled her hands into fists, resting them on her knees. "This isn't going to come out right, and there's probably not a right way to ask this, but—"

"You want to test yourself. With me."

He didn't sound shocked or angry. That encouraged her. "Nothing as clinical as that. I mean, it may sound like I'm being clinical, but I'm not. And I'm not saying that we should date or anything, just explore the attraction we feel."

"You're attracted to me?"

"Oh yeah," she answered, surprised that he sounded surprised. "I think you're amazing."

When he remained silent, she hurried on. "We're both adults. We can rationally decide how we relate to each other without bringing drama into it."

"Aren't you concerned about your reputation, about any rumors that could start?"

"I'm more worried about you," she answered truthfully. "I don't know if I can move beyond kisses, but I want to try with you. I know it's an unusual request, but I figured it would be best to be upfront about this rather than try to seduce you."

He coughed. "I appreciate that."

"Not that I'd be any good at that. Either way, this isn't all that fair to you, especially if I panic in the middle of-of something important."

He huffed. Willow realized it was his version of a laugh. "Oh my God, you're laughing. Hey wait—you're laughing at me!"

"No, at the situation. You can see the irony in this, right? Me helping you? That's pretty damn funny."

Her sudden anger evaporated as she considered his words. She knew he had issues, even though he hadn't mentioned them. She was supposed to be the one who fixed issues, but here she was, asking for his help. At least he laughed, a better reaction than indignation or anger.

"I know, it's a case of 'physician, heal yourself.' You'll definitely have the upper hand."

"Maybe that's the problem." He sobered. "Maybe it's just that you've never felt like you could control the situation. If you set the ground rules, then nothing can happen that you don't want."

Her mind latched onto the idea as he pulled up to her gate. She had given the same advice to a variety of her patients. The first step to surviving a tragedy was to claim it. If she laid out the ground rules for an encounter with Brandt, she'd control the situation, and hopefully control her fears.

She shifted to face him as he lowered the window to enter her security code for the gate. "Are you saying that you'd let me control you? Like it could really happen?"

"I know what discipline is," he said easily. He raised the window as the gates swung open, and she remembered how she'd returned home the previous night, sprawled on the backseat of her car. "I can control myself. I won't do anything you don't ask me to do. Up to a point."

That made her uneasy. "What point is that?"

"Depends on how successful you are. Some things are humanly impossible to control."

Heat burned her cheeks, making her grateful for the dark interior. She knew exactly what he meant. The thought of being that successful made her momentarily breathless.

"So you'll help me?"

He pulled the truck into the double garage. "Yeah, if Mack doesn't kill me."

Mack. She hadn't thought about what her brother might do or think if his friend and his sister got together. "This is a personal matter just between us," she said, her voice even. "I don't think we need to bring anyone else into it, do you?"

"Your rules, Willow. Your decisions." He killed the headlights, then the engine before extracting the keys.

She hadn't expected him to agree so easily to her half-formed plan. Why had he agreed so easily? "So, uhm, what do we do now?" she asked, fighting a case of nerves.

He got out of the truck, then opened the rear door to release Boscoe. "You're going to go inside and think about the rules of engagement, what you want and if you want it," he said, wrapping the dog's leash around one fist. "Boscoe and I are going to do a quick turn around the grounds, then I'm coming in and going to bed. We can talk in the morning, if you want."

Meaning nothing would happen that night. She didn't know whether to feel relief or disappointment, and felt a curious mixture of both as she got out of the truck and headed for the door that opened onto a coatroom off the kitchen.

CHAPTER SIXTEEN

"I can't make the fundraiser tonight."

"Can't make it?" Willow stared at the phone in disbelief. Mack wouldn't do this to her. She couldn't go there alone. She couldn't go in front of five hundred people who expected her to razzle and dazzle them, and not have her brother there for moral support. "What do you mean, you can't make it?" she asked, trying to keep her voice from hitching.

Mack must have heard it anyway. "Wil, you know if it wasn't important law enforcement business, I would be there."

"I know. It's just…" Willow forced her breathing to remain even. Mack just didn't realize how much she depended on him for support. She'd never told him about the panic attacks she sometimes got speaking in front of large groups, the fear that one day someone in the crowd would stand up and call her out as a hypocrite.

"I'm sure Pattie will love to go," Mack said in blissful ignorance of her concerns.

"She's not here," Willow all but moaned. "I sent her on a weeklong cruise to the Bahamas for her anniversary. She won't be back for two days!" She'd also told her assistant she was more than capable of holding down the fort. *Liar.*

"I bet Brandt will take my place."

"What?" Air left her lungs in a rush of surprise. "Brandt?"

"It's an excellent idea," Mack went on, not letting her get a word in. "I'll call him and tell him what's up. He'll be happy to stand in." He disconnected.

Willow stared at the receiver for long moments before replacing it in its cradle. How could she go to the fundraiser with Brandt? He did- n't seem like a man who would enjoy putting on a tux to go eat tasteless, $250-a-plate food and listen to supposed dignitaries drone on about community involvement and the importance of second chances.

Still, he'd look amazing in a tux. She could pretend it was a date, pretend that they were having an L.A.-style night on the town instead of attending a fundraiser. Maybe they'd even kiss again, maybe more.

She couldn't deny her attraction for him, and found that she didn't want to. She wanted to run her hands over his chest and arms to see if his muscles were as hard as they looked, his skin as smooth as it seemed. She wanted to feel those gorgeous lips sliding over her skin.

She wanted the man more and more every day. Yet she hadn't taken another step towards that goal. Fear kept her rooted in inaction, fear that she'd try and fail. If she didn't try, at least she'd be in the same place.

If she tried intimacy and failed, things would get awkward. She'd start avoiding him, and he'd throw up a barrier between them again. They'd be back to square one, with no hope of moving forward. How would she help him if she couldn't face him?

She still hadn't considered the idea that she would succeed. What if being with Brandt was as wonderful and freeing as the romances she occasionally read described it? What would happen then?

Fifteen minutes later, Brandt came to her office. Covered in sawdust and sweat, he remained in the doorway. "Mack said you needed an escort to some fundraiser tonight."

"Yes." He was just too damn fine for her peace of mind. Willow took a deep breath and prepared to give him an out. "I don't expect you to—"

"He said it was black tie."

She nodded, fascinated by the way his biceps molded his skin, delineated by the woodshavings that clung to him. The T-shirt hugging his washboard abs wasn't damp with sweat, making her wonder if he'd had it off while working in the chapel.

The image almost made her whimper. She really, really wanted to know what it would be like to be stretched out beside him, to feel his skin beneath her hands. She wanted to know the feel of his hands moving over her skin, cupping her breasts, shaping her as gently and as surely as a piece of mahogany.

He moved slightly, causing her to shift her focus, look at his face instead. Sweat beaded on his forehead, and she felt a ridiculous urge to wipe it away for him.

"I'll take you."

Thank goodness for dark skin. He couldn't see the flush that swept up her cheeks as she suppressed her sensual thoughts. Feeling guilty, she tried again to let him off the hook. "Look, I'm sure Mack must have called in a pretty big favor, but really, you don't have to do this."

"What if I want to?"

His unexpected answer made Willow's mouth drop open. "Really?"

"Really." His lips quirked in the closest thing she'd ever seen to a smile from him. "I'm good for more than carving wood, you know. It'll be a good change of pace, if you're up for it."

"Oh." He wanted to go to the fundraiser with her. She sure as heck would get up for it. "All right then. Uhm, there'll be a couple of stylists here early this afternoon, to help me get ready. I just want to warn you so you're not walking around in just a towel."

She groaned aloud at the instant picture in her head, and got even more flustered. "Not that you ever do," she hurried on, wondering when the air conditioner had switched off. "I mean, I wouldn't know if you did or not because it's not like I'm trying to catch you in just a towel or anything."

Lord, have mercy. "Not that there's anything wrong with that, you being in a towel. In fact, there's nothing wrong with that at all, you should feel free to walk around however you want to. It's just that—aw, hell."

She took a deep breath and stared at a spot over his shoulder, certain that he was laughing at her expense, except that he never laughed. "If I manage to get my foot out of my mouth in time, the car will be here around seven to pick us up. The fundraiser starts at eight, but there's a half-hour of small talk and networking beforehand."

"I'll be ready." He turned, then paused, looking back at her. "Don't worry, I'll make sure no one who shouldn't sees me in a towel." He left without another word.

Willow sat back in her chair, completely flummoxed. Brandt Hughes wanted to go to the fundraiser. With her. What was she supposed to make of that?

Nothing. She was too busy imagining him walking around in just a towel.

Brandt stood in his room, staring at his reflection in the mirror. As he adjusted the black silk of his borrowed tie, he wondered for the umpteenth time why he'd agreed to escort Willow to her fundraiser. He finally settled on curiosity.

Oh, he was curious about Willow Zane all right. Curious to see how she reacted to being in the spotlight. It had been easy to forget that she was a celebrity, that she was a glamorous woman with movie stars on speed dial. All he could think about was how flustered she'd gotten after warning him not to walk around in a towel, and how cute she was when she stammered. He'd had half a mind to walk into her suite in said towel, but luckily a cool shower and the presence of the stylists had prevailed.

It was probably a mistake, but he couldn't help thinking that the night was something more than it seemed. He was essentially taking Willow out on a date, albeit it a date with five hundred of her closest friends. If he thought that way, what was going through Willow's mind?

Anticipation swam through him, feeding the need that had been growing for days. Work-related issues had them working harder and longer hours than they usually did, meaning the opportunities for intimacy had been slim to none. This would be the first time in days that they'd have a break from their schedules. He wasn't going to push Willow; his father had taught him better than that. There was nothing wrong with testing the waters, however, to see if she felt the same longing he did.

A chime announced the limousine's arrival at the gated entrance. He stepped into the hall. "I'll get it," he said loudly, since the door to Willow's master suite was firmly closed. Making his way downstairs, he checked the security display trained on the main gate, saw the limousine, then pressed the button that would allow the car to drive through. She actually had a state-of-the-art security system, with intercoms and LCDs throughout the house, sensors around the grounds. If only he could get her to use it regularly.

He entered the great room, an area more in keeping with what the public expected of Dr. Willow Zane: formal, designer serene, and aesthetically pleasing. Completely at odds with the shabby-chic comfort of the rest of the house, or the Zen-like simplicity of her master suite.

That was the true Willow, he'd discovered. Serene, sleek even, complicated in her simplicity. Just like the king-sized bed that dominated her bedroom suite. The woodworker in him coveted her rosewood bed with its hand-carved, aged finish. It had to be two hundred years old, and he wanted to run his hands over every line and curve. Not as badly as he wanted to run his hands over Willow, but close enough.

He heard her coming, quick but muffled footsteps on the thick slate blue carpet of the upper level. He turned to the stairway expectantly, waiting for her to make her entrance.

What an entrance it was.

Toes painted the color of burgundy wine peeked at him from a strappy silver sandal, the spiked heel showing her trim ankle to advantage. Her bare shin disappeared in a satiny sweep of pewter-toned silk.

She revealed more of herself with each step she descended, and he couldn't, wouldn't, ruin the moment by greedily lifting his gaze. The gown hugged her close above the thigh, hinting at the high roundness of her hips, the flatness of her stomach. Silver embroidery and crystals skipped across the top that just cradled her breasts, causing his blood to heat and his heart to stutter. She held a small silver clutch bag in one hand, and a length of pewter material that he supposed served as a wrap hung from her elbows. Distantly he wondered what it would feel like sliding across bare skin.

He dimly noted a diamond eternity pendant and teardrop earrings that skimmed her bare shoulders. She'd pulled her braids back and atop her head, and a few curling strands softly framed her face.

She reached the last step and paused, staring at him with wide-eyed wonder and parted lips the color of blackberries. He had to swallow twice before he could speak. "You look—you look—" He didn't know words adequate to describe how fine she looked.

"Thank you," she answered, her voice a bare breath as she continued to stare at him. "You look…" She searched for a word, then finally settled on, "Wow."

Her reaction pleased him. He'd taken extra care, knowing how important the night was for her. Wishing he'd had time to send for his own tux back in Atlanta, he'd had a hurried fitting for Mack's tux. They were close enough in size that, except for a little looseness in the shoulders, the tux fit him impeccably. He'd gone shopping on Beach Avenue and paired the black suit with his own gleaming white shirt and cufflinks.

He finally remembered his manners and offered her his arm. "You sure clean up real nice, Dr. Zane," he drawled.

Laughing, she curled a hand around his elbow. "I guess it was worth it then, to have the house overrun with stylists and makeup artists. And may I say, you clean up mighty fine yourself."

"I try." He led her towards the front entrance. "Boscoe caged?"

She nodded. "With his blankie and favorite chew toy. He makes a good excuse against staying out late, though I'm pretty sure we'll be home before midnight."

"The famous Dr. Zane, psychologist to the stars, not a party animal?" He set the alarm before closing and locking the door. "I don't believe it."

A sleek white limousine sat in the curve of the drive, engine softly humming. The driver tipped his hat to them before opening the rear passenger door. "Good evening, ma'am, sir."

Willow greeted him before Brandt handed her inside, then climbed in himself. She sat on the far side of the seat, staring out the window, but she'd left enough room for him to sit beside her. He took the seat opposite instead. He was lightheaded enough without the bird's eye view of her cleavage.

The chauffeur shut the door, leaving them alone. Brandt noticed that the privacy divider was in place, making him doubly grateful that he sat opposite Willow instead of beside her. The car slipped into gear, then, like a boat pulling away from dock, they headed for the gate and the highway beyond.

"I should have asked, is this a mix and mingle type of event, or an 'I can't believe we paid this much for rubbery chicken' type of event?"

Willow turned to him, her smile a little strained. "The best of both, or the worst of both, depending on how you view it," she said. "After the reception, there's a small presentation during dinner before I speak."

"What is your speech about?"

She shifted on the charcoal-colored leather. "The importance of second chances. It's the unofficial slogan of Serena Bay, the 'City of Second Chances.' Then, if I don't put everyone to sleep, we'll announce the total raised for the community center."

"'City of second chances,' huh?" He ignored the sudden tightness in his chest.

"Everyone, at some point in their lives, needs a second chance," she said softly. Dark eyes focused on him, reading him. "The question becomes, What will you do with it."

She knew. He could see it in her eyes. Before he could think of anything to say, before he could become angry or afraid, she dropped her gaze. "That's the gist of my speech, which is essentially a condensed version of my current work in progress."

Willow watched Brandt relax by degrees. He'd tensed up so completely when she'd mentioned second chances that she couldn't confess that she already knew about his wife and son. She'd let him keep his secret a while longer, but she'd help him eventually.

If she could. Maybe she wouldn't be able to help him, and he'd leave with the same burden he'd arrived with. Maybe she was fooling herself that she could help people. Maybe all her success was just a fluke of cosmic proportions.

Her stomach knotted. Would this be the night she'd get called out? Would someone stand up and call her a hypocrite before all of Serena Bay's elite? These people would know the truth, if anyone did. Even though most people believed she'd run away from home just before prom night, a handful had known that she'd actually left town with Antonio Salazar two months after graduation, a graduation she hadn't attended.

No one had approached her about it since she'd returned to Serena Bay, but someone kept sending her threatening letters. Did her mysterious stalker know about her past? Why not ask for money, instead of demanding that she leave? Who would want her to leave her hometown?

"Hey, got any tissue in that microscopic excuse for a purse?"

She looked up, surprised to find Brandt sitting beside her. How had she not noticed him move, not noticed him beside her? Her radar was usually better than that. "You'd be surprised what I can fit in this thing," she said, grateful for the change of subject. "Cell phone, keys, credit card, lipstick and a few dollars."

"Tissue?"

"Yes, some tissue. Why?"

"Because I'd really like to kiss you right now, but I'm not eager to look like I've been eating blackberries."

At his words, Willow's nervous stomach did a backflip. She remembered all too well what it had felt like to kiss him, because she'd replayed each moment repeatedly in her imagination like a hormone-stoked teenager.

She looked at him through narrowed eyes. "You're trying to distract me, aren't you?"

"Yep. Is it working?"

"Yep." She opened her clutch, took out a travel pack of tissue. Pulling one loose, she blotted at her lips. "Better?"

"Let me see." He reached out, tilting her chin with a lift of his fore-finger. His thumb brushed across her bottom lip, sending a tendril of hunger curling through her. She shocked herself by darting her tongue out, touching the tip against the rough pad of his thumb.

He swallowed, audibly. "I think…I think you got it all."

"Are you sure?" Her voice sounded weak to her ears, as if she could-n't breathe.

"I'll find out." His lips touched hers, gentle, testing. Controlled.

That wasn't the kind of kiss she wanted from him. She cupped her hand to the back of his neck, deepening the kiss. He responded instant-ly, parting his lips, silently demanding that she reciprocate. She did, feeling a heady rush of desire as their tongues met, tasted, tempted.

All too soon, he pulled away. "We have to stop, Wil."

Dazed, she opened her eyes, focused on him. He'd moved to the other side of the car again. "Why?"

He shifted on the seat with a wry twist of his lips. "I need time to calm down," he explained. "Your condition could be explained by air conditioning, but I don't think people will cut me that much slack."

Her eyes immediately dropped to his crotch. Hastily she looked toward the window instead. "Maybe we should do another ice cream run."

"Will you be satisfied with that?" he asked, his voice careful. "I'd have thought you'd be hungrier than that. I know I am."

His voice slid over her senses like silk on bare skin, causing her stomach to clench, and not because it was empty. She knew they weren't talking about food.

"Tonight." She licked her lips, started again. "Tonight, I think I could go for something a little more…filling."

He sucked in a deep breath that became a groan as he closed his eyes. "God, I hope we're not talking about food."

She laughed then, the sudden tension breaking. "Not even close. Actually, I could compare your effect on me to the alcohol content of a couple of *mojitos.*"

He opened his eyes, his features relaxing into a ghost of a smile. "I'll take that as a compliment."

"You should." He was hot, gorgeous, sexy, strong, artistic, and good with his hands. And, God help her, he had a sense of humor and a caring heart under all that muscle. She'd have to be stupid not to want him.

At that moment, she felt like a genius.

"Willow? Looking at me like that isn't helping."

She blinked, focused on his eyes. "How am I looking at you?"

For answer, he leaned back, stared at her. Heat wrapped around her as he gave her a look that made her stomach jump and her breath shallow.

"That's the look you're giving me right now," he said, gray eyes alight. "If you expect me to be able to walk normally when we get out of this car, you need to stop. Please."

"Oh. Okay." How could she not look at him? He sat there, absolutely gorgeous in his tuxedo, with the promise of pleasure in his eyes.

She had to remember that, aside from a hurricane tracking well east and north of them, the fundraiser was the biggest news in Serena Bay. The society reporter from the newspaper would certainly be attending the fundraiser. All she'd need would be for a photo to be taken at the wrong time, and an incident would be created. Tonight was about publicity for the community center, not her.

"I'll just not look at you for the rest of the evening," she said, shifting her gaze to the darkened window. "I'll look in your general direction if I need to. How's that?"

"Better," Brandt said, as the limousine slowed, then stopped. "Looks like we're here."

Brandt watched as Willow sat back, taking a deep breath and closing her eyes. As the driver opened the rear door, she opened her eyes again. It seemed as if a switch had been thrown. Suddenly she was more…*more*. He didn't know how else to explain it as a cheer went up from what sounded close to a mob.

Remembering his escort duties, he came to his senses and exited the limo. People called Willow's name, lights flashed, and the energy level rose exponentially. Willow smiled and waved as press and regular people called to her for photos and autographs.

This was *the* Dr. Willow Zane, psychologist to the stars, that he'd been expecting all along. It amazed him, how different she seemed now. This was a confident, dazzling celebrity who could charm birds from trees. Not that the at-home Willow wasn't all those things, but this was like going from a string quartet to an entire symphony. Wow.

Just as he was beginning to feel out of place, even as dressed-up bodyguard, Willow turned that high-wattage smile on him. It might as well have been a Taser, because he felt the jolt all the way to his toes. Then she put her hand in the crook of his elbow, and he took that as his cue to step forward and guide her into the building.

They entered the reception area, crowded with glittering people in tuxes and gowns who wanted pictures with Willow. She obliged with energetic grace, chatting and shaking hands with a politician's skill. She sailed through the reception like a sparkling jewel, owning the room and putting every other woman to shame.

Brandt found himself looking at Willow differently as the night progressed. He was completely captured, mesmerized. He didn't taste his dinner, didn't hear the mayor welcome other dignitaries of business and politics. He only noticed Willow, watching her as she approached the podium, a small stack of index cards in her hands. She adjusted the microphone as the lights dimmed, as the audience quieted in expectation. He saw her hesitate, glance around the room. Her eyes seemed to pick him out in the darkness, rest on him for a moment. Then she smiled and began to speak.

Passionate conviction filled her expression and her voice as she talked about the power of second chances, about the need to allow oneself the chance, like the phoenix, to be honed in the fires of failure in order to become a brilliant, successful being.

Her eyes rested on him frequently as she spoke, giving him a jolt each time. It didn't matter whether she knew about his heartbreak or not. Her words reached into his soul, saw how he wanted to stop, and encouraged him to continue, to find the strength inside. She made him believe anything was possible, if he wanted it badly enough.

He did want. He wanted her. It had been too long since he'd wanted to be close to someone, wanted to connect. The kisses and embraces they'd shared were too few and far between to satisfy him.

He had to wonder, however, if he could handle it, handle being with her. This confident, dynamic woman didn't gel with the sweet, sexually shy woman struggling with writer's block and enervating migraines. Why in the world would this woman pick him to be with, a nobody carpenter with issues of his own?

Brandt shook his head. He didn't need or want to know the reasons. There was a lot to be said for blissful ignorance. Besides, his male ego relished the knowledge that she'd chosen him. Whatever her reasons, he'd make damn sure she didn't regret her choice.

CHAPTER SEVENTEEN

"The hometown girl certainly has done good," Zee said, a glass of champagne hovering at her lips. She looked her usual stunning self in a Valencia orange strapless gown that showed her tan and flawless skin to advantage. "I don't think we've ever had a fundraiser this successful."

"I had a little help, Zee," Willow said modestly, trying not to search the ballroom for Brandt. With her speech over, the opportune time to attempt to harm or embarrass her had passed. Her feelings of anxiety had lessened, but anticipation had increased tenfold. All she could think about was slipping out of her spiked heels and form-fitting dress and slipping into Brandt's arms.

"Everybody in the Serena Bay Chamber of Commerce and even a few private citizens pitched in to fund the community center. I think it's great that we won't have to have a bond referendum on it. Tony will be able to keep his campaign promise of not raising taxes for another year. I'm just glad people didn't get tired of me begging them for money."

Monica sipped her champagne. "I'm surprised no one told you to pay for it out of your own pocket. I was sure old man Conners would tell you to take a long walk off the lighthouse pier."

Willow laughed. "Old man Conners was one of the top five contributors. Said he'd pay anything to keep kids from hanging out in his orange trees."

"I'm sure that's not the only thing he said," Zee murmured.

Willow turned to her, about to ask what she meant, when she caught sight of Brandt moving towards her. In the crowded, glittering room, he moved like a force of nature, a law unto himself. People parted before him whether they wanted to or not, as if they couldn't help stepping aside.

He was amazing.

Monica caught her gaze and turned. "He's intimidating, isn't he?"

"Not at all. He's nice, once you get to know him," Willow said, not wanting anyone, not even her friend, to speak ill of Brandt.

Monica didn't look convinced. "What's nice to a man like that? I still can't believe you're letting him stay in your house. Aren't you worried about him being there? I mean, he hasn't tried anything, has he?"

"Please." Willow rolled her eyes at Zee's melodramatics. "He's Mack's best friend. I'm just as safe with him as I am with my brother."

"If you say so," Monica said doubtfully. "I for one would be scared to death."

"Well, you're not me, are you?"

Brandt closed the distance between them. Willow watched in amazement as Zee straightened and pasted on a dazzling smile. "Mr. Hughes," she purred, sticking out a hand adorned with nails the same color as her dress. "Monica Zanteras-Salazar, though friends call me Zee. Willow's been telling me all about you, but she certainly didn't tell me how dashing you are in a tux. And here I thought you were just a carpenter."

Brandt shook her hand quickly, and just as quickly dropped it. His expression betrayed nothing of his thoughts. "I am just a carpenter, ma'am," he said.

"Really?" Tony took that moment to show up, looking as dashing as any spy in his tuxedo. "Seems to me that you're also a boarder, and now you're an escort. Is there anything you won't do?"

"I do whatever Willow wants," Brandt said evenly, not looking at Zee or Tony. "She's the boss."

"Is she now?" Monica raised a perfectly arched eyebrow. "That's certainly…interesting. Don't you think so, Antonio?"

Tony's face darkened like a hard-forming thunderstorm, promising all manner of fireworks.

Willow took the hint. "And the boss thinks it's time to get home," she said, glancing at her watch. "Boscoe's been in his cage for more than three hours."

Brandt took her elbow. "Y'all heard the lady," he said. "If we don't leave now, she might make me the janitor. Nice to meet you, ma'am. Good night, Mayor."

"I've got to meet with the development group about all the pledges and donations, then I'll call Anna to schedule a formal meeting with you and the city council," Willow said to Tony. "Zee, I'll catch up with you later."

Tony clearly thought better of whatever he wanted to say. Monica gave her a brilliant smile and waved with her free hand before asking Tony for another glass of champagne.

Willow let Brandt guide her through the crowd, pausing to thank and be thanked by several people along the way. Once they were outside and a valet had signaled for their driver, Willow turned to him. "Thank you."

"For what?"

"For being my escort tonight. I really appreciate you being there."

He looked at her briefly before returning his attention to the crowd. "I take my job as bodyguard very seriously."

Hhm. He obviously wasn't thrilled with her friends' comments. Then again, she wasn't bowled over either. She'd talk to both of them tomorrow.

The car arrived. He opened the door before their driver could get out of the car, handing her inside before climbing in beside her and closing the door.

She waited until they'd pulled away before speaking again. "That's not what I meant."

"What did you mean?"

She reached over, bolder than she felt, and gathered his hand to hold in her lap. "I appreciated having you there as my friend," she told him. "It helped when I gave my speech, knowing you were out there."

He grunted, but at least he didn't try to pull away. "You didn't need me there. You knocked them out all by yourself."

"Yeah. I think I overcompensated."

"For what?"

She rested her temple against his shoulder. "Speaking engagements tend to make my nerves go haywire. It's why I always drag Mack or Pattie along to events like this. That's the deal. If they want to go to star-studded events, they also have to go to ones where I'm the main draw. So thank you for agreeing to come along."

He relaxed by degrees; she could feel it in the loosening of his arm, and the way he turned his hand to capture hers. "I told you, I didn't mind. I actually enjoyed most of it. You were something else."

His casual compliment warmed her insides, causing her to squeeze his hand. "Thanks."

"So, you consider me a friend?"

"Of course I do," she replied.

"Good to know. This could get awkward if you thought of me as a second brother."

At the deepening of his voice, she lifted her head. He was giving her that look, the one he'd told her to stop using before. The one that promised all sorts of wild and delightful things. The one that made her insides turn cartwheels. The one that made her want him, very, very much.

He lowered his head to hers. No sooner did their lips touch than they heard the squeal of brakes followed by a muted thud.

Brandt broke away from her, his gaze jerking to the tinted window. He slammed his hand down on the intercom button on the console beside him. "Stop the car!"

The driver, hearing the bark of command in Brandt's voice, instantly obeyed, pulling the car over into the emergency lane. Brandt leapt from the car almost before it stopped, leaving Willow alone and stunned.

Shaking off her surprise, she slid out of the car just in time to see him dashing through oncoming traffic to get to the other side of the road. Her heart jumped to her throat, choking off her scream. Good Lord, he could have been killed!

Since her ice gray dress reflected the row of orange streetlamps better than his black tux, Willow made it over to the median unscathed but far from unfazed. She found Brandt kneeling beside a dark object. He raised his face, and the expression carved into his features tore her heart. "Someone hit her," he said, his voice mangled. "The bastard hit her and kept going."

"Oh God." Willow felt tears spring to her eyes as she realized he knelt beside a large dog, her left hind leg dangling at an unnatural angle. "Is she…?"

"No." He stripped off his tuxedo jacket, wrapping it around the injured animal. "And it's not going to happen, not if I can do anything about it. Is there an emergency vet around here?"

"I know where one is." She yanked at her hem, ripping off a strip of sheer fabric. "Tie this around her muzzle before you lift her, so she doesn't snap at you."

Brandt took it from her with shaking fingers. "Easy there, girl," he said to the dog, placing his hand on her muzzle. With careful movements he wrapped the strip of cloth around the dog's jaws. "We're here to help you. It's going to hurt, but if you just hang on, we're going to take care of you."

The large dog whimpered as Brandt gently gathered her close, mindful of the shattered leg, then stood. "We have to hurry," he said to Willow, his features drawn. "I probably did more damage just by lifting her."

"It's not that far," she promised, lifting her skirts and hurrying to match his ground-eating stride. "We can get there in five minutes."

She stepped into traffic ahead of him, using her glittering dress and outstretched arms to stop traffic. The story would probably be all over the papers the next morning, but she didn't care. Tomorrow would have to take care of itself.

The limousine driver balked as they approached. "You can't put that thing in my car!"

Brandt barely spared the man a glance as Willow held the door open for him. "Watch me."

"That mutt's gonna bleed all over the leather."

"Then I'll buy the damn car!" Brandt and Willow shouted together. They looked at each other in perfect understanding, then Brandt carefully slid into the back.

Willow narrowed her eyes at the driver. "Get in, or I'll drive off and leave you where you stand."

The driver got behind the wheel without another word. Willow slid into the back, reaching for her evening bag as she gave the driver directions to the animal hospital. She pulled her phone out of the tiny bag, flipped it open. "Vet," she said, and the phone dialed the animal hospital.

Quickly she informed the nurse of their arrival, aware of Brandt's voice, low and strained, comforting the poor dog, urging her to hold on.

Within minutes they screeched to a halt in front of the hospital. People were already waiting for them. Brandt placed the animal on the stretcher held by two women while Willow explained what had happened. Everyone moved quickly and efficiently, and within moments of arriving, the dog was whisked away for surgery, leaving Brandt and Willow to begin the waiting process.

Brandt stalked the open area in front of the receptionist desk like a caged tiger. Blood marred his hands, his shirt. Remembering all too clearly what he'd been through with his wife and child, Willow knew she had to do something before he erupted.

She approached the receptionist. The woman had the phone stuck to her ear, whispering in a low voice. "Yeah, she's here, all dressed up. Some guy's with her. No, I don't know who he is; he looks like a football player. He's got blood all over him. I think they hit a dog."

Willow narrowed her eyes. "Excuse me."

The woman looked up, her mouth dropping open as she noticed Willow standing in front of her. She immediately hung up the phone. "Yes, ma'am?"

"I believe you have some forms I need to complete?" Willow asked, her voice icy.

"Yes, ma'am." She hurriedly pulled out a clipboard with a sheaf of paperwork attached to it, then handed it over. "You can just have a seat over there," she said, waving at the hard plastic chairs near the glass doors.

Before she could refuse, Brandt leaned over the desk, deliberately intimidating. "Is there a more private area where Dr. Zane can wait and freshen up?"

The receptionist swallowed, staring at the swath of blood staining his tuxedo shirt. "Yes sir, there's an exam room right here that you can use."

She scrambled from behind the desk, leading them down a short hall to an exam room. "I'll let the doctor know you're here," she said after letting them in. Then she left them alone.

Brandt slumped into a chair, blood drying his shirt and hands to the color of rust. Willow ached for him. She knew it was more than just a dog to him, that it was every life that he'd cherished, and lost.

Somehow she found her voice. "Come on, Brandt, we should clean up."

"It doesn't come out," he said, his voice hollow.

"What doesn't?"

"The blood." He held up his hands. "It never comes off. No matter how much you scrub at it, it seeps into your skin and stays there."

She swallowed, spoke past the sudden hard lump in her throat. "Let's give it a try anyway, all right?"

He dutifully rose to his feet as she tossed the clipboard onto the exam table. Like an examination room for people, this one had a counter and cabinets along one wall that held a sink, paper towels, and hand cleaner. While he washed and dried his hands she looked through cabinets, finding a couple of white cotton towels.

She wet half of one of them, then began to dab at one of the dark brown streaks high on his chest. He stopped her, his hands clasping her wrists. "Don't worry about it," he said. "It's ruined anyway."

He let her go, then returned to the chair, leaning his head back against the wall as he closed his eyes. She let him have the silence for a moment even though all she wanted to do was comfort him, try to find comfort herself. What would she do if the dog didn't make it? What would Brandt do?

Tears welled in her eyes, but she blinked them back. She couldn't fall to pieces now, not if Brandt needed her. Instead, she picked up the clipboard and began filling in part of the forms.

"I'm sorry."

She looked over at him. His hands were fisted on his knees, his jaw clenched. "For what?"

"I was too late," he whispered. "Too damn late, again."

"Brandt." She crossed to him then, cupping his face between her hands. "Brandt. Don't do this. Stay with me. Just stay with me."

"So much blood," he said, his voice empty. "How does a body lose so much blood so fast? How will I ever be forgiven for that much blood?"

He meant the dog, but so much more. Her heart thumped in fear for him. She sat on his lap, trying to tilt his chin down so that their eyes were level. "Brandt. Look at me. Look at me."

She watched him blink, struggle to focus. His beautiful gray eyes stared at her, darkened to charcoal by pain and memories. His hands lifted, wrapped around her waist as if she were a life preserver.

He took a deep, shuddering breath. "Willow. You should move. I'm covered in bl-blood."

"So am I." Her only movement was to wrap her arms around his shoulders. "I'm not going anywhere."

Against his will, she pulled him close, cradling his head against her chest, aware of his cheek resting against the bare expanse of skin above her neckline. Without thinking, she brushed feather-light kisses on his forehead. He stiffened, his head jerking upward. Her fingers curved around his cheeks like warm feathers, then she kissed him again.

Willow was unprepared for the change in him. He shuddered, once and then his lips moved insistently against hers, almost brutal with demand, as his arms engulfed her, crushing her close. Panic sliced into her lungs, driving out compassion.

She pushed against his shoulders. "Brandt, let go."

He didn't seem to hear her, his mouth moving roughly along her throat. Fighting growing fear, she tried to twist away. His fingers immediately locked onto her upper arms, digging into her flesh.

All at once she remembered her senior prom, Porter Garrick pawing at her dress. When she'd swung at him, he'd swung back, making her see stars before dragging her into a dark room.

She had to get away.

She struggled, her heart slamming against her ribcage. Working one hand free, she slapped Brandt with all her might. "I said, let go!"

He froze, staring at her. The emptiness in his eyes caused ice to slick her stomach. Then he blinked.

"Willow?" Surprise colored his voice. "Oh, God."

Abruptly he released her. She stumbled to her feet, putting the exam table between them. He stared down at his hands in horror. "I almost—I didn't mean—God."

Brandt slumped in the chair, head and shoulders bowed as if in pain. "God," he breathed, sounding like he was praying, begging for help. "God."

He lifted his head, staring at her with a hopeless expression it hurt her to her soul to see. "I wouldn't hurt you, Willow." His words crawled from him, desperate, as if he'd give anything for her to believe him. "I swear to God I wouldn't hurt you."

"I know." He wouldn't, not intentionally. But he had hurt her, whatever his intentions had been. She could still feel the imprint of his fingers on her arms.

"Brandt, I—"

She jumped as a knock sounded on the door just before it opened. A young, pale-haired man in blue scrubs carrying a clipboard entered the room. "Dr. Zane?"

"Yes?" She drew in a deep breath as Brandt climbed slowly to his feet, introduced himself.

"I'm Dr. Vernon," he said, shaking their hands. "I just wanted to let you know that we've managed to stop the bleeding, but it's too early to make a prognosis. I paged our on-call surgeon, Dr. Conyers, and she should be here in the next few minutes."

"How is she?" Brandt's voice sounded thick, foreign.

"I'm not going to lie to you," the young doctor said. "She wasn't in the best physical condition to begin with, which could hamper her recovery. It's also entirely possible that the dog could lose her leg, which is the least of my concerns. We'll monitor her to make sure there are no further complications like bruising to organs or internal bleeding. That's just the start of a very long, very expensive process. You might want to consider other options if the cost is prohibitive. She's a stray, right?"

"I don't care if she is a stray," Brandt said, his voice heavy, resolved. "If no one else claims her, I will. What you have to do will help more than hurt, right? She'll be able to have a decent quality of life if you take the leg?"

"Yes, sir. She's getting stabilized for now, and although she's experiencing some pain, she's not suffering. Depending on what the surgeon says, it's entirely possible that the amputation won't negatively impact her."

"Then I don't care how much it costs," Brandt cut in. He reached into his pants pocket, dug out his wallet. His hands shook as he extracted two platinum credit cards and a wad of cash. "You do everything you can to save her. You treat her like she's your child, and you save her life."

"We'll do everything we can, sir," the doctor said. "By the way, your driver's still outside. Why don't you folks go on home and get some rest? We'll call you if there's any change in the dog's condition."

"Thank you for all your help." Willow followed the vet to the door, then paused as she realized Brandt didn't follow. "Brandt?"

He picked up the clipboard, focused on the forms. "I'll see you to the car," he said, "but I'm going to stay here, make sure the dog's going to make it."

"You need to come home, change your clothes," she pointed out, wishing he'd look at her. The air conditioner had nothing to do with the chill that had settled into her bones. She sensed that if she didn't get him to return with her then, he wouldn't ever go back. "We can come right back. I'll come with you."

He exhaled, a defeated sound. "Okay. I need to go set up billing arrangements first."

It was a small victory, and Willow cherished it, but she knew the battle was far from over.

CHAPTER EIGHTEEN

Brandt headed for the stairs as soon as he'd locked the door behind him. All he wanted was to strip the bloody remnants of the tux off and take a long shower.

Willow's voice stopped him. "I need to let Boscoe out of his cage and just hug him for a moment," she said to his back. "I want to go back to the vet's with you, but I want a shower first."

He nodded, unable to look at her, and spoke his first words since they'd left the animal hospital. "All right. I'll just meet you back down here in half an hour or so."

He didn't wait for a response, just climbed the stairs to his bedroom. Immediately he headed for the shower. If he was smart, he'd take advantage of the time she spent in her room to pack and get the hell out. He had no choice but to leave, but knew she'd worry if he just disappeared. On the long, silent ride home, he'd felt her concern wrap around him like an oversized comforter.

He didn't deserve her concern. Remembering how roughly he'd grabbed her in the exam room made him sick. Another mark against him. She was the one person on this earth who could help him, and he'd hurt her instead. She'd been hurt before, he could tell. Maybe not Salazar, but someone had hurt her bad enough that she preferred being alone. Being intimate unnerved her.

He stood under the stinging cold shower spray, cursing himself bitterly. Warmth had spread through him at her touch, blowing the darkness away. Soothing his soul, thawing his heart. She'd been trying to comfort him and he'd twisted it.

He couldn't even explain it to her. How in the hell could he explain that he had to save the dog because he couldn't save his son, didn't save his wife? He'd craved the comfort she'd offered the way a drowning man craved solid ground, and he'd clutched at it with all his strength, terrifying her.

He toweled dry and dressed with quick, vicious movements. He'd had a couple of good months down here, and just when he thought he could relax, could begin to breathe again, he'd had to go and screw it up. Then again, he'd screwed up his life royally four years ago.

He dragged his duffle bag out of the closet. No need to expect things to be different just because he was in Serena Bay with her. Restoring a chapel wouldn't save him, wouldn't wash the blood off his hands.

A light tap on his open door announced Willow's presence. "Boscoe thinks Mommy's crazy," she said as she entered the room, wearing jeans and a yellow t-shirt. "I just had to hug him for a while."

She stopped in her tracks, taking in his oversized black leather duffle, the open closet. "What are you doing?"

"Packing," he answered, steeling himself for her reaction. He had no idea what that reaction would be, only that he had to prepare for it. He already knew he had precious few defenses against her, and he needed all the preparation he could get. "Gonna find a hotel." He shoved a stack of jeans into the duffel.

She folded her arms. When she spoke, her voice reeked of polite calm. "Would you mind telling me why?"

Crossing the room, he yanked open a drawer on the oak paneled dresser, removed a pile of t-shirts. "You know why."

"If I knew why, I wouldn't have asked," she said, her voice still polite, almost analytical. "Why do you want to go to a hotel?"

"Dammit, Wil!" He threw the shirts onto the bed, feeling his control fray with every question she asked. "How can you ask me that, after what happened? What else should I do?"

"You should stay here and deal with the situation. That's what I'm going to do."

"I scared you. More than that, I hurt you, something I swore I'd never do." He stared down at the bed. "Mack would want me gone."

She moved closer, the only sound the soft swish of her jeans. A ridiculous thought came to him: he'd never seen her in jeans before.

"Mack isn't going to know," she told him. "And even if he did know, he'd trust us to work it out together."

"Yeah, right. Mack would beat my ass six ways to Sunday, and you know it. I'd even let him."

"Brandt." She clasped her hands together, took a deep breath. "Yes, you scared me. I wasn't prepared for that sort of reaction from you, given where we were. I panicked. I didn't mean to, and I certainly didn't want to. I couldn't help it."

"Don't even think about blaming yourself for this," he bit out, suddenly angry with her. "You wouldn't have panicked if I hadn't grabbed you."

"And you wouldn't be trying to leave if I hadn't freaked out," she informed him. "Were you even going to tell me, or were you just going to sneak out while I was in the shower?"

That hurt. "I wouldn't have done that," he insisted. "I was going to tell you after I finished packing." He shoved the shirts into his bag.

"You're still going to leave?" she asked, disbelief causing her voice to rise.

He nodded, not looking at her. He didn't know what to say to convince her that he had to do this, for both of them. It would be impossible to stay, to sleep down the hall from her, to pretend that things hadn't changed between them, that she wouldn't treat him differently from now on.

"I'll take the next few days to arrange care for the dog, see if I can adopt her. You don't have to worry about the chapel, either. It's to a point where someone else can take over. My father could come down and finish it. Or I could recommend someone else for you."

"I see." Her voice sounded hollow. "Are you punishing me, or are you just running away?"

He did look at her then, noting the way her arms were folded across her chest, as if she were freezing. "What?"

"It's got to be one of those reasons," she said, her voice cracking. "I kiss you for comfort, your control slips because you need that comfort. I panic, and you decide you have to leave. You're either punishing me for my problems or you're running away from yours."

That hit too close to home. "You don't know a damn thing about my problems."

"I don't need to know about your problems." She stepped closer to him. "What I do know is that you're hurting. I can feel it. Will you talk to me, please?"

He wanted to. He wanted to sink to his knees, wrap his arms around her waist, and spill his sorry guts out. It was bad enough that she thought he was off his rocker. It would be worse to give her proof. "No, Dr. Zane. I don't think I can afford you."

She sucked in a breath as if he'd struck her. "Don't do this," she whispered, her voice intense. "Don't throw my profession between us. I'm not standing here as a doctor, but as a friend."

He shook his head, not understanding her. She should have been glad to get rid of him. She should have kicked him out and dumped his stuff on the lawn, then called Mack to lock him up. "Why do you think you can fix this? Why would you even want to try?"

She reached up, cupped his cheeks. He flinched, but didn't try to pull away. "Because seeing you in this kind of pain rips my heart out."

God help him, he was screwed up *and* pathetic. Why else would her words make him choke up?

"Willow." His arms automatically lifted, but he checked the impulse, stepping away from her before the temptation to pull her close overpowered his common sense again. "I'm sorry. There's no excuse for grabbing you like that. I just—trying to save that dog upset me more than I'd expected, and I wanted, I needed…"

He took a deep breath. "There's a light in you, a light I don't have. I've been in the dark so long, I just wanted a little of it to shine on me."

It was all the explanation he could trust himself to give her. Any more, and the darkness and memories would break through his fragile control, roaring to life and ready to consume him. He couldn't tell her how desperately he'd needed to feel her goodness, the kindness that came so naturally to her.

He didn't have to. "You were hurting," she said softly, dark eyes watching him. "You needed to connect. You wanted something to hold on to. I understand that."

"How can you understand that?" he demanded, angry with himself for wanting her, for needing to reach out to her. "How can you accept this?"

"Because sometimes people need people. Sometimes people just need someone to hold them close and tell them that everything will be all right, even if you don't know how to make it right. People need to know that they're not alone, even if just for a little while, that there's someone there with them. People need to know that they're not beyond redemption, that they're not being punished and pushed away. People need hope, that one day the pain won't be so bad, that the crash and burn part is over and the rebuilding can start."

The gentle words, spoken for herself as much as for him, flayed him. "Willow, you know it's not you."

"No, I don't know that." She stepped closer, her eyes glittering with unshed tears. "I can blame myself just as easily and as harshly as you're blaming yourself. All it's going to do is make us hurt more."

She wiped at her eyes. "I don't want to hurt anymore, Brandt. I don't want you to hurt anymore. I just want to hold you and have you hold me. Hopefully we'll feel that everything's going to be all right, even if it's just for a little while."

"Willow." How could he refuse her, even if he wanted to? He opened his arms and she stepped into them, thrusting her arms around his waist before resting her cheek against his chest.

Her trust and acceptance floored him. Slowly he lifted a trembling hand to touch his fingers to her cheek, whisking her tears away. Finally he dropped his hands to her back, carefully holding her close. Closing his eyes, he rested his cheek against the top of her head and just breathed her in while the world settled around them.

CHAPTER NINETEEN

Willow held onto him tight, as tight as she dared. She knew exactly how Brandt had felt at the vet's because she felt that way now. Fear spiked through her, calling out desperately for comfort. She was afraid of the anguish that rode Brandt, and the guilt that made him believe he had to leave her to protect her. The pounding of his heart was slowly returning to a normal rhythm, helping to ease her own anxiety.

Feeling so many emotions in so short a time unnerved her. Since college, logic and intellect had saved her when emotion had threatened to destroy her. Thinking things through, analyzing everything, had been a part of her life for so long, she didn't know how to do anything else.

Since Brandt's arrival, she'd had to confront emotion more than once. She'd come face to face with her own fears. Now she could see how those fears had directed her life, even her success. She had to let that fear go, obliterate it so that it could never haunt her again. She had to follow her own advice and climb out of the ashes.

Taking a deep breath, she lifted her face, staring up at his always-so-serious features. "I need you here, Brandt. I don't want someone else. I want you. You've put your heart and soul into the chapel. It's your cause, your heart. It won't have the same life if you leave it. It needs you here. I need you here."

Rising to her toes, she kissed him. He stopped breathing, holding himself still, neither giving nor taking. It wasn't enough. "I need you," she repeated against his mouth. "Kiss me. Please."

He did, his lips moving over hers with a light yet sensual thoroughness that made her head spin. Heat thickened inside her, and she had to grip his forearms in an effort to keep grounded. Then she realized that being grounded was the last thing she wanted or needed to do.

Instead, she did what she'd dreamed of doing for weeks: she tugged up his t-shirt so that she could run her hands over his chest.

He sucked in a breath. "Willow."

"Hhm?"

"Are you sure you want to do this?"

"Yes." He had the most amazing skin, like cinnamon or brown sugar with a dollop of honey thrown in. Thinking of him as food brought a sudden, nervous giggle to her lips as against all reason she wondered what he'd taste like. "May I?"

"Hell, yes."

She tugged at his t-shirt again. "Take your shirt off. Please."

He stepped back from her, his eyes fastened to her face. Slowly he gripped the hem of his shirt, and just as slowly pulled it up, over his head. Her mouth went dry as she watched his perfectly formed muscles flex beneath his skin. Something flared inside her, something new yet not quite tentative. The sweet sensation thrummed through her like the tide coming in, and she realized it for what it was: desire.

It had been building for a couple of weeks now, growing stronger with every kiss she shared with Brandt. It hadn't been that way with any of the others she'd dated, none of this heavy, heady anticipation that tightened her insides. That Brandt felt it but didn't push her had given her confidence.

She put that confidence to use now, pulling her own t-shirt over her head despite the wild hammering of her heart. After all, he'd seen her in her swimsuit several times, as she liked to go for a swim after their workouts. Still, a racer style swimsuit didn't compare to the beige lace that now cupped her breasts, and the harsh breath Brandt took proved it.

Yet he made no move to touch her, and that made her bold. She stepped closer, admiring the way his pieces fit. Muscles flexed beneath the smooth bronze of his shoulders as she lightly ran her hands over them and down his chest. A gasp of appreciation followed her movement, but she had no idea which one of them made the sound. His body fascinated her, had since the day they'd met, and she gave herself over to the joy of discovering it.

The small, hard male nipples with whorls of dark hair encircling them caught her attention. She ran her fingertips over them lightly, pleased when they puckered beneath her touch. Tension filled the muscles beneath her fingers, and his breathing deepened. Still he made no move to touch her.

She'd have to remedy that.

She stroked her hands up his chest to his shoulders, then down his arms to his hands. "You have amazing hands," she breathed, lifting his right hand between hers. She stroked his skin again, feeling the roughness of his fingertips. A thrill of anticipation shot through her, stuttering her breath as she imagined his fingers stroking her skin, her breasts.

She pressed his palm against her collarbone, feeling the heat of his skin seeping into hers. "You make such beautiful things with your hands."

"Nothing as beautiful as you," he replied, his voice as rough as the pads of his fingers stroking the pulse beating wildly at the base of her throat.

The raw desire in his voice sent a thrill shooting down her spine. "Your hands. Will you touch me like I'm touching you?"

His fingers twitched against her collarbone as fire sparked deep in his eyes. "Only if you kiss me again."

She smiled up at him, giddy. "I can do that."

This time when she lifted her head, he met her halfway, his lips gentle but insistent, coaxing a response from her. Respond she did, threading her arms around his neck, the movement lifting her breasts into his hands. She couldn't suppress a moan as his hands cupped her through the lace of her bra. Her nipples tightened instantly as his thumbs caressed her, but it wasn't enough. She had to feel his hands on her bare skin. She had to.

The straps slipped off her shoulders. "Take it off me," she demanded against his mouth. "I need to feel your skin against mine."

His fingers trailed back up to her throat, to her shoulders. As her head tilted back, his lips followed the curve of her jaw, down her throat, following her collarbone to her shoulder. So focused was she on his lips that she didn't realize he'd unhooked her bra until it loosened, slipping down her arms. She eased her hold on him long enough to let the garment fall to the floor, then pressed close again.

God, he felt good, like a living generator. She had to close her eyes against the sensory overload. It amazed her that she could be like this with him, half-naked with him, and still feel the need for more. Her breasts ached, felt full, heavy, and ultra sensitive as her nipples brushed against the hair covering his chest. Her whole body felt prickly, sensitized, almost as if she'd stayed too long on the beach baking in the sun.

Yet coastal heat cooled in comparison to Brandt's expert mouth and magical hands. When his fingers finally brushed over her bare nipples, her entire being stiffened.

At once he stopped. "Wil? Is this okay?"

She remembered how to breathe. "Okay? This is, this is incredible. I love the way your hands feel on me."

The pads of his thumbs scraped over the swollen tips of her breasts, sending currents of energy to pool low in her belly. She sucked in a breath as heat poured into her body, radiating from the deepest part of her. "Brandt."

"More?" His teeth nipped lightly at her bottom lip.

"Yes," she breathed, simmering now. Her entire existence seemed to be made of this moment, composed of the areas ruled by his lips and hands, twin signal fires on a dark night.

Brandt shifted, one hand splaying against her back. She groaned a protest that sifted to a moan as he trailed light, nipping kisses down her throat to the hollow between her breasts. She held her breath, anticipation coiling inside her.

As if sensing the exact moment she'd demand it, his mouth closed on the dark peak of her right breast. At once she shuddered, his name a hot sigh on her lips as she arched backward. This…this was heaven, even though she burned with a deep ache, an elemental fire of need.

He drew on her gently but surely, and she felt an answering pull down to her toes. Her hands gripped his shoulders, short nails digging into his skin in an effort to keep from spinning out of control.

"Brandt."

In answer to her faint call he switched his magical mouth to her left breast. She made a gargling noise deep in her throat, a sound she'd never heard herself make. A sound of pure, warm satisfaction and pleasure. Brandt's hands and mouth expertly stoked the flame of sensual pleasure, causing everything inside her to flare to life.

He lifted his head. "More?"

His hands skimmed across the flatness of her stomach, leaving sparks in their wake. She'd gone from simmer to steaming, all thanks to Brandt. "Please."

Slowly he knelt before her, his large hands splaying around her waist, just above the waistband of her jeans. His hands burned her skin, stealing her breath. He lifted his face to hers, and she could swear that she felt the heaviness of his gaze, hot and hungry, caressing her.

Then his lips pressed against her stomach. Her hands clamped down on his shoulders, not to push away, but to hold on. "Brandt."

"Tell me what you want," he whispered against her navel, his voice low, hypnotic. "Show me what you want."

Promise filled his voice, pure sin, enticing her. Unable to refuse the husky command, she fumbled for the button of her jeans, her fingers made clumsy with need. She'd never felt this kind of heat before, this driving, insistent, and burning desire for a man's hand. This man's hand.

She wanted his hands on her, his mouth on her. She wanted it so badly she didn't know how to form the words.

Brandt pinned her with a heavy-lidded gaze, his hands stoking the embers inside her by slowly gliding from her breasts to her navel and back again. "Tell me, Willow," he said, his voice as dark as his eyes. "You have to tell me what you want."

He wouldn't do anything she didn't want him to do, tell him to do. The power, the decision, was hers.

With a hard swallow, she tugged at the zipper that held her jeans closed. A tremble coursed through her that had nothing to do with cold or fear and everything to do with desire. She could feel her insides melting, feel the heat pooling between her thighs, a delicious ache.

"Help me," she said, her voice husky. "I need to feel your hands touching me. I want to feel your mouth on me."

Those magic hands skimmed up her jeans-covered legs. He held her gaze as he hooked his fingers into the waistband and slowly began to pull the heavy cotton down.

One word, and he would stop. One sound, one tremor born of anything other than desire, and he would stop. She read his intent, his will, clearly shining through the hunger in his eyes. Even with passion firing through them both, he maintained rigid control.

Her wrists framed his face as she rested both hands on his shoulders for support while he pulled her sandals and jeans off. Even as she struggled for balance he turned his head so that he could kiss one wrist, then the other.

The simple gesture fragmented one last corner of resistance inside her. She needed him. "Touch me," she demanded. "Touch me now."

He obliged her, stroking his thumb over the damp triangle of cotton that covered her. She gasped as sensations she'd never experienced before slammed into her. He stroked again, with increased pressure, his entire will focused on the center of her body. Her whole body burned for him, for what he promised, and she had to have it before the flames completely consumed her.

Lifting one hand, she tugged at her waistband, impatient with the fabric barrier. She felt his fingers curl around the elastic at the top of her panties, and she had to close her eyes as he pulled the fabric down and away. Blindly she stepped out of them, her heart pounding furiously, her insides liquid fire as she waited for him to touch her.

He didn't.

Her eyes snapped open. He stared up at her, eyes darkened with need. His hands, resting on her hips, seared her skin. He wanted to touch her, she could see that clearly, but he waited for her.

"Brandt." She licked moisture onto her lips, found the words. "I want your hand. Please."

Sparks flared in the depths of his eyes. The work-roughened pads of his fingers slid over her skin, moving towards her heated core. She wanted to look, but his eyes held hers.

Then she felt it, felt his blunt fingers slowly pushing against her. The reality of the moment stuttered her breath, but she widened her eyes against the urge to close them, and focused on his face, his hands. Brandt.

Shifting, she widened her stance, allowing his fingers to find their way inside. Sensation flared deep within her, burning her senses, forcing a moan from her lips. She couldn't help it, she had to close her eyes to prevent sensory overload as his fingers retreated, then advanced in a slow, decadent dance.

"Brandt." Her nails dug into his massive shoulders as her hips instinctively pushed forward, searching for more, burning for more.

Then he kissed her.

Her knees instantly buckled at the unexpected eruption of pleasure. His hands guided her, and she found herself lying on the edge of the bed.

This time he didn't ask, launching an offensive with mouth and fingers that scorched her entire being. If she thought his hands were wonderful, she didn't know adjectives good enough to describe his mouth. Wave after wave of sensation roiled through her as he stroked deep inside her with his tongue, teased the engorged ridge of pleasure that centered her. She burned, she bucked, and she blasphemed as her body suddenly, violently exploded into red-hot orgasm.

Once there, he wouldn't let her come down. She couldn't catch her breath as he worked memorable magic, his mouth suckling her as his fingers delved deep, then curved upward. Her hips lifted off the bed again, incoherent words tearing from her as electric sensations zapped every nerve ending. The heat built again, flames licking higher and higher, stoked by velvet caresses. She tried to hold on, tried to stay in the moment. Pleasure blazed through her again, causing her to cry out, to fly out of control into a brilliant, shattering release.

CHAPTER TWENTY

Brandt pulled the sheet over Willow, then moved up to stretch out beside her. She didn't move or open her eyes; it seemed to be taking all of her energy just to breathe. A smile pulled at his lips. She'd come apart at least twice, and he felt more than a little male satisfaction that he'd been the one to do that for her.

Looking at the satiated smile on her face, Brandt felt his own need clawing through him. God, he wanted her. Wanted to feel her tremble and shimmer around him, wanted to hear those incredibly sexy moans as he moved inside her. He wanted her so badly it shook him.

He made no move towards her, though. Despite what he'd just given her—or maybe because of it—she still had a right to say no, and he'd honor that right. She'd trusted him this far, and he'd prove himself worthy of that trust even if it killed him.

Shame hit him again as he recalled her reaction at the animal hospital. She'd been afraid of him, afraid of what he'd do to her. He'd rather die than have her look at him like that ever again. It stabbed him to the core that she'd believed, even for a heartbeat, that he was capable of doing something so heinous. He had enough sin at his feet without adding that to the pile dragging him down.

She turned to him then, or rather, rolled her head so that she could see him. A languid smile lit her eyes as she lifted a hand to stroke his cheek. "Brandt. I…you…God."

He laughed then, not because it was expected, but because he actually felt like it. Thankful for that gift, he captured her hand, pressing a kiss to her wrist. "Ditto."

She tilted her head. "Do you think…will I feel the same when you're inside me?"

Breath left him in a rush. She'd said when, not if. His whole body jumped in response, in promise, but he quelled it, knowing he had to answer truthfully. "It'll feel different, because I'm, uhm, larger than my fingers."

She shifted onto her side. "Let me see."

He hadn't expected that. He stared down into her eyes, trying to read her expression, to understand. Curiosity stared back. Did he imagine anticipation, or was it just wishful thinking?

She pulled her hand free of his to hook into his waistband. "Show me."

Before he could question it, he rolled off the bed. Keeping his eyes fastened to hers, he unzipped his jeans, then pushed them and his briefs off his hips. Freed at last, his erection jutted proud and undeniable between them.

He felt her gaze like a caress, sliding down to the aching part of him. Her eyes widened, then she licked her lips. He jumped in response.

She giggled. She actually giggled. "Yeah, you're definitely more than two fingers," she agreed, her voice husky.

He didn't know what to make of her or her words. The suspense was killing him. "I know you said it's been a while, but we can prob—"

She stroked him.

His thoughts evaporated, his voice stuttering to a halt as her fingers wrapped around him. His hips slipped forward, pushing his penis through the warmth of her hand. "That feels good," he told her. "Better than good." It was the only thing he could think of to say, but it was true.

She sat up, the sheet slipping from her breasts. She didn't seem to notice or care, so focused was she on her hand. So was he for that matter. "Do you have condoms? I didn't think to get any."

The bluntness of her words contrasting with the soft stroking of her hand made him feel as if he'd been drugged, or zapped into an alternate reality. A wave of heat coursed over his body. "Yeah, I bought some," he admitted, his voice gruff as he gritted his teeth against sweet sensation.

Control, he had to stay in control. He sensed that she wasn't completely ready for the next step, despite the bravado of her words. He tried to give her a way out. "Wil, we don't have to do this." *And I won't be able to walk for a week.*

With a gentle tug, she pulled him closer. "Yeah, we do."

She reached up, kissed him then, her hand still stroking him. Someone moaned, but he didn't know who. He held her gently, but couldn't stop the need to sweep his tongue into her mouth, thrusting in counterpoint to the movement of his hips. By sheer will alone, he slowed his movements, taking her lips with a slow, almost lazy exploration while he barely moved in her hand. He wanted her hot for him, burning for him, needing him inside her as badly as he wanted to be there.

She tightened her grip, capturing his attention. "Go get the condoms," she ordered, her voice raspy. "Now."

He complied, feeling as prickly and urgent as a teen experiencing his first time. As soon as he could, he draped himself over her, skimming his hands over her skin because he simply had to.

She pressed against him, kissing him with all the encouragement he needed. He pushed against her, feeling heat, slick resistance. The sensation fired his senses, leaving him wanting more. Shaking, he pushed forward until he'd buried himself to the hilt.

He wanted to remain still, wanted to give her the moment she needed to adjust to him filling her. His hips had other ideas, flexing against her, pushing him through the satiny heat. A sharp breath caught his attention, only because it didn't sound like passion. It sounded like pain.

He opened eyes he didn't realize he'd closed. Willow stared past his shoulder, her eyes wide with something perilously close to fear. Her entire body was stiff, her hands pressing against his chest in silent entreaty to be let up as her chest heaved with the need for air.

Gripping her hips in his hands, Brandt rolled them over until she rose above him. His hands immediately fell away from her, digging into the sheets as she relaxed enough to straighten. She shifted—

"Don't. Move. Yet." He didn't even recognize his voice. It was all he could do to breathe, close his eyes, and struggle to maintain control. Finally he eased his grip on the mattress, and opened his eyes.

Uncertainty shadowed her wide-eyed gaze, stealing whatever pleasure he'd seen there minutes before. He couldn't help wondering what else had happened to her before now. Surely bad sex with the mayor couldn't cause this sort of reaction.

"Willow." He swallowed, then tried again. "Sweetheart, it's all right. If you need to stop this, it's okay. But you have to be the one. Leave now, and I swear to God I'll let you."

He waited, still rock-hard inside her, maintaining an increasingly thin veneer of control. Willow needed to decide soon. Immediately. He was trying to help her, trying to keep his promise to her. No matter what, he never wanted her to look at him in fear again.

"Willow. Please."

Something flickered in her eyes, something that locked his lungs. Slowly she spread her hands on his ribcage, then lifted off him. Disappointment forced his eyes shut. She'd warned him this would happen, and he'd already experienced more with her than he'd expected—

She lowered herself again, surrounding him with moist heat. His eyes snapped open, searching for hers.

"I want this," she said shakily, raising her hips again. "I want you. You do know that, don't you?"

He blew out a breath as she settled onto him again. No, he hadn't known that, not until that moment. Something inside him eased, melted. "Willow."

"You have to help me," she said then, her voice strained. "We both need this, but I need you to help me."

He looked into those beautiful dark eyes and was instantly lost. Once again he rolled, until she was beneath him again. When she stiffened, would have closed her eyes, he kissed her.

"Look at me," he urged her. "See me, here with you."

She nodded, wide eyes locked to his, arms tentative around his neck. "Wrap your legs around my waist," he whispered against her mouth. She complied, immediately settling him deeper.

He withdrew, slowly, and just as slowly reentered. Her breath caught, but her hands skimmed down his back, causing him to shiver. Mindful of crushing her or triggering a panic, he leveraged away from her, giving her space to breathe. Only their hips and legs touched, but it was more than enough.

He wanted to take his time, wanted her wild for him, wanted to drive into her soft heat until he became a part of her. Sweat slicked his back as he slowly increased the pace, determined to soothe her while sending them both over the edge.

She moved beneath him, legs stroking against his hips, his thighs. Her hands roamed over his skin in a restless dance, leaving fire in their wake. Staring down into her eyes was an erotic sensation all its own. He saw the exact moment that passion overrode everything else, her lips parting, her back arching. When her nails sank into his shoulders, he increased the pace yet again, surging into her repeatedly in overpowering need.

He slipped a hand between their colliding bodies, stroking her. She responded instantly, humming with pleasure, hips arching upward. She was close; he could see it flaring in her eyes, enflaming him.

Suddenly her hands clamped down on his buttocks, her inner muscles gripping him as his name broke on her lips. Her whole body clenched around him as she cried out. Half a heartbeat later he exploded, his body rigid with the intensity of one long, shuddering release.

Breathing heavily, he pulled away from her, reluctantly fighting the desire to stay buried in her soft heat. She had her eyes closed, struggling to catch her breath. Leaning over, he dropped a kiss on her cheek. "I'll be right back."

He quickly cleaned up, then returned, carrying a damp washcloth for her. What he saw stopped him cold. Willow lay on her back, hands over her face as her body shook.

She was crying.

A cold, sick feeling formed in the pit of his stomach. How could he have been mistaken, how could he have thought he was pleasing her when he'd really been hurting her instead?

He dropped to his knees beside the bed. "Tell me what's wrong, sweetheart. Tell me what I need to do to make this right."

She dragged her hands away from her face. "If you make this any more right, I'll die."

"You're not upset?"

"Upset?" She beamed at him through the moisture sparkling in her lashes. "I'm nowhere near upset. I just had no idea it could be so—that you would be so, so—"

She lifted up, raining kisses all over his forehead, cheeks, lips. The kisses became slower, more thorough, until he was lightheaded and hot-blooded again. His heart hammered in his chest as he took her hand, pressed a kiss into the back of it because he couldn't think of anything to say, any words to describe what she'd given him.

Her eyes softened as her free hand lifted, fingers trailing over his face. "You're smiling. That's like a bonus on top of a bonus." She held up the sheet. "Come here."

He slid into bed beside her, tucking her into the curve of his arm as she rested her head on his chest. Her fingers moved in lazy circles over his heart as she yawned. "Hope you don't mind, but I think I'm gonna fall asleep right here."

"I don't mind." He didn't mind a bit. For a long moment he just lay there, feeling her body next to his, still amazed that she was there. "Thank you," he whispered to her, "for this."

"Thank me when I wake up with sleep in my eyes and dragon breath," she said, yawning again as she snuggled closer.

"Promise, as long as you're still okay with this in the morning."

"You know what? You talk too much," she mumbled, then promptly fell asleep.

For the first time in years, Brandt Hughes fell asleep smiling.

CHAPTER TWENTY-ONE

Willow wondered where she'd left her mind. Obviously in the same pile as her clothes.

She'd awakened to Boscoe's whines and Brandt's soft snoring, a situation so foreign she'd thought she was dreaming. The reality of her naked body, full bladder, and Brant's heavy arm around her waist told her she was very much awake. How she'd managed to slip out of bed and gather her clothes without waking him, she had no idea. All she knew was that she still wasn't quite ready to face him yet. She needed time to absorb what had happened, and why.

She quickly padded downstairs to let her overeager mutt out the side door, then started a pot of coffee before heading back upstairs to a long shower. Her analytical mind poured over her experience, examining it from every angle with clinical detachment.

The results were the same, no matter how she approached it. She didn't regret sleeping with Brandt. Even now, with hot water soothing foreign aches, she felt too good for it to be wrong.

If she had any regret, it was that they'd gone about being intimate the wrong way. Going to bed with Brandt should have been easy, instigated by nothing but the pure desire they'd shared in the limousine ride to the fundraiser. Instead, there'd been this desperate, driving need to comfort and be comforted. Sure, desperation had changed to desire quickly enough, but the fact remained that they'd slept with each other for the wrong reasons.

She'd had to apologize to him for that. That, and for panicking on him again. She didn't have to be a psychologist to know that it had taken a great deal of control for Brandt to give her space and let her make the choice they'd both needed. She was grateful for that, and grateful for making the right choice. It had been worth it, more than worth it. He'd taken her to a place she couldn't take herself. She'd even go so far as to admit that she felt as if she'd been reborn. Next time would be even better.

She paused, the towel slipping off her shoulders. Was she really thinking about the next time already? She skimmed her hand across her throat, remembering the feel of Brandt's hands, Brandt's mouth. Want puckered her nipples, and confusion stopped her hand.

How could she already want to be intimate with Brandt again, after so many years of avoiding intimacy? One night, even a night as magical as the previous one, couldn't negate more than a decade of phobia, could it? Fear of intimacy had been a part of her psyche for so long it had become instinctive. Tony had borne the brunt of her phobia, and so had other potential relationships.

Why was Brandt different? More importantly, why would she think Brandt was different?

Her private line was ringing when she reentered her bedroom. She pulled her robe tighter, pushing away memories of pleasure and multiple orgasms. Since it was just after nine, either Tony or Mack had to be the first call of the day. Might as well end the suspense. "Hello?"

"Have you seen the paper?"

"Good morning to you, too, Tony." She sat on the edge of the bed. "No, I haven't seen the paper yet. Anything interesting happen?"

"You know damn well something interesting happened," Tony retorted. "There's a picture of you standing behind your bloody carpenter-bodyguard, and you're both looking like you've been through the wringer."

"Please don't tell me this bumped coverage of the fundraiser," Willow said, rubbing at her forehead.

"Your little rescue made the front page. I can't believe you risked your life stepping out into traffic like that. Don't you realize your life is more important than a dog's?"

Willow pulled the towel from her hair. "What you should be outraged about is that someone hit a dog and just drove away. You should be outraged that someone abandoned their pet to become a stray and be put into danger. Don't get mad at me because Brandt decided to help that poor dog and I decided to help him."

"It always comes back to him, doesn't it?" Tony said, his voice bitter. "What is this guy to you?"

"A friend," Willow answered simply, knowing it was true. "He's a good friend."

There was a pause on the other end of the line before Tony spoke again, his voice just above a whisper. "He's more than that now, isn't he?"

Willow closed her eyes. "I don't know," she answered, telling the truth. She had no idea what she was to Brandt or what he was to her. Friends didn't seem to cover it, yet saying they were lovers didn't seem to fit either.

"I saw you two together last night," Tony said, interrupting her thoughts. "I saw how you kept looking at him all through the fundraiser. You can't tell me that there's nothing going on."

This conversation had to happen at some point, she knew, just as she knew she would have lied just to make Tony realize he couldn't wait for her anymore. "You're right. I can't tell you that."

She heard him sigh, a small defeated sound. "I guess I shouldn't be surprised," he said then, his voice stranger than she'd ever heard it. "Do you know what you're getting into with him? Do you even know what happened to his wife and child?"

Willow closed her eyes, wanting to curl into her pillows for the rest of the day. She understood Tony's concern, but she'd been making her own decisions for a long time. "Yes, to both questions. I'm going into this, whatever this is, with my eyes open, Tony. I really am."

She heard him clear his throat. "Well, then. I guess there isn't anything else to say."

"I guess not," she managed through a tight throat.

"Take care of yourself, Willow. If you need anything, well, you know where I am." Tony disconnected.

Willow replaced the phone in its cradle, then went to get dressed. She couldn't shake the feeling that her friendship with Tony had just suffered a mortal blow. She'd trusted Tony with her life, with her darkest secret. Since high school, he'd been the one she'd turned to during every major event in her life. She would always think of him with affection.

Yet even now she couldn't imagine being with him the way she'd been with Brandt. Just as she didn't think she could share with Brandt everything that Tony knew about her. She knew that whatever this was with Brandt, as new and fragile as it was, it probably didn't have a long life. She couldn't help wondering what would happen to each of them when Brandt returned to his life in Atlanta.

Her heart heavy in her chest, Willow stepped into the hallway, heading for the stairs and her office. At the door to Brandt's bedroom, she paused. She'd left it open a crack when she'd left, but now it stood closed.

Realizing that Brandt was awake caused a skittering of nerves up her spine. What would it be like to face Brandt for the first time? Would he think she'd sneaked out of his bedroom to avoid waking up with him? Did he have regrets, or did he want to be together again as much as she did?

One thing for certain, she wouldn't get answers lurking outside his door. She headed down the stairs to her office. Any answers she wanted would have to wait. With the incident with the dog making the paper, she'd have to make some sort of formal statement, especially if she and Brandt returned to the animal hospital to check up on the dog.

Telling herself that she wasn't a coward, she entered her office and put the morning-after worries out of her mind.

"Hughes."

"You've got five seconds to tell me why I shouldn't drive over there and arrest you."

Brandt winced at the anger in Mack's voice. "Couldn't this wait until I get coffee?"

"No."

Great. He sat on the edge of his bed. "So the word's out, huh?"

"The word, as you put it, made the front page," Mack informed him. "Are you out of your freakin' mind, putting Willow in danger like that?"

"I thought she'd stay in the damn limo," Brandt said, knowing it was a sorry excuse for an erstwhile bodyguard. "I didn't think she'd follow me into traffic."

"Which goes to show that you know nothing about my sister at all."

"So I'm learning." Willow was even more complicated than he'd thought. Way the hell more complicated. She had more layers than an onion. "Have you talked to her yet?"

"She's next. You're both lucky I didn't drive over there first thing this morning."

Considering where Willow had been first thing that morning, Brandt knew exactly how lucky he was. "She's all right, I think," he said, fudging the truth. "It wasn't exactly the best night for either of us."

A harsh sigh answered him. "You did a good job trying to keep her from being photographed, but you look like you went ten rounds with Muhammad Ali."

Brandt snorted. "Thanks for giving me the whole ten."

"I hear the dog's doing well, thanks to you," Mack said. "It was a good thing you did. Stupid, but good. Then again, I seem to recall you doing something similar out in the sand pit."

"Yeah, well." Brandt hunched his shoulders at the wartime memory. "Mama never claimed me as the smart one. I couldn't leave the dog out there to just die. I wouldn't."

"I know." Mack's tone sounded sympathetic, and Brandt wondered if his friend recalled the same images of dust and blood and sand as he did.

"How did Willow handle it?"

"You mean me or the dog?"

"Both."

Brandt hesitated, searching for the right words. His gaze fell to the bed, the rumpled sheets. His fingers moved over the spot where Willow had been, an absent-minded gesture. He certainly couldn't tell Mack what had happened at the hospital and after they'd returned home. How do you tell your best friend that you slept with his sister, and would do it again at the first opportunity?

"I don't understand her," he said, finally settling on a truth, if not the whole truth. Memory caused acid to fill his stomach as he confessed, "I didn't handle it nearly as well as she did. Saving the dog brought back some things, and I didn't react all that well. She forgave me anyway."

"That's my little sister," Mack said with obvious affection. "Her heart's way too big. Lord knows she didn't get that from our parents. But listen," he added, "I'm only going to say this once, then I won't mention it again. You should talk to her, about what happened."

Brandt knuckled the phone, his chest tightening. "No."

"Willow's not stupid," Mack said quietly. "If dealing with the dog brought back things as you said, Willow noticed. She knows you're dealing with something, even if she doesn't know exactly what it is. She's good at what she does. If you let her, she'll help you."

"I know." At the vet's, he'd felt himself sliding into darkness, a darkness so deep and complete he couldn't see his way out. She'd been there for him, her touch and her voice guiding him back. She didn't know how much darkness churned inside him, though, and he meant to keep it that way.

He tried to deflect Mack's attention. "Have you talked to her? Professionally, I mean."

"Hell no," Mack said. "She doesn't have me on a high pedestal as it is. I certainly don't need to be knocked off completely by letting her know how screwed up I really am. Besides, we're talking about you, not me."

Brandt's hand fisted the sheet. "I can't talk to her," he managed to say. "Not about that." Hell, she already pitied him enough. If she knew everything about him, the stain on his soul—

"Do you really think she'd treat you differently?" Mack asked.

Brandt rubbed at his forehead. Of course Mack would know what he was thinking. "Everyone else did."

"I'll say it again. You obviously know nothing about her. I suggest you learn."

"Is that an order?"

"No, just a friendly public service announcement. Why don't you tell me about the fundraiser? Anything unusual happen there?"

Since they were done discussing his state of mind, Brandt relaxed. "Nothing unusual, but I definitely got a strange vibe from the Salazars."

"Really?" Mack sounded intrigued. "Like what?"

"Well, the mayor definitely wasn't happy to see me last night. I guess he's still smarting from whatever Willow said to him after his surprise visit here a couple of weeks ago. As for the sister-in-law—"

"Fine, ain't she?"

"If you like them dangerous," Brandt said. "She's like a barracuda in a thousand-dollar dress. She's got a cold streak a mile wide. She didn't like the fact that Salazar was all bent out of shape over me being there with Willow."

"You think Monica has a thing for the mayor?"

"That's like saying Liz Taylor has a thing for diamonds," Brandt retorted. "I don't think it's mutual since the mayor still has it bad for Willow, but a jealous woman can be a dangerous thing."

"I hear you. Has anything happened around there lately?"

"It's been quiet since I gave you that last letter," Brandt answered. "Willow's been so deep in writing and clients that she hasn't seen either one of them in the last two weeks. I use dinner as an excuse to get her to come back to the house before dark, so she hasn't been in the mission at night. Even with Pattie gone, things have been smooth. We're probably due for something."

"You think it's one of the Salazars? Her best friends?"

"If those are the best friends Willow's got, you should worry," Brandt said. "Neither one of them treated her very friendly last night. If it's not Monica being the other woman, then it's the mayor wanting Willow for himself. You need to watch them both."

"Great." Mack blew out a breath. "How in the hell am I supposed to quietly investigate two of Serena Bay's most prominent citizens?"

"I could help." The thought of sticking it to the mayor made Brandt smile.

"You just keep on doing what you're doing and protect Willow," Mack retorted. "Last thing I need is for my best friend to be caught breaking and entering. Let me know if anything happens that I should know about."

There was a bunch that Mack needed to know about, Brandt thought as he got dressed. His gaze returned again and again to the bed, his mind replaying every moment spent with Willow, every sound she'd made, the way she'd felt, the way she'd tasted.

He told himself there was a reasonable explanation for her to sneak out of his bedroom. He knew her schedule well enough to know she always got up early to let Boscoe out. He certainly couldn't expect her to come back to bed with him, as much as he would have enjoyed it. He certainly couldn't expect her to be completely comfortable lying naked with him, especially after the difficulties she'd had. It had been enough that she'd fallen asleep snuggled beside him.

That was last night, however. Morning had a way of making people see things differently. Would she regret sleeping with him?

He hoped not. He opened his door and stepped into the hallway. The door to Willow's master suite stood open, so he headed for the stairs. In being with her, he'd found something he didn't even know he'd been missing. He wanted to experience that again, and he wanted to experience it with her.

The aroma of caffeine drew him to the kitchen. Only two cups' worth had been poured from the carafe, he noted, snagging a mug to pour a cup. That meant Willow hadn't gone to the mission yet. It always took three cups to get her moving towards her office in the other building.

Determined to see her, he headed past the great room for her office. He hadn't gone two steps before his cell phone rang. Pulling it free of his belt clip, he glanced at the readout and immediately groaned. Steeling himself, he flipped open the phone and spoke. "Hey, Maya. What's up?"

"What do you mean, what's up? We see a picture of you on national news, in a tux and walking with Willow Zane, and you don't call your family? Mom flipped out."

Brandt suppressed a groan. Mom flipping out wasn't pretty. He was suddenly glad that he wasn't in Atlanta. "Tell Mom that it wasn't a big deal. She needed an escort to a fundraiser, so I stepped in to help her out. That's all."

"That's all." Disbelief came over the phone line loud and clear. "Like you escort celebrities to star-studded events all the time."

"It wasn't a star-studded event. It was a local fundraiser for a county community center. I don't even know why it would make the national news."

"Oh, do you think it might have had something to do with the dramatic rescue of an injured dog on a busy highway?" Maya asked sweetly.

"That made it too?" Brandt groaned again. "Mom's not the only one who's going to flip. Willow's going to hit the roof."

"And you just happen to be on a first-name basis with this particular client?" Maya nearly purred with excitement. "You've been holding out on me."

"No, I haven't," he disagreed quickly, even as his mind flashed back to early this morning and Willow naked in his bed.

"Uh-hunh," Maya snorted in patent disbelief. "Well, I guess I'll just have to see for myself, won't I?"

Brandt straightened. "What do you mean, see for yourself?"

"We're taking Taylor and Zack down to spend a little time with Nick's parents," Maya explained. "I thought it would be nice to take a side trip and see how you're doing."

"No," he said, and immediately winced, wishing he could take it back.

"Why not?" Maya's voice radiated reasonable sweetness, which meant she was up to something. "Mom thought it was a great idea, especially since we won't be all that far from Serena Bay."

"All that far?" he echoed. "Orlando's almost four hours away!"

"What's time and space to family? You convince me that you're fine, and I'll report back to Mom and Dad." She paused. "It's either that or Mom shows up down there herself."

Brandt rested his forehead in his hand. The thought of his little Vietnamese mother running rampant around Serena Bay filled his stomach with acid. The poor town wouldn't stand a chance.

He didn't have a choice and he knew it. "When will you be here?"

CHAPTER TWENTY-TWO

"I just wanted to stop by and make sure you were all right," Zee said from beneath her broad-rimmed hat. She looked like some '40s film icon with her dark sunglasses and white halter dress showing her olive skin to advantage. Willow wondered again, for the umpteenth time, why Monica had chosen to stay in Serena Bay after Ricardo died.

"I'm fine," Willow said, taking a seat on the stone bench in one of the alcoves that dotted the serenity garden. She sat gingerly; some parts of her were still a little tender.

"I still can't believe you risked your life crossing A1A to save a half-dead dog," Monica exclaimed. "Are you out of your mind?"

"Take a number on reading me the riot act, Zee," Willow said, her irritation mounting. Her early morning good humor had evaporated with the first phone call of the morning, and not seeing Brandt yet had only served to make her more edgy. Getting some air by taking a walk in the serenity garden had seemed like a good idea at the time, until she'd gotten the call that Monica was at the front gate. "I've already had enough yelling from Tony. I don't need it from you."

"Come on, Willow," Monica said with a small laugh. "It was just a dog. It's not like a child got hurt."

"Have you had a pet, Zee? They're members of the family. If something happened to Boscoe, I'd be devastated."

Monica lowered her sunglasses. "This from someone who didn't come home for her father's funeral, but returned to bury a nun. Though if I'd known I was getting a choice piece of real estate out of the deal, I'd have come running, too."

Shocked to stillness, Willow could only stare at her friend, though she had to wonder if a real friend would say the sort of things that

Monica just had. "You've got a lot of nerve, Zee. I can't believe you could say something like that!"

Monica gave another one of her light laughs, a sound Willow was beginning to dislike. "I was kidding, Willow. Okay, I admit it was in poor taste, but even you have to admit that your timing was a little suspect."

"I don't have to admit anything," Willow retorted, grinding her teeth against the urge to raise her voice. "And I sure as hell don't have to explain anything to someone who's supposed to be my friend!"

The smile slipped from Monica's face. "I wouldn't be a good friend if all I did was say 'that's great' to every little thing you do, just because you're rich and famous."

"I wouldn't expect a friend to do that," Willow retorted, climbing to her feet. "Then again, I wouldn't expect a friend to take jabs at me every time we get together."

"I apologize," Monica said, her voice stiff. "I didn't realize you had such thin skin where your father was concerned."

That was it. Willow settled her hands on her hips, suddenly glad she hadn't invited Monica into the house. "You know what? I think it's time for you to leave. I need to go back to work."

"What? I can't be blunt with you?" Monica sounded hurt, but her expression was angry. "I understand why you'd take it from Mack, but why would you let Tony tell it like it is, and get all upset when I try?"

"Tony and I have been friends for a lot longer, Monica, since before we were 'rich and famous,' as you put it. I love him to death, and I've never once had to question our friendship."

"I see." Monica settled her sunglasses into place. "All I've done is try to be the voice of reason in the little fairy-tale view you have of life. If you don't want a real friend, fine. But don't think for a second that Tony doesn't have ulterior motives for being your friend."

Monica stalked away. Willow let her have the last word simply because she wanted the woman off her property. She exhaled slowly, then headed for the path that led to her side of the grounds. She needed to stand on her private beach.

It took a couple of tries to get the passcode entered, but she finally made it through the gate and down the path to the ocean. She kicked off her sandals and kept walking until she was up to her thighs in the warm saltwater. Only then was she able to take a breath in, to allow herself to feel the sadness and surprising elation.

The late morning sky flowed with streaks of clouds, driven by the same breeze that raked through her hair. Deep inside she knew she didn't need a friend who criticized more than supported. She hadn't gone to Monica's in a couple of weeks due to her busy schedule, and she found she didn't miss the banana nut bread or the company nearly as much as she'd thought she would. She certainly didn't miss the barbs casually disguised as jokes. Why hadn't she noticed before how not nice Monica was?

Probably because she'd been desperate for a friend, a female friend, in Serena Bay. She could count on one hand the people she called friends: Pattie, Isis, Tony. Though Pattie had been working for her for a few years and treated her like a daughter, Willow couldn't confide everything to her.

Since she'd returned to Serena Bay, she rarely saw Isis. Both their assistants had worked hard to coordinate the spa and shopping weekends she and Isis had religiously taken when they both lived in L.A. Willow missed Isis's dry wit and sharp mind, her confidence as bright as the trademark shade of red she always wore. Even with Isis, though, there were some things that Willow didn't share, just as she was sure there were things the ultra-driven talk-show star didn't share with her psychologist friend.

Willow realized that she'd tried to find a surrogate friend in Monica. That had been a mistake, a mistake that had corrected itself. She found herself mourning the loss of a friendship more than the loss of Monica's friendship.

Tony's friendship was a different matter. Tony had been a part of her life for so long that she couldn't imagine life without him. He alone knew everything about her, and stood with her anyway. She'd meant it when she told Monica that she loved Tony. She'd always love him, as a friend, like a brother.

She wasn't in love with him, and that was what he deserved. The thought that he might have missed out on finding the right woman because he'd waited for her crushed Willow's heart.

A tennis ball sailed past her, followed by her dog. Both landed with a splash. She quickly wiped at her eyes, then turned to see Brandt striding towards her. He looked different, and she couldn't figure out why until she realized that he didn't have on his tool belt or the jeans and workboots she'd grown accustomed too. Instead he wore sneakers, loose fitting navy shorts, and a Georgetown t-shirt.

Her heart gave a funny leap in her chest. Brandt was her friend, or at least she thought so. Maybe more, but she couldn't wonder about that. Surely she meant something more than duty to him, after last night. Surely he felt the same longing she did. Even knowing that he'd leave sooner rather than later didn't lessen the desire. She wanted as much time in Brandt's arms as she could get, storing up the memories to keep her company after he left.

She waded through the water towards him, not caring about lifting her skirt, just caring about getting to him. Boscoe beat her to him, but Brandt quickly palmed the ball and threw it into the ocean again. His expression changed as he watched her, became fierce, but he held out his arms, and she walked straight into them.

Pressing her face against his heart, she closed her eyes and just stopped, stopped being a celebrity psychologist, stopped being someone with dubious friendships, stopped being anything other than a woman on a beach being held by a gorgeous man.

Brandt held her close, one large hand rubbing her back in a soothing gesture. She didn't know what it was about him, his size, his strength, or the resolve in his eyes, but he made her feel safe. He made her feel at ease in her own skin in a way that no one else ever had.

He tilted his head, his lips grazing her left ear. "I thought you might be feeling some regrets about last night."

"About us? No. The only thing I regret is that it wasn't just desire between us. I wanted it to be simple."

"It's never simple," he replied, and his voice sounded as if he was mentally far away. "You just hope that you don't overcomplicate things."

"Then let's not complicate things," she said into his chest. "Lord knows, life is complicated enough."

His left hand settled at her waist. "Busy morning?"

"You could say that. After fielding so many phone calls, I needed to clear my head."

"I thought you were walking in the gardens with your friend." He didn't seem to be in a hurry to let her go, and she wasn't in a hurry to make him.

"I was." Since he was holding her, she felt free to shift her hands lower, just above his back pockets. "But I don't think she's my friend any more. We had a big argument before I asked her to leave. And I don't know what to think about Tony. I'm trying to figure out why I'm not more upset."

She felt him hesitate, and she realized he was searching for words. Finally he spoke. "I don't know much about friendship anymore. Mack's one of the last ones I've managed to not screw up, and that's more thanks to him than to me. Maybe you're not all that upset about Monica because you know, on some level, that she wasn't that much of a friend."

That was the conclusion she was reaching, but it surprised her that Brandt knew that after one meeting with Monica. "Why do you say that?"

He stared out at the sea. "I'm just saying that for friends, neither seems all that friendly towards you. I mean, the mayor has his reasons, but I don't see why Monica Salazar doesn't like you, unless she's jealous."

"Do you really think Monica doesn't like me, that she's jealous of me?"

"Why wouldn't she be?"

"Why would she be?" she countered. "She's beautiful. She went into modeling right out of high school. She also got lots of money when her husband died. Why in the world would Monica be jealous of me?"

"You have one thing she doesn't."

Willow pulled back, just enough to stare up at his face. What in the world do I have that Monica doesn't?"

"The mayor's attention."

"I-I..." She didn't know what to say to that for a moment. "Tony's not going to go there. She was married to his brother. He wouldn't think it was right, even if he liked her that way. And the whole town would flip if they did hook up."

"That's your take on it. Monica might think differently."

Willow mulled over his words, and her friendships. She'd never in any way given Monica reason to think her relationship with Tony was anything more than platonic. On top of that, she'd never told Monica about leaving Serena Bay with Tony or their brief engagement during college.

She remembered how Monica had looked beside Tony last night, all decked out. She had to admit that they looked good together. Both were tall, athletic, beautiful, and looked as if they'd just stepped off a yacht in South Beach.

Given what she'd discovered of Monica's personality, there was no way in the world that she'd encourage them towards each other. Tony was a good man, more than a good man. He deserved to be the center of someone's universe, because that was how he'd treat the right woman.

Maybe she was wrong about him, though. She'd certainly been wrong about Monica, and there was some truth to Monica's parting comment. Tony hadn't stayed close to her simply because he wanted her friendship, but because he wanted more. She should have been flattered; instead, she felt betrayed, as if their friendship were an illusion.

"It's funny," she said, her voice barely above the pounding of the surf. "I can diagnose a paranoid-schizophrenic with no problem, yet I can't tell when people closest to me are lying to me."

She felt him stiffen, remembered that he was keeping things from her. Then again, she hadn't been completely truthful with him, either.

To hell with it, she thought. "You know what? I'm done thinking about friendships. This is a beautiful day, and it would be a shame to spoil it with heavy thinking." She stepped back, not enough to break his hold, but to look into the rain-cloud gray of his eyes. "I think I'm going to play hooky."

He squinted down at her. "Can you take time out of your schedule?"

"Well, there are things I should be doing, and there are things I want to be doing," she replied, looking out at the water. "I've got some notes I need to transcribe, even though those can wait for Pattie, I suppose. I've got some prep work to do before I call a couple of clients Monday, and of course, there's the manuscript. And I still want to go back to the animal hospital. But really, I think I'd like to play hooky, forget about all my issues and problems for a while." She looked up at him. "Would you like to play hooky with me?"

His eyes sparked, a veneer of a smile just curving his generous lips. "I thought you'd never ask."

He stepped back from her as Boscoe lumbered out of the water. As if realizing they were headed for the house, he shook himself, sending seawater flying, soaking her and Brandt both.

She laughed in spite of herself, her somber mood breaking. Brandt narrowed his eyes at her. "Oh, you think that's funny, do you?"

She read his intention and made a break for it, shrieking. "Oh no you don't!"

He immediately gave chase, Boscoe urging him on. He caught her easily, one muscular arm snaking around her waist, lifting her off her feet and over his shoulder. Screaming with laughter, she half-heartedly tried to break free as he strode into the water up to his thighs, Boscoe barking at his heels.

She gasped, trying to speak through giggles. "You dunk me, you're going to be in big trouble, mister."

"It doesn't sound threatening when you're laughing your ass off." He spun in a dizzying circle.

"Stop before I throw up!" She gripped his back pockets with both hands, her braids dangling centimeters above the waves. "Boscoe, aren't you going to defend your mommy?" she demanded, only to have her mutt look at her as if she were crazy.

"Boscoe knows better," Brandt said, tightening his grip on her legs. "Us menfolk have to stick together."

"We'll see about that." She reached into his waistband. "How would you like a wedgie?"

He froze. "You wouldn't."

"Really? Dump me in the water and find out."

"Okay, maybe you would, especially after the whole making you dizzy thing." He slowly lowered her to her feet. "How about I make lunch to make up for it?"

"I say that sounds like a plan."

They waded out of the water arm in arm, pausing so that she could grab her sandals. She vowed not to think about friends, responsibilities, reporters, or even her actions. She'd think of nothing but the man beside her and this moment, this current heartbeat, and spending it with him.

They moved from the beach to the mixture of scrub grass, sea-grapes and royal palms that served as a privacy barrier to her deck. She was paying an hellacious mortgage for transforming the rectory into a showplace, and the insurance premiums were killing her, but there were days when she felt it was worth it. This was one of those days.

The builder had worked the deck into the natural treeline and ringed it with tall lanterns that blended into the vegetation. The deck was a two-tier split level that wrapped around towards the pool and sauna on the far side of the house, away from the mission.

"Are you hungry?" Brandt asked as they stepped onto the larger bottom deck.

"Yes, but I won't make you fix lunch. We can just order something in."

"After I went to all this trouble?" They stepped onto the second deck. The teak patio table had been set for two, and he'd set out a pitcher of her newest addiction, sweet tea, to brew in the sun.

He smiled at her as she stared up at him in surprise. "I've got a couple of salmon steaks marinating, I made a salad, and there's a sorbet for dessert."

Willow felt her mouth drop open, and closed it long enough to ask, "When did you have time to do this?"

"While you were fielding calls from everyone in creation," he explained. "I thought you'd probably appreciate a break."

She squeezed the curve of his arm, unable to speak. He'd done this for her, for no other reason than he'd thought she needed it. Having such a gesture on the heels of her earlier depressing thoughts of friendship tightened her throat.

"Thank you," she whispered. "I really appreciate this. You're wonderful for doing this for me."

"It's nothing," he said with his characteristic modest dismissal. "You need to eat."

"You're right." She patted her stomach. "But I think we should take a shower first."

He stopped in his tracks, looked down at her. "By saying 'we,' then 'a shower,' do you mean one apiece, or just one?"

"Just one," she answered. "We're under a water restriction, you know."

He smiled. "God forbid I should be responsible for you getting fined by the county. One shower it is."

CHAPTER TWENTY-THREE

"Stay, boy," Brandt ordered Boscoe, then took Willow's hand, leading her through the sliding glass door and into the house. Seeing Willow standing unmoving in the ocean had stabbed at him. In that moment, she'd seemed more lonely than alone, solitary by fate instead of by choice.

The lost look in her eyes had torn at him, and he knew he'd give almost anything, even his self-imposed aloofness, to make her smile.

She dragged him to a halt in the kitchen. "Wait."

He paused, telling himself that if she needed time, he'd give it to her. If she needed convincing, he'd give her that too. "What's up?"

"We're soaking wet. I don't want to track seawater all through the house."

"You've got a point," he said, then forgot whatever he'd planned to say next as she pulled her dress over her head then tossed it to the floor.

"Come on," she wheedled as he stood there gawking at her peach-colored panties and matching bra. "The sooner you get out of those wet clothes, the sooner I can get my back scrubbed."

His entire body jerked in response. "You're something else, you know that?"

That instantly shut her down. "I'm sorry, I know I'm coming on too strong. I don't know if I can explain it, because I don't know if I understand it. That's a hard thing for the doctor in me to admit. All I know is that you gave me the most incredible night of my life, and I now find myself being greedy. I want to make up for lost time. I want as many moments as I can for as long as I can. Don't you want that too?"

"God, yes," he breathed. To level the playing field, he kicked off his sneakers, then all but ripped his shirt over his head, tossing it to the floor. "Last night was incredible. You, me, us…it's never been like that."

She lifted her head just a notch, staring at him through a curtain of braids. "Never?"

"Never," he confirmed, sending his shorts the way of his shirt. His erection tented his boxers, eager to come out and play. "I really want to know if we can make it happen again."

Her smile returned as she pushed her hair back. "Me too. But I really want that shower. I want to feel your hands spreading soap all over my body. I've thought about your hands a lot."

His insides warmed as he stepped closer to her. "Really?"

Her head bobbed in affirmation. "Sometimes I'd watch you work," she confessed. "I'd watch how you'd take a piece of wood, shape it, make it into what you want. Every day since we agreed to, uhm, get to know each other better, I've thought about what it would feel like to have your hands on me. Now I know."

His fingers lightly trailed down her cheek to her throat. "And what do you think?"

He watched her swallow as his fingers paused at her collarbone. "I think you're an artist. Your hands are pure magic."

His fingers slid across her shoulder, then down her arm to capture her hand, lifting it to his lips. "Thank you. I've been inspired lately."

His breath warmed the inside of her wrist. "And you," his lips moved to the bend of her elbow, "are my," he grazed her throat, "muse."

His lips captured hers. She responded instantly, quick as a lightning strike and just as intense. Gripping her behind in his palms, he dragged her high against him, wanting her, needing her. She moaned into his mouth, her legs circling his waist, drawing her closer. A dance of lips, tongues, and teeth had him shuddering with white-hot demand.

It took bumping into the kitchen island for him to break his hold, to draw back from the desire that roared through him. "It's still there, whatever it is."

"Yeah it is," she gasped, fanning herself with one hand. "Maybe, maybe we should shower afterwards."

"Good idea." He picked her up, tossing her over his shoulder yet again. Somehow he managed not to break into a run, or bump her as he took the stairs. Maybe it had something to do with her rump balanced on his shoulder. With his left hand trapping her knees, he was free to glide his right hand over then under the cotton bikini that hid her from him. Dimly he heard her say his name, a whisper of sound.

He didn't stop until he reached her bedroom. Placing her back on her feet, he dashed to his bedroom to grab the box of condoms. Racing back down the hall to her master suite, he stepped inside the door, then froze.

She stood before him completely nude, hands at her sides, braids pulled back in a ponytail. Serenity warred with vulnerability in her eyes, the proud tilt of her chin, the set of her shoulders. He knew then that he'd have to attempt to capture that moment in wood, Willow as regal as any African princess. He'd probably fail, but he'd try anyway.

Something soft filled his chest. He stepped into the room, swallowed to find his voice. "You're beyond the word beautiful."

She smiled at him, soft and pleased. "Come here."

In answer, he dragged her close, his mouth covering hers in crystalline need. A dance of mouths, limbs, and clothes followed, and then they were sprawled naked beside each other on the king-sized bed.

Before he could reach for her, she kissed and nipped her way down his body. He gasped as her braids slid over his skin, and heard her answering laugh, feminine and satisfied. She was discovering that she had power over him, this kind of power over him. What would she do with it?

Her mouth blazed an unerring trail past his navel. He hissed when she lifted her head, her hair teasing his erection. When she wrapped a hand around his thickness, his entire body jerked in response. Then he felt her tongue along his balls, and had to grind his teeth in a fight for control.

"Turn this way," he demanded in a harsh whisper. She complied instantly, allowing him to cup her buttocks, then slide his fingers between her thighs. With a murmur of appreciation, she rocked against his hand, mimicking the motion on his erection with her hand, and finally, her mouth.

She was driving him crazy, and it was a hell of a ride.

"Come here," he said, needing more of her. He lifted her until she straddled him, until he could taste her as fully as she tasted him.

"Brandt."

His fingers stroked her skin even as his tongue stroked her center, deliberately testing, teasing, tending. He could feel her tensing, feel her tightening, as she struggled against the encroaching wave. "Not yet," she pleaded.

"No. Let go." His fingers sank deep as he suckled.

She shuddered apart instantly, arching back as his name tore from her lips. He continued the sensual onslaught, not releasing her until she peaked again.

She poured off him in a boneless puddle. "No fair," she gasped as he shifted to face her "I want to make you happy, too."

"I am," he said, realizing with a jolt that it was true. Being with her was the best thing that had happened to him in a long while. Maybe he'd pay for it later, but he didn't care. All that mattered at that moment was getting inside her and holding on until he let go.

Covering her, he took his time, lightly rubbing the head of his penis against her. She moaned, her eyes slitting as she shifted, trying to settle him. Finally, when the waiting became unbearable, he slowly pushed himself inside her. She drew in a sharp breath, then exhaled as he lodged himself completely. Keeping his gaze locked to hers, he withdrew, then filled her again with that same deliberate pace.

"Kiss me," he demanded, sinking into her again.

She did, her mouth hot and open against his. He growled with the need to let go, to drive into her over and over until the frantic ache disappeared. When her breath hitched, when she whispered his name, when she wrapped herself around him, he wondered if the ache he felt for her would ever truly go away.

He stared down at her, into that beautiful face, and wanted to give her everything. "Take it. Whatever you need, however you need it. Take it."

"I'll take you." Her hands framed his cheeks as she smiled, that sexy, secret woman's smile. "With me this time."

He nodded, unable to speak as her heat wrapped around him. Grabbing her hands, he laced their fingers together, high above her head. She circled her legs high around his waist as he deepened his strokes, as she lifted her hips to meet him. As the passion ignited, grew, devoured.

He thought he was in control, guiding the pleasure, the completion. Then her inner muscles clenched around him, snapping his control. Burying his face into the crook of her neck, he drove into her, hard and fast and deep, as his blood burned and heart pounded. She pulled her hands free of his to run her hands over his back, her nails scoring his skin in pleasure-pain.

"Now." Her legs tightened around him. "Come now."

He felt her inner muscles grip him a heartbeat before she trembled, called his name, then fell apart. Digging his fingers into the mattress, he drove into her, then up and over into white-hot ecstasy.

CHAPTER TWENTY-FOUR

"I have something to tell you."

Willow looked up from her salad at the seriousness of Brandt's tone. He fiddled with his glass of tea, a sure sign of nerves from a man who controlled his every action and reaction. "There's someone else, right?"

He looked up, startled. "What?"

"I wondered what the worst thing was that you could tell me right now, and that's what I came up with," she said. "Am I right?"

"No. I already told you, I'm not seeing anyone." He leaned forward. "Is that really the worst you could think of?"

"At the moment, yeah." She relaxed. "What else could there be?"

"My sister Maya and her family are coming down to visit me."

"That's great! I'm sure you'll be happy to see them." Except that he didn't look happy. "When are they coming?"

"Tomorrow."

"Tomorrow." Her stomach gave a nervous leap, driving away the last of her post-orgasmic haze. "As in the day after today? As in, in less than twenty-four hours they'll be on the doorstep?"

He nodded, clearly miserable. "She called this morning. Apparently the incident with the dog became a national soundbite. They were already coming to Florida to take my niece to visit her paternal grandparents, and Maya decided to take a detour."

Willow ignored the explanation and focused on the timeline. "You've known since this morning?"

He hunched his shoulders guiltily. "You were busy," he pointed out. "Then we were busy. There wasn't a good opportunity before now."

"What, you couldn't tell me on the beach? How about in the shower? Or in bed?" She dropped her forehead into her hands. "God, the cleaning lady's not scheduled until Wednesday. I need to scrub the house, and oh my God, I've got to put clean linens on the beds, the smell of sex is everywhere."

"Willow!"

She raised her head. "What?"

"You don't have to go to all that trouble. They're my family, not yours. I'll just put them up in a hotel near here."

"Oh." She sat back, feeling as if he'd slapped her. "I guess I overreacted."

"Just a little." He gave a brief smile. "I would like to show them the mission, if it's not too much trouble."

"Of course. You should show it off to them." Did he not want her to meet his family? She swallowed the disappointment, hoping he wouldn't notice, and concentrated on being polite instead. "I'll make sure to keep out of your hair. I have some errands I need to run anyway, and tomorrow's as good a day as any."

He noticed anyway, and frowned. "What is it?"

"You know, you should take a couple of days off, spend time with your family," she said. She reached for her tea, taking the opportunity to break his gaze. "You haven't taken time off since you got here. You could invite them to a cookout here tomorrow or the day after, and have free rein of the beach. If you don't want to spend the day here, there's a public beach about three miles up A1A."

"Willow."

"What?"

He reached across the table, stopping her fingers from drumming against the smooth glass surface. "Maya would never forgive me if I didn't introduce you, but I could live with that, if I thought it would make you uncomfortable."

"You think I'd be uncomfortable meeting your sister and her family?" He was concerned about her?

"You're a private person," he told her. "I know how much you like your privacy. My family never learned the meaning of the word quiet. Even when it's only a couple of us getting together, we tend to be loud. I didn't think you'd want them trooping all over your house, and I certainly don't expect you to put them up."

"There's plenty of room," she said, warming at his obvious concern. "I don't mind if you don't mind."

"Are you sure it wouldn't be putting you out? Because you'd basically be making Maya's dream come true, letting them stay here."

"I'm sure," Willow said, smiling now. "I just want to run into town for a few things, make sure we have everything we need. If you come with me, we can even stop by the animal hospital, and check in on the dog."

"Zadie. I've decided to call her Zadie."

"All right, we'll check in on Zadie, then we'll make sure we have everything we need for Maya and her family. There are just two children, right?"

"Taylor's nine now, almost ten, and Zachary's almost two."

"So we'll need a couple of kid-friendly movies, in case they'd like to watch the big screen," she said. "I'll invite Mack; he'll definitely show up for free food. We'll get the house ready tonight, and then I'll relax in the hot tub as a reward. Parts of me could really use the soak."

"I'm not going to apologize." He squeezed her hand. "Are you sure about this?"

"It'll be fun. Like having a giant sleepover."

He just looked at her. "Remember you said that."

It'll be fun, Willow reminded herself as she stood at her kitchen counter, a cookbook open in front of her. She'd crawled out of Brandt's arms just before dawn, too keyed up to sleep despite an energetic night spent discovering his every erogenous zone. A case of nerves or writer's block meant the same thing—she went to the kitchen and began to cook.

Brandt stumbled in fifteen minutes later. "I should have known you weren't going for water," he said, yawning and looking too sexy for his own good in a pair of checked boxers and a gray t-shirt. "Guess I can't convince you to come back to bed?"

"Are you kidding? I've got a lot of work to do. Besides, aren't you sore by now?"

"I won't be able to walk right for a week. But you're probably the one who's really sore," he pointed out. "All that 'making up for lost time' stuff."

"The last two times were your fault," she reminded him, stirring the bowl of batter with more force than needed. "Though I appreciate learning what sleepy, pre-dawn sex is like."

"You're welcome," he said, stretching as he headed for the coffeepot. "But I'd like to beat you out of bed just once, if you don't mind."

Willow almost dropped the bowl. Brandt was still too sleep-fuzzed to realize what he'd said, the promise inherent in his words. They implied that there would be plenty of opportunities, plenty of mornings after for them.

"Not my fault that you're a lazybones," she said quickly, before he wondered at her silence. She appreciated this early morning camaraderie far more than he knew. He looked perfectly at home as he measured the coffee, and she didn't mind at all. If every morning could start this way, she would be one happy woman.

"Lazybones," he muttered, flipping the switch on the coffeepot. "Woman rides me like we're in the Kentucky Derby, and she has the nerve to call me lazybones."

Before she could think about it, she put down the bowl, crossed to him, and threw her arms around his waist.

"Hey, now, don't start something that I can't finish," he said, taking her by the shoulders.

Laughing, she cupped his beard-roughened cheeks in her hands. "You are the most amazing man."

He avoided her gaze. "Yeah, well, don't tell anybody, all right? I've got a reputation to maintain."

Realizing he was uncomfortable, she loosened her grip. He brought her back by snagging a handful of braids. "You don't have to do all of this, you know," he told her. "Maya will be thrilled just to meet you."

Her turn to be uncomfortable. She pulled her hair out of his grip, then returned to her batter. "They'll want to eat. If there's nothing else to talk about, we can always talk about food. Why don't you make yourself useful and make the frosting for this coffee cake?"

He made his way to the counter, snagging the recipe book she'd balanced on a bag of oranges. "You want me to make orange zest frosting? For God's sake, Willow, it's just my sister, not the president!"

She thumped a good portion of the batter into a greased baking dish. "So? Can't I make a homemade dessert for my guests? Besides, after you zest the oranges, you can make fresh-squeezed juice."

"You're nervous," he said, brows lifting in surprise. "Why in the world would you be nervous?"

She looked away. "Just want to make a good impression, that's all," she muttered. "Maybe I should have called a caterer."

"Willow." Hands came down on her shoulders, turned her around. "You've already made an impression on Maya, with your books. I really want her to meet you, not the doctor. Just relax and be yourself, okay?"

"She's not all that interesting. Pretty boring, actually."

"I disagree. I think she's very interesting."

Looking up into those serious, determined eyes, she believed him. "Thank you," she said, meaning more than the compliment.

"You're welcome." He dropped a quick kiss to her forehead before stepping away. "And if I don't say it enough over the next two days, thanks for inviting Maya and her family to stay here."

"I'm glad to do it. You're very lucky, you know." Her voice softened as she looked away. "To have such a close-knit family."

"Yeah, I know." He opened a cabinet, removed a mixing bowl. "Which is why I'm gonna make orange zest frosting."

Willow hid a grin. "I guess you're as close to Maya as I am to Mack," she said, pouring the remaining batter into the baking pan. "Actually, you're probably closer."

"Maybe. She's right after me in the line-up, so we've been close since we were kids. Though that's eased off some, now that she's got a family of her own."

"Maybe your sister can convince my brother of the joys of marriage and parenting. I really want to be an aunt."

He turned to her, an orange balanced in one hand. "You don't want kids of your own?" he asked in surprise.

"I don't think that's meant for me," she said, a shrug deflecting the weight of her words. She crossed to the oven, slipped the coffee cake inside. "I'm pretty sure I'd be a better aunt than I would a mother."

"If you wanted to be a mother, you'd be good at it," Brandt said.

She looked up, clearly surprised. "Really?"

He nodded. "You care about people. I mean, you do everything you can to make sure the people around you are happy, whether they deserve it or not."

She wondered whether he was talking about himself, then decided it didn't matter. "Well, I for one think everyone deserves to be happy."

"Which is probably why you're successful at what you do," he said, adding ingredients to his bowl. "No matter how badly people crash and burn, as you say in your books, it's part of the process of going through the fire to refine the spirit and emerge from the ashes as something better."

He'd read her books.

It was something she'd wondered for weeks, ever since he'd told her about his sister. Now she knew.

And she realized then that she knew how to help him.

CHAPTER TWENTY-FIVE

"Uncle Brandt!"

Willow watched as a young girl with dark pigtails and stunning blue eyes dashed from the rental car and up the stairs, launching herself at Brandt. He caught her easily, swinging her around in an exuberant circle. Willow wasn't sure which surprised her more, the girl or Brandt's easy laughter.

A slender dark-haired woman emerged from the front passenger side. She looked to be in her mid-thirties, with Brandt's coloring and the same curve to her eyes. "Taylor Marissa Whitfield, where are your manners? You're too old to be treating your uncle like a human jungle gym!"

Brandt grinned as he set his niece back on her feet. "What, you want her interested in boys?"

"On second thought, climb away," the woman ordered.

A man exited the driver's side, a tall slender man with a golf tan, dark wavy hair and eyes as stunning a blue as those of the preteen balanced on Brandt's back.

Brandt turned to face her, giving Willow an easy grin she hadn't seen before. "This is my niece, Taylor," he said, turning so that she could wave at the child.

The sound of a car door shutting caught her attention, and she turned to see the couple coming up the stairs together. Willow caught a glimpse of a little tawny-shade boy with thick dark curls in Maya's arms.

"Willow, this is my brother-in-law, Nick Whitfield, M.D. That's my sister Maya, and this—" he plucked the toddler from his sister's arms— "is Zachary."

The incongruence of the happy, chubby-cheeked toddler and the stern, hard-planed man made something flip flop in Willow's stomach. He must have been a wonderful father.

Willow shook hands, caught between being herself and the Dr. Willow Zane everyone expected to see.

Maya beamed at her. "It's such a pleasure to meet you, Dr. Zane. Your books have been a tremendous help to me."

The young girl, now back on her feet, stepped forward. "Uncle Brandt says you're famous," the young girl said. "Are you famous?"

"Taylor," her father admonished.

"I just wanted to know," Taylor said, but obediently fell silent.

Nick then turned a sheepish grin on Willow. "Sorry about that, Dr. Zane."

Willow smiled, her shell cracking. "It's all right, and please, call me Willow." She bent towards the little girl. "I guess you could say I'm famous, but there's a whole lot of people more famous than I am."

Taylor bobbed her head. "Sweet."

She straightened. "Why don't you all come in? I'm sure you could use some refreshments after driving all the way from Orlando."

"And after flying into Orlando from Atlanta yesterday," Maya answered. "The kids' paternal grandparents live there, but we decided on a quick side trip to see what Brandt was up to."

"Most of the time, I'd say he was up to his elbows in sawdust," Willow joked, leading them into the house. "I'm sure Brandt will show you the fantastic work he's done on the chapel later. My brother will be stopping by for lunch, but there's plenty of stuff to munch on now, and you can either relax in your rooms or head straight out to the beach."

"Beach!" Taylor exclaimed, hopping up and down.

"Beach," Zachary parroted, clapping his hands.

"Looks like we're headed for the beach," Nick observed. "I'll get our suitcases."

"And I'll make sure our kids act like they've got home training," Maya said.

"Are you my uncle's girlfriend?"

Willow choked on her fruit juice. "Ah, no. We're just friends. He's my brother's best friend."

"Do you want to be his girlfriend?"

Why hadn't Brandt warned her about Taylor's directness? "I'm glad to be his friend, Taylor," she said casually. "But I live here and your uncle lives in Atlanta."

Taylor thought about that. "I'm glad Uncle Brandt lives in Atlanta, but if you were his girlfriend and he moved down here, I could come visit, right?"

"You can come visit anyway," Willow said. "Especially if your mom and dad say it's okay."

"Thank you," Taylor said politely.

"You must really love your uncle," Willow observed.

"He's the best," Taylor said. "It was just me and my dad until we married Mom. Then I got two aunts and four uncles, but I love Uncle Brandt the most. I was really scared when Mom went into the hospital to have Zach, but Uncle Brandt made me feel better."

Willow could imagine it. Brandt had calmed her fears on more than one occasion. "He's a good man, your uncle."

"Taylor." Maya crossed the deck and joined them. "Why don't you go play with your uncle and leave Ms. Willow alone?"

"But Mom," the child pouted, "I was just asking questions."

"And I know what kind of questions you ask. Go on now. Princesses aren't supposed to be nosey."

"All right." Still pouting, Taylor bounced off the deck and into the sand, Boscoe trailing after.

"Sorry about that," Maya said with a rueful laugh, taking the empty lounge beside Willow. "My daughter's going to be the next Barbara Walters."

"It's all right. She's actually better than Barbara."

"God." Maya adjusted her hat. "For a moment there, I forgot who you are."

"I'd just as soon have you completely forget," Willow said, reaching for her iced tea. "I'm really not all that Hollywood."

"I know, and I've been good, haven't I? I haven't once asked you to dish the dirt on any famous people. You wouldn't do that." She sat up, lifted her sunglasses. "Would you?"

Willow laughed despite herself. "Sorry."

Maya laughed with her as she slipped her sunglasses back into place. "That's what I thought. Didn't hurt to try, though."

They sat in companionable silence for a while, enjoying the summer breeze. Finally Maya spoke. "I just want to thank you for opening your home to my family."

"It's no problem, really. I'm glad you're enjoying yourselves."

"We are. So's Brandt. I don't think I've seen him this happy since...well, I can't remember." Maya smiled. "So I have something else to thank you for."

"I haven't done anything."

"You wrote your book." Maya leaned closer to her. "Your first book helped me. It took a long time for me to stop being a victim when my first husband left me, thinking I couldn't have children. I took control of my life, and got to a place where I felt like I could live again. I met Taylor and her father, and I wouldn't have dared attempt to make a family with them if not for the lessons I learned in your book."

She laughed self-consciously. "I've had a few rough spots, of course, but the happiness I feel, the life I have right now, I wouldn't trade it for anything in the world. So from the bottom of my heart, thank you."

Willow didn't know what to say. "You're welcome" seemed so inadequate, but she said it anyway. "I'm glad I was able to help you."

"You did. Now I'm hoping you can help Brandt."

Willow's eyes strayed to him. He stood chest deep in the ocean, letting Taylor use him as a human diving board. She noticed that he watched her like a hawk, having her jump into the shallower water on the beach side, always there to pull her back. Knowing how he'd lost his son, Willow couldn't help wondering what it took for him to play with his niece in the ocean like that. She also noticed that while Maya's husband played in the sand with their son, the toddler went nowhere near the water.

"I gave him a copy of your first book a couple of years ago, and I thought it helped, but lately things have been so hard for him," Maya said quietly. "When Brandt told me what he was working on down here, and who he was working for, I thought it was a miracle. I know he's in the one place with the one person who can help him."

"He doesn't want my help," Willow said, her gaze locked on the man who kept his emotions wrapped tighter than she'd thought possible. "I promised him that I wouldn't try to psychoanalyze him."

"He told you what happened?"

Willow shook her head. "No, he hasn't, and you can't tell me either. It has to come from him."

"So, you won't help him then?" Maya sounded crestfallen.

"I said I wouldn't be his therapist. I never said anything about not helping him." Willow tore her gaze away from Brandt and turned back to Maya. "He's a good man, and he deserves to be happy. He's just forgotten that."

"Thank you." Maya reached over and hugged her. "Thank you so much."

Surprised, Willow remained still for several heartbeats. Then, feeling awkward, she reached around to give the other woman a quick pat on her shoulders. She wanted to put Maya at ease, but she knew she'd have her hands full trying to help Brandt without making it obvious that she was helping him.

CHAPTER TWENTY-SIX

Brandt stood at the edge of the ocean, hands shoved in his pockets. Far out in the dark water, lights twinkled, representing boats headed for Miami. Stars winked overhead as the sea sang its unending song.

He could understand why Willow would want this. Sometimes he'd watch her, not walking the beach, but standing at the edge of forever, staring into the darkness. He'd often thought that she meditated or maybe even thought out a tricky passage in her manuscript. Now he knew better.

This was hearing the lonely cry of the sea, calling endlessly. This was feeling the loneliness inside answering that call. This was standing on the shore alone, in order to feel less alone.

It wasn't working.

Maya and her family hadn't been gone two hours, and he missed them. He missed holding Zach, talking to Taylor. He missed the happiness on Maya's face and the quiet contentment that Nick exuded whenever he looked at his little family.

Familiar loneliness crawled through him, sharp and bitter. Loneliness that he hadn't felt in the months since he'd been in Serena Bay. For a short time, he hadn't been lonely. For a short time, he hadn't been aching. For a short time, he'd felt peaceful.

Willow had given him that. Willow, with her easy smiles and giving heart, had eased the pain that he'd endured for the last four years. Even Maya had noticed.

Maya wanted him to talk to Willow, to tell her how he'd lost Brady and Sarah. He knew his sister wanted him to heal, to find whatever happiness he could. She wanted him to have his second chance, the way she'd gotten hers.

He clenched his hands into fists, struggling against memory, against guilt. Maybe he'd been brought here to help Willow, and in helping Willow, to help himself. He could almost believe that he'd been sent to Willow so that he could finally begin the long road to healing.

What he couldn't do was believe that this was his second chance, that she was his second chance. The thought of staying in Serena Bay, staying with Willow, filled him with a sticky panic.

What the hell could he possibly offer her? Sex, certainly. They'd had two mind-blowing days together, and the more familiar they became with each other, the better it became. If it got any better, he'd have a heart attack.

Eventually though, Willow would want more than sex. Eventually she'd want the emotional to go with the physical. He couldn't give it to her, and she'd want to know why. She'd find out why, and she'd realize he wasn't the right choice for her. She was a celebrity doctor with a full calendar and a fuller bank account. She could have any man she wanted, if she wanted. She certainly didn't need a broken man who'd thought more than once that salvation was a bullet with his name on it.

Pain flared in his chest, bright and burning. He couldn't fool himself. People like him didn't get second chances. Even if he did, he knew he'd already screwed that one up too. He'd failed to save Brady, and he'd failed Sarah. Two lives, two chances, both gone.

Brady. Thinking about his son caused his heart to tighten with pain. He should have followed Brady, as he'd promised. He'd stayed behind because he'd thought people needed him. His family, especially Maya, had been his reason for hanging on, for getting up each morning and going to sleep each night. Maya had needed him, but no longer, causing him to feel restless, adrift.

Until he'd come to Serena Bay, that is. Until he'd seen the chapel, and Willow. He had a purpose now, a cause that kept him going. He'd bought himself some time.

But he was running out of time now. The chapel was all but complete, with the final inspection due in less than two weeks. Willow's mysterious stalker had apparently stopped as abruptly as he'd begun. She wouldn't need Brandt's protection for much longer, and she certainly would realize that she didn't need his body either.

What did he have left?

He tried to recall an image of Brady, riding on his tricycle. He tried to recall the sound of his son's laughter as it gurgled out of him.

Neither came, and it scared him. Panic hit his heart, setting it pounding. *He couldn't remember his son's face.* The only image he could recall was a bright red ball floating in the pool.

He turned and ran, not towards the house, not to Willow, but towards the chapel. His heart threatened to explode in his chest as he stumbled across the sand to the gate. After missing the code, he pounded on the metal bars in trapped frustration before trying again and succeeding.

Breath scrubbed through his lungs as he finally, finally, made his way into the mission, through the chapel. The serenity he'd sweated so diligently to bring to the chamber pressed in on him as he ran down the center aisle to his workshop. He ignored his tools, carving complete and in progress, and dug for his sketchpad.

A silent desperation roughened his breath as he cleared room on his workbench by sweeping everything aside. Then a frantic search for charcoal before his trembling fingers found a clean sheet.

He moved the pencil across the thick paper almost blindly. Yes, he could have reached for his wallet, could have extracted the faded and folded photo of Brady holding his favorite toy, the bright red ball. But that would be cheating, and he'd promised his son, his only child, that he'd always remember. Always. One parent had failed him already; Brandt refused to make it two.

Boscoe's barking finally urged Willow to toss her book down and go in search of Brandt. She'd known he'd take his family's leaving hard. The doctor in her had tried to give him space; the woman in her had other ideas. She followed Boscoe to the glass door, in time to see light-ning fork the sky.

Concern gripped her in an iron fist as she pulled the sliding door open and stepped out onto the deck. The air thickened around her with the pregnant promise of the electrical storm to come. She could-n't focus on that. Instead she focused on her dog, who hated thunder-storms yet dashed onto the deck, then down to the path leading to the mission. Boscoe had an uncanny ability to sense when someone need-ed comfort.

Brandt.

Her heart in her throat, she ran after her dog, unmindful of the sudden rain pelting her like pennies. She wasn't even aware of going through the gate, losing a shoe on the path. Brandt had to be in the mission, in the chapel. The knowledge didn't slow her pace or her pulse as she ran along the gravel path to the front door of the mission.

Maybe he was just working, making up for the past two days. Maybe he was just sitting in the chapel, hoping for an answer from on high. Maybe she was just overreacting. Either way, she had to see for herself.

The main door to the mission was unlocked; Brandt had to be there. Willow pulled the heavy door open, then entered with Boscoe squeezing in with her. The vestibule stood dark and silent, and she needed a moment to get her bearings. Boscoe however, headed straight for the chapel. It was then that she noticed the faint light coming through the small windows set in the doors. Hesitant now, conscious of the silence, she hooked her fingers into Boscoe's collar, then let pushed open the sanctuary doors.

Darkness and heat greeted her, clinging to the rain on her skin. The dim light came from the room behind the pulpit, and she moved forward, cautious. Brandt had claimed it as his office, and she, respect-ing the need for personal space, hadn't entered it since. She thought about calling out to him, but curiosity got the better of her, so she qui-etly stepped to the doorway.

Brandt hunched over a wooden worktable, the sound of pencil moving across paper frantic to her ears. The sound failed to cover his low words, repeated like a mantra. "I won't forget. I swear, I won't forget."

She knew he meant his family, the one he'd lost. Her heart broke for him, for this powerful man who held himself so carefully apart.

Suddenly feeling like an intruder, Willow turned to go. Her eyes caught an odd wooden shape. She gasped, unable to control her reaction to the carvings.

Magnificent agony radiated from each. A four-foot tall angel with a broken wing, head downcast with both arms raised to ward off another blow. A man on his knees, back bowed with grief and suffering, raising anguished face and arms heavenwards in a silent, unanswered plea for mercy.

Tears blurred her vision. The sheer, tortured beauty of these works of art stunned her, overwhelmed her. Her heart lurched inside her chest, pounding with the desire to wrap her arms around the carvings, to ease the obvious pain reverberating through the polished veins of wood.

Brandt had carved these. This was the expression of his grief, his way of mourning his lost wife and child.

"Brandt?"

The pencil stopped, but he didn't turn around. "You should get back to the house, Willow. There's a storm brewing outside."

"Not without you," she said, hearing the anguish in his voice. The anguish that had created these magnificent, heartbreaking carvings.

Boscoe broke her grip and moved to Brandt's side, whining. Brandt dropped a hand to the dog's head. "I can't go back with you, Wil. I was starting to think—I was starting to feel happy. I started to forget, and I can't do that. I can't."

She wanted to go to him, but knew it would be the wrong thing to do. Determination to help him dried her tears. "No one believes you should forget. But there's nothing wrong with being happy, with finding some contentment in your life. Don't you think people deserve to be happy?"

"Not me."

Willow took a step towards him then, she couldn't help it. Her entire being longed to hold him, to ease the heartache in his voice, the guilt bowing his shoulders. "Why not you, Brandt?" she asked quietly. "Why don't you deserve to be happy?"

A sigh lifted his shoulders. With precise movements, he put down the pencil, closed the sketchpad. Finally he turned to face her, his eyes dark and tormented.

"Because I let my wife kill my son. And then I let her kill herself."

His words fell around them, shards of brittle memories. She knew what had happened, but not his version, how he'd blamed himself.

"I don't believe that," she said, keeping her voice neutral. He needed to talk about what had happened, just as she needed to help him face it, then overcome it. "I'm sure your family doesn't believe it either. How can you believe that of yourself?"

His face drained of all emotion, leaving behind the hard, stoic man she'd first seen standing in her meditation garden. "It doesn't matter if you believe it or not. It's the truth."

"Then talk to me about it. Let me decide for myself."

"I met Sarah about two years after I left the service." He looked down at the floor. "We should never have gotten married. She was fragile, I know that now, but back then I thought she was just sweet. After doing stints in the Middle East and Africa, I'd needed that. Don't get me wrong—I did what I had to do to protect the people in my unit, to make sure Mack would get home to look for you. And I'd do it again, no matter what it would cost me. Knowing that didn't stop the memories or make me feel better. I thought if someone that sweet could fall in love with me, then maybe I wasn't so bad after all."

He paused, swallowed. "We had a couple of good years, then Brady came along. My boy, the best thing I'd ever been a part of. Sarah started to change after that. Nothing made her happy. She found fault with everything. I tried, I swear to God that I tried, but everything I did to try to help just made her more snappish, angrier. Counseling didn't help either. Finally all we did when we were together was argue.

"I finally had enough. I went to see a lawyer, filed divorce papers seeking full custody of Brady. He was four then. To this day I can't remember why I left him at home with her, why I didn't take him to my mother's. When I got home, I found her on the couch, passed out and stinking of liquor. I was pissed, but I was afraid too. I shook her, God I shook her so hard, but she wouldn't wake up. Then I started looking for Brady. I went through the house calling for him, telling him everything would be all right, Daddy was going to take him someplace safe, all he had to do was come out. But I couldn't find him.

"I went back downstairs, into the kitchen, and that's when I noticed the sliding door open. I looked out the door, saw the gate to the pool, the gate that locked with a key, standing open. I ran. I knocked the glass door off its track, and glass went flying. I didn't care, because I knew. I knew where Brady was."

His hands clenched. "At first I saw just a red ball. His favorite ball that he took everywhere. It was floating in the deep end of the pool. Then I saw—it didn't even look like a person, just a large doll floating in the water. I dove in, even though I knew. I got him out and I tried, I tried to bring him back, tried to beg God to send him back, that I would make it all better if he just came back.

"I don't know how long I did CPR before the paramedics stopped me. My neighbors had called them because they heard me screaming. Sarah didn't even wake up until the cops broke down the front door, but my neighbors heard me. I didn't want to let him go, I couldn't let my boy go, but they pulled him out of my arms."

He held his hands up, staring blindly. "They said he'd been in the pool for about forty-five minutes, maybe an hour. Forty-five minutes that I'd spent arranging for a place to stay, when I should have been home saving my son.

"They arrested Sarah. They were going to arrest me too, and I didn't care. I couldn't care about anything because it felt like my goddamn heart had been ripped out of my chest."

He clenched his hands repeatedly, a futile gesture that tore at her heart. "Everything was a blur after that, questions with no answers, apologies with no forgiveness, sympathy with no relief. The next thing I remember was the funeral. Brady, he-he didn't look like himself, like a doll made to look like my son. I remember putting that red ball in beside him and kissing him, and telling him that Daddy would be with him soon."

"When I straightened, I looked right at Sarah. She was out of jail, under the supervision of her parents, so she could attend. I looked right at her, saw the gun, my gun, in her hand. I thought she was going to shoot me, and I intended to let her. But when she lifted the gun, she looked at me and screamed that it was all my fault, I had done this to her and to Brady. When I realized what she intended I lunged for her but I was too late. I stood there, covered in her blood and guilt, and watched her die."

He looked down at his hands. "I wanted to die. More than that, I thought I needed to die. It was the only way to make things right. If it wasn't for my family, especially my mother and Maya... They needed me for the stupidest things, but I needed some sort of purpose to replace what I'd lost. I threw myself into the business, taking on more restoration jobs, spending the hours away from work on my carvings."

He reached out a hand, touching the wing of the fallen angel. "One day Maya gave me a copy of your first book. At first I thought it was a stupid idea, that bad things had to happen to people, that people had to go through tragedy. One night I had a really bad time, nightmares that wouldn't end, and I started reading your book. I read the damn thing dog-eared, and some of it started sinking in, making some sense. And after a long time, it got easier to breathe.

"Carving helped. Besides your book, it was the only thing that did. For four years I started each day the same. I'd wake up, surprised to find myself still alive. Then I'd lay out my gun, and I'd lay out my carving tools, and I'd wait to see which one won."

No. Willow covered her mouth, trying to hold back the gasp, the denial. He faced that every day?

Clenching his hands into fists, he turned to face her fully. Heaviness filled his voice as he made his final confession. "The day Mack called me about the chapel was the day before Brady's eighth birthday. That day," he took a deep breath, "that day, my gun won."

CHAPTER TWENTY-SEVEN

Unable to bear it, Willow wrapped her arms around Brandt's waist. "I'm so glad," she managed, pressing her face against his chest. "I'm so glad Mack called you."

For a long moment he stood unmoving. Then, wrapping his arms around her, he buried his face into the crook of her neck and held on for dear life.

Willow felt the shudder pass through him and tightened her hold, her heart breaking for him. Brandt didn't recognize his worth, his goodness, but she did. She saw it in the way he cared for his sister and her family, the depth of his grief for his son and the wife he'd wanted to leave in order to protect his child. She saw it in the way he nursed a wounded dog, and the patience he had with her as she struggled to manage her sexual fears and desires.

He was the most amazing man she'd ever known, and it hurt her to her soul to see him in so much pain. To think that he'd been so overwhelmed by guilt and grief that he'd almost lost the battle to survive.

Fresh tears pricked her eyes and she clung even harder to him. She wanted nothing more than to crawl inside his heart and drop-kick every shred of remorse and self-condemnation he carried. To push out all the negativity until only peace remained.

She realized then that she was on the verge of falling in love with him. It made her determined to help him heal, if it was the last thing she did.

Lifting her head, she stepped back, capturing his gaze. He sucked in a breath. "How can you look at me like that?"

"Like what?" she whispered.

He looked away. "Like you—like I'm something better than I am."

"Brandt." She reached up to cup his cheek. "Sometimes you break my heart. You are so much better than you think you are. You're a good man with a good heart. Look at the work you've done on the chapel. Look at how you rescued Zadie, how you've helped me. Doesn't that show you how good you are?"

He shook his head, as if unwilling to believe it. "You're just saying that because you have to."

"No, I don't have to, and that's the difference. I'm not one of your sisters. I don't have to stand by you no matter what."

She leaned against him. "But I choose to stand by you, Brandt. I choose to go to the wire with you. And I choose to do whatever I can to prove to you that you're a good person and deserve every happiness."

He fisted his hands, closed his eyes as he struggled with her words. She wanted to hold him close, to take him somewhere where they could simply be a man and a woman with no tragedies between them. She wanted to free him as truly as he'd freed her.

"Brandt." Her free hand reached up until she framed his face. He dragged his eyes open, staring at her with a desperate need that stole her breath. He couldn't understand why she would want to fight for him, she knew, just as she knew it took everything in him to fight for himself. She knew why, she just had to convince him.

"Brandt, I know what you're thinking. I know you think that you should be punished, or at the very least blamed for what happened to your wife and son. I know you think that you don't deserve to be happy. And I know you think that you're beyond redemption."

He shuddered, just once, and finally put his hands to her waist, as if he didn't dare hold her tight again. She placed her palm flat against his chest. His heart pounded a fierce rhythm beneath her fingers.

"You're wrong. You suffered a horrible, horrible tragedy. You couldn't predict it, couldn't control it, and it's not your fault. Even if you don't believe you deserve some joy, I believe it. I'll believe it enough for both of us, until you finally believe it for yourself."

"How?" His voice cracked on the word. "How can you not be bothered by the stain on my soul?"

"Because your soul isn't stained," she choked out, her vision blurred with tears as she wrapped her arms around his neck. "Because you wouldn't be suffering like this if you weren't a good man."

She caught his face in her hands, then kissed him. She'd intended it to be soft, comforting. Instead she pressed against him, wanting to crawl inside and shed light on all his dark places.

He wrapped his arms around her, lifted her off her feet. She held him just as tightly, not caring how the strength in his arms made her lungs protest. "Willow." He said her name as if it were the only word he knew. "Willow."

"Let go, Brandt," she whispered against his cheek. "Just let go."

He did, returning her kisses with a ferocity that left her breathless. Then his hands went to her skirt, bunching the hem, pulling at her panties. She helped by stepping out of them, knowing what he needed, that need feeding her own.

She wrapped her legs around his waist as he freed his erection. He placed her on the edge of his worktable, then thrust into her, filling her suddenly and completely. She groaned softly at the abruptness of it, then lost her breath as he buried his face into the crook of her neck and drove into her wildly.

Before she could adjust, he stopped as suddenly as he began, locked to her. A tremor went through him, then again, and he drew a deep, gasping breath. "I...I'm sorry," he whispered, his voice fractured. "God, I should be shot."

"Don't say that!" She held on to him, arms and legs holding him as he tried to withdraw. She could tell that he hadn't released, that he'd stopped as if he'd fought his way back from someplace dark and frightening.

Hot tears scalded her neck. "I need you, Willow," he said, his voice raw. "I need you so damned much it scares me."

"I know," she said, closing her eyes against her own tears. "I need you too, Brandt. I need this. Let go. Please. Just let it go."

She held him, running her hands over his back, soothing him. He shuddered, then drew back, resting his forehead against hers. Then he kissed her, a soft, apologetic brush against her mouth.

They moved together in a slow dance of sensual comfort, focused on giving. The tempo increased in slow increments as comfort deepened into the thrumming bass of desire. Murmuring her name, Brandt lifted her off the table, hands guiding her as she rode him. She entwined her arms about his neck, eyes locked to his, mouth against his as pleasure rolled through them as deep and profound as the thunder crashing outside.

It took a long while for individuality to return, for Willow to lift her head from his shoulder. "Let's go home."

He cupped her face in his hands, his eyes clear but solemn as he stared down at her. "Yes," he said, "let's go home."

CHAPTER TWENTY-EIGHT

The shriek of the phone had Willow jerking her eyes open in surprise. She stared down at Brandt, frozen. Before she could clear passion from her senses, Brandt snaked an arm out, answering the phone. "Hello."

She felt him stiffen, and not in a good way. "It's Mack," he said, his expression apologetic.

Willow groaned. She hadn't envisioned Mack finding out about her and Brandt this way, but there probably wasn't a right way to let her brother know she was sleeping with his best friend. She scrambled off Brandt, already missing the feel of him, then reached for the handset. The clock on her nightstand read one thirty-five. Mack wouldn't call her unless something had happened, something bad.

"Mack?" She heard the breathlessness in her voice, winced. "What's going on?"

"I could ask you the same question, but we can have a heart to heart later." Her brother sounded tired, and more than that, mad. "I need your help."

She sprang to her feet, heading for her closet. A call this late from her brother meant he needed her professional help. "What's happened?"

"Her name's Deana. Sexual assault, multiple perpetrators. We've got two suspects in custody, but when EMTs arrived on scene, she locked herself into a bedroom and refused to come out. Anytime anyone goes near, she starts screaming, threatening to harm herself. I don't know if she's got a weapon, and I don't want to jeopardize her or any of my people by using force. We need to talk her out."

Willow grabbed a pair of pants off a hanger, tossed them over her shoulder. "Where are you?"

"Apartment complex on East Fairview," he replied. "Fairview Shoals. Wil, this won't be pretty."

"I understand." More than her brother knew. She dropped the phone on the bed, then strode over to her dresser in search of underwear and a bra.

"What happened?" Brandt had already pulled his jeans on. They'd been sharing a bed since the night his sister left. Willow had gotten so used to his presence there over the last two weeks that she hadn't thought to grab for the telephone before he did.

"Assault." She pulled on panties then the pair of khakis, then shoved her feet into a pair of tennis shoes. "Mack needs me to counsel the woman." She donned the bra quickly, then pulled a knit blouse over her head.

He pulled on a t-shirt. "I'll drive you."

"No." The word came out harsher than she intended. "This is my job, Brandt. I can handle it."

"I know. But I still don't want you driving off into the middle of the night by yourself. Let me drive you. Please."

The "please" got her, and she didn't have time to argue with him. "All right."

The drive was a longer one than their usual excursions around Serena Bay, taking them farther away from the coast to where the air hung thick with humidity and mosquitoes. Swirling red and blue lights announced their destination before they reached it.

Willow left the truck as soon as Brandt pulled to a stop. Mack met her halfway up the sidewalk, his features cool as he looked over her shoulder.

"Where is she?" Willow asked, cutting off whatever remark her brother was about to make. They had more important things to do than discuss her private life.

"Upstairs unit," he said, holding a Kevlar vest for her to shoulder into. "I wouldn't expose you to this, but—"

"I told you that I'd help whenever the department needed it," she reminded him, fastening the straps while climbing the metal and concrete stairway to the upper level. "What's her name?"

Mack paused outside of what was left of the door of unit 2-A. "Deana. Deana Richards." He looked at her then, righteous anger burning in his eyes. "She's about sixteen."

Willow paused on the threshold. Sixteen. She'd only been a year older when she—

"Wil?"

She shook the memories away, meeting her brother's concerned stare. "Give me a pair of gloves if you don't want me to touch anything. Which room is it?"

"Last one on the right."

"Okay. Keep your people out of sight for now. I've got to be the only one she sees at first."

Taking a deep breath, she entered the living room. Plaster peeled from the formerly white walls, and a brown stain spread like a moldy fan from one corner of the popcorn ceiling. A striped couch that hadn't been pretty when it was new crouched behind a scarred faux wood coffee table littered with beer bottles, cigarette butts and used matches. The air, stale and stinking, settled heavily in her lungs.

It was a hard room, and hard lives had obviously been lived in it. Still, it wasn't an excuse or a reason to hurt others. She knew enough people who'd faced the same bleak existence but made different choices, who'd managed to pull themselves up through sheer will and timely help. All they needed was a chance, and if they'd already had one, then a second chance. She vowed that she'd move heaven and hell to give this girl another opportunity.

Blinking rapidly to dry the moisture lining her eyes, Willow accepted a pair of thin surgical-grade gloves from her brother, conscious of Brandt standing in the shadows even though no one else seemed to notice him. Mack wasn't going to be happy with him, with her, but she couldn't think about that just now, couldn't think about them on a personal level, couldn't think about the explanation that would need to be given. The sheriff and her carpenter-bodyguard would be dealt with later.

Pulling on the gloves, she stepped carefully through the debris that covered a linoleum floor that might have once been beige but cowered now in a color like dirty mop water. She passed an open doorway, saw a thin mattress in the center of the floor surrounded by police tape and stained with she didn't know what. At the end of the hallway she stopped at a closed door, turned to give the sheriff a questioning glance. He nodded, and she waved everyone back a discreet distance.

She knocked once. "Deana."

"Go away!"

The voice, thin and hysterical, ripped through Willow. The girl sounded younger than sixteen, and scared.

"I can't do that, Deana," Willow said soothingly. "My name's Willow, Willow Zane. I'm here to help you."

"I don't need no help."

"Okay, we can just talk." She squatted beside the door. "The sheriff called me because he's worried about you. He wanted me to make sure you're all right."

"I don't wanna come out."

"I know you're scared, Deana," she said, putting as much reassurance as she could into her voice. "I'm the only one here right now, and I'm only going to help you if you say it's okay, all right?"

"Y-yes, ma'am."

"Call me Willow. Can you do that for me?"

"O-okay, Willow."

She waited out that small victory. "Deana, will you open the door?"

"I can't."

"Why not, sweetheart?"

"I don't want nobody to see me."

"It's just me here right now, Deana. No one else will come in until you say it's okay. It's up to you, all right?"

Silence. "Deana, you know I want to help you, right? It's the only reason I'm here, to help you. Please open the door."

"Everything hurts. I wish I was dead."

"I know sweetheart." Willow closed her eyes for a brief, pain-filled moment. "I know you're hurting. There are people here, people who want to help you, to keep you from hurting anymore. My brother is the sheriff, and he already took the men who hurt you and put them in jail. With your help, they'll stay there for a very long time."

"Did he take my momma?"

No. Willow swallowed, found a way to force the question out. "Why would the sheriff need to take your mother away?"

"Momma gave me to them. She made me come here with her, but I didn't wanna. She didn't even say anything when they dragged me in the bedroom."

Willow could feel the girl's hysteria rising, trapped behind the door and frantically searching for an outlet. "Deana, please open the door. I swear I just want to help you. I'm going to do everything I can to make sure no else hurts you again, I promise. But I need you to trust me, and I need you to open the door, so we can make sure you're all right."

Willow held her breath, waiting. Then she heard a faint scuffling noise, then the doorknob turned. She felt rather than heard movement behind her, and sharply waved them away. The girl would panic if she saw anyone other than Willow, not to mention the fact that it would break whatever trust they'd created.

The door opened just a crack, just enough for Willow to see a bloody slice of the girl's face. It was enough. Somehow she kept her expression neutral as she saw the swollen eye, the blood caked in the corner of her lip.

"You really are Dr. Willow," the girl said. "You came to my school and said that we could be anything we wanted."

Willow swallowed. "I remember." She'd spoken at Serena Bay Middle School, before summer break. How old was this child?

"I don't wanna be scared," Deana said, opening the door wider. "I wanna be just like you."

"You'll be better than me," Willow choked out. "You'll be stronger. You'll show everyone that hurt you that you're a survivor and you're not going to let them ruin your life. You have the power to make sure all of them go to jail for a very long time, Deana. You do that, and you'll be better than me."

She wrapped her arms around thin shoulders. "I know exactly what you're going through. But you're not alone, okay? I'll be right there with you, I promise. Right now, there are people outside who want to help you. If you say it's okay, I'll call them in. You just hold on to me."

She gained her feet, pulling the girl up with her, trying not to notice the bruises and the blood, the smell and the damage. Wrestling her anger and memories under control, she focused on getting Deana to put one foot in front of the other. They'd gained the hallway when Deana's knees buckled.

"Mack, she's going into shock!"

Two large forms blocked the hallway, Mack and Brandt, the paramedics close behind. Her brother scooped up the child, put her on the stretcher. The medics began their work even as they moved the stretcher out of the hallway and towards the living room.

Her brother and her lover turned towards her like twin monoliths, concern, horror, and anger lining their features. They spoke in unison. "Are you all right?"

No, she wasn't. She blinked back a red rage. "Her mother," she ground out, her hands fisting. "Her own mother gave her to them."

Mack immediately barked an order into his radio. Deana's mother wouldn't be going home.

Brandt hovered near her, stretching a hand between them before pulling back. "Are you sure you're okay?"

"I'm fine. If you could do me a favor, go back to the house and get me a change of clothes, I would appreciate it. Mack's going to need mine for trace evidence, right?"

Mack nodded. She turned back to Brandt, kept her voice crisp, professional. They didn't need to see how much this had devastated her, how close the memories were to breaking through. "The hospital's just off Grove and Hacienda. I'm going to ride in the ambulance with Deana, stay with her while they do the kit. Mack, do you have a counselor on standby, or do you want me to raise one?"

"One of my officers can—" he began, but Willow cut him off.

"You need someone from the Crisis Center," she said, heading for the door. "I'll make the call. Have one of the female officers come to the hospital with us. I'll stay with Deana until the counselor gets there."

She paused at the door, knowing the sirens and flashing lights had attracted onlookers and possible media.

Mack paused beside her. "Willow, this isn't your job. You don't have to do this."

She turned to look at him, at the concern spreading across his face, then glanced over his shoulder at Brandt. Even in the blue and red glare she could see the speculation in his eyes. He was putting the pieces together.

"This is what I came back home for," she said to Mack. "So yes, I do have to do this. Besides, Deana trusts me now. I promised her."

Straightening her shoulders, she stepped out into the night.

CHAPTER TWENTY-NINE

By the time they returned home from the hospital, Willow was at a breaking point. Deana's condition was bad enough that she'd been admitted to the hospital, and the doctors had given her a sedative. She'd been remarkably brave through her examination and questioning. Before the child slid into sleep, Willow had promised to return as soon as she could.

She was grateful that Brandt had been there, simply because she didn't think she could have driven herself home. At the same time, she wished she'd been with someone else, because now she had to pretend that she wasn't devastated inside, that she wasn't flashing back to fifteen years ago.

It was giving up her clothes that had done it. Folding her shirt and pants into the brown paper bag, handing it to the female officer as evidence. She'd kept her underwear, but it had reminded her of where she'd been, what she'd been doing when Mack had called.

She noticed how carefully Brandt watched her, and she really couldn't blame him. He was waiting for her to fly apart, to break down, but she wouldn't do that. She was a professional. Even though she wrote books, she still had her practice. Logic and knowledge allowed her to help people; logic and knowledge would help her help herself.

"Can I do something for you?" Brandt asked as they entered the house. "Is there anything you need?"

Boscoe came thudding down the stairs. Just seeing him almost broke her. Her mutt knew when people needed comforting and went charging into the fray like a bulldozer with fur.

She backed away from him, away from both of them. "Can you let Boscoe outside? I need to take a shower."

He gave her an odd look, but hooked a hand into Boscoe's collar, keeping the dog from getting to her. She moved up the staircase, trying not to hurry, fighting the urge to break into a run. Her skin crawled with the need to get clean, even though none of Deana's blood had touched her skin.

She had to take a shower immediately.

Urgency had her stripping before she hit her bedroom door, her shirt flying, then her bra, kicking off her shoes before hopping out of her jeans and underwear. She all but ran into her bathroom, opened the shower door, and wrenched the knob for hot water. One small sane part of her mind made her give the cold water knob a half-hearted turn. With steam billowing like fog, she stepped inside, letting the scalding water batter her back. She reached for the soap, dropped it twice. Clutching it in both hands, she started to scrub.

And scrub. And scrub.

She heard a loud, muffled sound that could have been Brandt's voice, except that she'd never heard him use such an angry, aching tone. Then the shower door opened. "Willow, I think that's enough."

It was Brandt. Even though she knew it was him, even though they'd shared the shower and each other's bodies numerous times, she still felt a wave of panic rising inside her. She stopped scrubbing to cover herself as best as she could, the lather on her face rendering her blind. "I-I'll be out in a minute."

"It's been almost sixty," he said, his voice gentle, more gentle than she'd ever heard it. "I think it's time to come out."

She felt tile pressing against her sides and realized that she'd backed herself into the corner. Half-crouching, she lifted a hand in a quick swipe at the suds stinging her eyes. "I haven't finished yet," she said, hoping that he'd go away. "I still need to scrub my back."

He made another sound, a trembling exhalation. "If you scrub any more, you'll start bleeding." He laid a hand on her shoulder.

She didn't intend to shriek as if he'd burned her. She didn't intend to jerk away from him, thumping the back of her head against the tile. She didn't intend it, but she ended up on her hands and knees struggling to breathe past the panic that threatened to fight free of her throat in a scream. If she let it loose, it wouldn't stop.

The shower shut off, then a large towel enveloped her. Gasping in relief, she pulled the edges around her body, searching for the ability to straighten her back and at the least, rise to her knees.

Another towel wiped at her face. She kept her eyes closed, her mouth, heart, and mind closed as Brandt wiped her cheeks, then carefully ran the towel over her hair. Her head hurt from knocking it against the wall, and she wondered if she'd have a bump. It was just one more in a line of hurts that formed a chain of pain.

A third towel layered her shoulders. "I want to help you up," Brandt said, his voice sounding as if it had been ground down to bits. "Give me your hand?"

Because he asked, she was able to pull one hand free of the knot holding the towel around her body. His arm slid beneath hers, his fingers grasping her elbow to lift her to her feet. When he eased his grip, she clutched his arm, illogically needing his touch. A tremor shook her, popping her eyes open. She focused on his t-shirt soaking his skin. He'd come in fully clothed to get her. To help her.

"Brandt." Something inside her crumbled like a dam breaking. Still, she tried to hold onto it, tried to keep it contained. She bit her lip, and when it wasn't enough, bit the heel of her hand. Despite her efforts the force of it broke through, a staccato shot of sound. A deep breath and the last of her control broke away, sobs tearing from her with the force of a landslide.

Arms swung around her, lifting, carrying. She found herself sitting in Brandt's lap, clinging to his neck, pressing her face against his chest. She felt his arms holding her, rocking her, one hand lightly stroking her hair. She heard the rumble of his voice, though she couldn't make out the words.

Finally, finally, the last sob left her, leaving lassitude behind. She could do nothing more than lean against him, accepting his presence and his warmth. When she finally found the courage to break the silence, she apologized.

He stopped rocking. "Don't ever apologize. You of all people shouldn't have to."

She lowered her head, swallowing the automatic apology for apologizing. She found a safer topic. "Is that coffee I smell?"

"Yeah. Coffee, with a side of Bailey's if you want, or rum and soda. I didn't know which you'd want more."

She let her forehead rest on his shoulder as she swallowed back a fresh set of tears. "Thanks."

Mortified for being caught defenseless, she moved off his lap, noticing for the first time that he sat on the edge of her bed. She'd turned to retrieve her robe when his voice stopped her. "Is he the one?"

The savage anger spun her around like a lodestone. "Who?"

"Salazar," he hissed, as dark, as dangerous, as she'd ever seen him. "Is he the one who hurt you?"

"Tony would never do anything like that."

"But someone did."

Her shoulders slumped. All her energy had vanished with her tears, leaving her exhausted in mind, body, and spirit. Turning away from him and his piercing gaze, she dropped the towels then pulled on her robe, trying not to react to being nearly naked in front of him. "Did you guess, or did you know?"

"I heard you talking to the girl," he said, his voice quiet. "I heard what you said to comfort her. I didn't know for sure until I saw you scrubbing yourself bloody in an hour-long shower."

Of course. Brandt would figure it out. "Tony's the only one who knows," she finally said, huddling in her robe, thankful for the oversized fit. "I never told Mack, or Isis or Pattie. It was the only thing I held back from you, Brandt, but I couldn't find the words to tell you."

"You can tell me now."

She didn't want to. Things would change; they always did. It had taken years for Tony to stop treating her like a porcelain doll. Only Sister Astencia had treated her normally, instead of as a victim. Brandt did deserve to know the truth, though, if only so that he would understand why being with him was such a gift for her.

She curled her hands into fists, struggling to push the emotion back into the firm control of her analytical brain. Forcing her fingers to relax, she crossed in front of him, choosing the rum and cola. Ice trembled against crystal as she lifted it to her lips, but she managed a large enough swallow. He'd been liberal with the rum, and it warmed her insides like liquid fire.

"It was my prom date," she said, her voice sounding loud and foreign in the room. "My father had forbidden me to go. I knew I'd get into trouble if he found out, so I pretended to go to bed early before sneaking out of the house."

She shook her head. "To this day, I think and rethink the choices I made that night. Defying my father, choosing a boy I hardly knew because he was popular instead of saying yes to Tony. Going into his house even though his parents weren't at home, choosing the upstairs bathroom."

A lump formed in her throat as tangled emotion years old swam to the surface. "I remember yelling, kicking, scratching. I remember being embarrassed because I lost control of my bladder.

"He got so mad. I think he kicked me a couple of times before dragging me to a room, locking me in, and saying he was going to go get his friends. The only way out was the window. I jumped out of a second-story window and I just ran. I don't know how long it took but I made it home, hoping that my dad wouldn't find me before I could call Tony to come and get me."

She folded her arms across her chest as ice pooled in her belly. "Dad did find me. He screamed at me. I'd never seen him so crazy mad, not even when he got drunk and would talk bad about my mother. He said I was a tramp just like my mother and if that's what I was, he'd damn sure treat me like one."

Brandt drew in a short, horrified breath. She ignored it, focusing on the sharp edges of her past as they raked over her psyche once again. "I ran again. I almost ran right into Tony's car. He took me to a hospital down near Miami. It's so humiliating, going through that process. And then they made phone calls. Garrick's friends backed his story that they were at the stadium drinking and didn't even know who I was. He was the deputy sheriff's son, and everybody believed him, especially when my father—"

She clenched her hands, stared down at the floor, breathed the emotion back in. "My father told everyone that I was loose, that I'd run away from home after stealing money from him. He told them not to believe me, and that he didn't want them to bring me back home. It basically became my word against the town. All Tony knew was what I'd told him, but he believed me. He was the only one who believed me. They were just going to ship me off to juvenile holding until Sister Astencia arrived."

She recalled the old nun's gentle eyes and soothing spirit, and smiled at last. "Tony and I would practically live at the mission during the summer and on weekends, helping out while staying away from our fathers. The sister was essentially a mother to us both. Tony had called her and she somehow convinced everyone that I should be released to her.

"So I stayed here with the sisters, waiting for the Next Terrible Thing. For a week I waited to die. Then I got my period and had to leave my room to ask for supplies. Sister Astencia asked me what I wanted to do. I chose to stay. She let me work in the garden and clean the mission, and at night I would go and stare at the ocean. Eventually I could breathe without crying.

"A month later, Sister Astencia called me to her office. She had a couple of large boxes filled with my things. My father had dumped them for garbage, and Tony had grabbed some of them. Again she asked me what I wanted to do, and again I said stay there. At the end of July I went back to her office. She had my high school diploma and an acceptance letter to USC. She told me that Tony had been accepted there as well. Again she asked me what I wanted to do, and I said—I said I wanted to help people like she'd helped me. Then she handed me a check to cover my first year's tuition and told me to go learn, live and love, and that I'd return when the time was right."

She stared at the floor, her vision unfocused. "It was the ticket to escape that I desperately needed, a chance to start over. By then, I was driven to understand what had happened, why it had happened, what I could do about it. That's how I became a psychologist, and why I wrote my books.

"Both Garrick and my father died while I was gone. Tony and I tried and failed, Mack found me but lost his little sister, and I became a best-selling hypocrite."

She listened to the silence, amazed at how loud it sounded. Not that she expected him to say anything, and really, what could he say? She was a trained professional, and even she didn't know what to say. Her crash and burn was fifteen years in the past. She had survived, she'd succeeded, and she'd returned home outwardly triumphant.

A thought came to her, had her spinning to face him. He looked horrified, though he blanked his expression quickly. But not quickly enough. "You have to swear to me that you won't tell Mack," she said, the ferocity in her voice surprising her. "He's punished himself enough, thinking I ran away because he left. He doesn't need to blame himself for this too."

"Mack would want to know," he said, sounding as if he'd just learned the words. "You shouldn't have to carry this alone."

"I don't. Tony knows, and now so do you. Nothing good can come from Mack knowing about this. All it will do is make him treat me differently, like a victim."

Anxiety had her stalking away, back. "This will devastate him, Brandt, after it's taken so long for us to grow close again. I'm begging you not to tell him."

"Fine." He looked away from her. "It's not my place."

Her shoulders slumped. "Thank you."

She looked at her balcony door, noticing how bright it was outside. The night had disappeared. Morning had come, and with it, more responsibilities.

"I need to get dressed," she said, for something to say to fill the heavy, dying silence. Even when they'd been strangers, the silence hadn't been this heavy breathing thing between them.

His expression tightened, as if he wanted to say something, then changed his mind. "Don't you think you should try to get some sleep? You've been through a lot in the last few hours."

He was treating her like a victim. The realization stung, but she had to shrug it off. He was out of his element, she told herself. What was a man supposed to say when he discovered his lover had been assaulted?

"I'll sleep later." She threw a mental switch, became the doctor. "I promised Deana I'd be there for her, and I need to make a report for Mack. Maybe I'll get some breakfast before I go."

"I'll make it," he said, climbing to his feet. "I'd better go put on dry clothes first."

He left. It wasn't until she was getting dressed that she realized it was the first time in weeks that he'd left her without kissing her.

CHAPTER THIRTY

Pattie's return was a godsend, and Willow busied herself answering email, scheduling appointments, and writing outlines for the various classes she wanted to hold. The paid workshops and counseling sessions would in turn fund the community outreach programs she wanted, especially the ones for young women.

Her thoughts turned to Deana, the young assault victim. Mack had located the girl's maternal grandparents in Tennessee. The district attorney had leveled so many charges against her mother and the two suspects that they wouldn't leave prison for quite some time, once they were convicted. There was no doubt in Willow's mind that they would be convicted, because Deana planned to testify.

Now that the chapel was finally complete, she could move ahead with scheduling the grand opening, opening the gardens up for free for nature lovers and anyone who wanted to walk the meditation path. All she needed was for the final inspection to be completed, and she could open Phoenix Haven.

The final inspection meant more than the ability to open Phoenix Haven, however. It meant the official end of Brandt's work on the chapel. Would he leave immediately or would he stay?

Could she ask him to stay?

She wanted to, but she didn't dare. Something had happened between them. He had changed when she'd told him about being assaulted. He still slept with her each night, but he didn't reach for her as he used to. If she initiated, he responded, and the sex was still wonderful, but he treated her with even more caution than he had their first night together.

It bothered her. Actually, it hurt. What had happened, had happened fifteen years in the past. Yes, she had issues she was working through, and had weathered a couple of bad episodes, but she'd moved past them. She didn't need reminders of how broken she'd been, but each time Brandt hesitated with her only drove the reminders deeper into her psyche.

Beyond that, she didn't know if Brandt would want to stay in Serena Bay. He had a large and supportive family back in Atlanta. His entire life was there. His son was buried there.

What could he do in Serena Bay if he stayed? Be her permanent carpenter? Her live-in bodyguard? He knew his job was almost done, yet he'd never said anything about the future. He certainly hadn't mentioned anything about a future in Serena Bay, or even if he had feelings for her.

She sighed, rubbing at her eyes. She'd been pushing herself too hard, getting the book done, getting Phoenix Haven ready, being there for Deana. Worrying about her relationship with Brandt, her friendships, her mysterious stalker. She needed a vacation, some time away from Serena Bay. Maybe she'd head out west, look in on Isis.

She couldn't take a break, though, until she got the revised manuscript back to her editor. Pushing away everything else, Willow opened her word processing program and accessed her manuscript. Just a few line edits separated her from final delivery, and she was more than anxious to send it out.

Symbols scrolled across her screen. Frowning, Willow closed the program, reopened it, then tried to access the file again. Same result. Changing the font didn't help, nor did accessing the document map or changing the view.

Her stomach flip-flopped as she closed the program and called up the file manager. As soon as she clicked on a file, the blue screen of death appeared.

"No, don't do this," she muttered, feeling acid bubble in her stomach. Not seeing another choice, she powered off her computer, waited a tense minute, then rebooted. She watched her monitor as the computer scanned files and directories, then stopped.

It just stopped. Willow's heart thudded in her chest as the display froze and the computer fell silent. She hit several keys, but nothing happened.

This could not be happening. "Pattie!" she called, fighting panic as she tapped her keyboard. "Pattie, are you out there?"

Neither her assistant nor the computer responded. Lurching to her feet, she headed for her office door. Pattie sat at her desk, staring at her monitor, an expression of shock freezing her face. "Pattie, didn't you hear me? Don't tell me your computer messed up too."

Pattie's gaze slowly traveled away from her screen. "Oh, Willow, why didn't you tell me?"

"Tell you what?" she demanded, stepping into the outer office.

"What happened to you." Emotion choked Pattie's voice.

"What are you talking about? My computer's on the fritz, and I need to pull up my manuscript. Can you access it for me?"

She stopped as tears streamed down Pattie's face. "Pattie?"

Her assistant turned the monitor, and Willow recognized her website. At least, it looked like her website. "Doctor Willow Zane: Fraud!" glared back at her. Testimonials and covers of her books had been replaced by what looked like a police report. Instead of her author photo, another image of her, younger, broken, and scared, stared back at her.

"Oh God." She remembered that photo, and the others that followed. Remembered the humiliation of their documenting her, even as they refused to believe her.

"Willow?"

"This was supposed to be sealed," she whispered, barely able to breathe. She looked at the web address, received another jolt. "This is my website. How did this happen?"

"I don't know."

"What do you mean, you don't know?" She stared at the train wreck that was her professional life, struggling to contain her anger, her fear. "How did you even know to look?"

"I go to the website everyday, checking the message boards and your blog," Pattie exclaimed, her eyes wide. "You don't think I had anything to do with this, do you?"

Willow bit her tongue, gripping the edge of the desk. Even though Pattie had access to her passwords and accounts, she hadn't known about the police reports. Hadn't even known to dig.

"Get my webmaster on the phone," she ordered, her voice thick. "I want this taken down, and I want to know how it got there in the first place."

The desk phone buzzed. Pattie answered it. Her eyes rounded as she stared at Willow. "Dr. Zane has no comment at this time. No. No."

She hung up. "That was a reporter from the *Serena Bay Herald*. They got a tip about the website."

"God." Willow staggered back, away from the image on the monitor. She felt victimized all over again.

"Willow, are you all right? I'll call Mack.'

"No!" She fought back a knife's edge of panic that threatened to slice her in two. She couldn't tell Mack.

"This has got to be some sort of crime," Pattie insisted. "Mack needs to find the son of a bitch who did this."

Willow sucked in a deep breath. Pattie was right. They needed to know how this happened. It had to be illegal to steal police files, especially ones that were supposedly sealed.

"I'll call Mack. You get on the phone with my webmaster."

Somehow she made it back to her office, to her desk. Her hands shook as she found her cell phone and forced herself to dial Mack's number.

"Wil, what's up?"

"Mack." Her throat closed up.

"What's wrong?"

"Someone hacked my website. They published photos and a copy of a police report from when—from when—" she couldn't say the words.

"I'll be right there." He disconnected.

Willow closed her phone, then all but collapsed into her chair. She had to think of something. She had to do something. Mack would be there soon, and she'd have to show him the site, the police report. She'd have to explain why it was such a big deal.

Her cell phone rang, causing her to jerk in reaction. She looked at the readout, saw Tony's number. She flipped open the phone with nerveless fingers. "Tony."

"What are you doing, Willow?" Tony wondered as soon as she answered. "I just got a call from a reporter, asking me about your website, and I go online and find a police report I thought I'd never see again. Couldn't you have discussed this with me before publishing it on the web for the entire world to see?"

"I didn't do this," she said, surprised that he would think so. "Do you really think I'd want this to come out, or that I'd choose this way to do this?"

"No, no you wouldn't," Tony said then. "But who would?"

"I don't know," she answered, desperation edging her voice. "And somehow my computer's screwed up and my manuscript is pure gibberish. Tony, why is this happening?"

"I don't know," he said, his voice grim. "But I'll try to find out. I'll be there as soon as I can."

Willow let the phone drop to her desk, burying her face in her hands. What in the world was happening, and why was it happening now?

Mack arrived within minutes, Brandt on his heels. She didn't want him there, didn't want him to see her barely hanging on, but she couldn't ask him to leave.

Willow and Pattie quickly related what they knew, which was precious little. Mack studied Willow's corrupted website, printed screens, including the police report. He approached it as he would any other case, and Willow appreciated the professional distance even though she knew they'd have to discuss it personally.

"Has anyone besides you and Pattie had access to your computers?" Mack asked.

Willow looked at her assistant, who shook her head. "No. No one's been around since we had the system installed."

Brandt folded his arms across his chest. "Wasn't that the day the mayor stopped by?"

"Yes, I guess it was," Willow said slowly, thinking back. "We were having some trouble with the wireless network. Tony took a look at it, got it up and running."

Mack pulled out a notepad, started making notes. "Did you see him add anything to either machine?"

"No. Wait, you think Tony did this?" She sat down, shocked at the implication.

"Antonio Salazar owns the local internet service provider," Mack reminded her. "He's responsible for wiring the entire city. And according to this report, he knew what happened to you."

Willow swallowed. "Yes, Tony was the one I called back then. He knows what happened, and he's kept it confidential for all these years. I don't believe he'd do this to me."

"Thanks for the vote of confidence."

They all turned as Antonio Salazar entered the outer office. Willow noticed the way Brandt stiffened and Mack climbed to his feet, stepping between them.

"Mayor, I'm surprised to see you here."

"You shouldn't be, Sheriff," Tony answered. "Despite recent events, I'm still Willow's friend. When I found out what happened, I came over to help."

"Just how did you find out?" Brandt asked.

"A reporter called me. My name's mentioned in the police report. I went to Willow's site, saw what had been done, and called her to find out how it happened and to offer my help."

"Help or clean up evidence?" Brandt demanded.

Tony regarded Brandt with flat, dark eyes. "Like the sheriff said, I wired this city. I made my own money during the technology boom. If I wanted to hack Willow's site or corrupt her PC, I wouldn't have to come here to do it."

"Mayor." Mack waited until Tony's attention shifted to him. "I'd like to ask you a few more questions, but you may want to call your lawyer."

"No need to bother her," Tony said, stripping off his jacket. "I have nothing to hide. Believe me, I'm as interested in discovering who's trying to harm Willow as you are. I can either help your investigation or I can conduct my own, but either way, I will find out who's doing this to Willow."

Mack stared at the mayor intently. "Fine. But you explain everything you're doing every step of the way. Got it?"

CHAPTER THIRTY-ONE

Three hours later, Mack went to secure several search warrants and Pattie went for food. Brandt had disappeared soon after, but Willow couldn't worry about him. She had to worry about Tony taking apart her computer and reassembling it with another hard drive controlling the original. If she was lucky, she'd be able to transfer her manuscript before Mack confiscated the machine as evidence.

"Do you think you'll be able to save it?" Willow asked for the umpteenth time.

"I'll do everything I can, you know that," Tony replied, also for the umpteenth time.

"I know," she whispered then, allowing the emotion she'd buried earlier to creep to the surface. Her hand tightened on his shoulder. "You were, and still are, my best friend. If it hadn't been for you, if you'd been so angry that you refused to help me—" She choked off, memories of that devastating night stealing her voice.

"Hey." He rose to his feet, pulling her against his chest. "I was never mad at you. Just the bastards who hurt you."

"Garrick? Or my dad?"

"Both." He ran his hand over her back, a comforting gesture. "But I was glad to be your hero, even for a little while."

He had been her hero, driving up in his dilapidated Honda in answer to her hysterical phone call. He was her hero now, though he'd long ago traded the Honda for a BMW.

"What am I going to do?" she wondered, taking comfort from him even though she knew it was the wrong thing to do. "What am I supposed to say about all of this? And how is this going to affect you?"

"I don't care how this looks for me," Tony said against her hair. "I'd do anything for you, I hope you know that," he said against her hair. "Especially if you'd marry me."

Willow stiffened before she could catch herself, knowing Tony felt it. She closed her eyes. Even if his tone had been teasing, they both knew that on some level he meant it.

"We tried the relationship thing, a long time ago," she said against his chest, her voice gentle and sad.

"I remember." His voice was a regretful rumble beneath her ear. "I was young and stupid, and I should have realized you were still deal-ing. I've learned a lot since then, enough to know that I'd treat you bet-ter this time around."

She looked up into that heart-stoppingly handsome face, those midnight black eyes, and wished that she could turn back time to near-ly two decades ago and go with him to the prom. If so, maybe now they'd be each other's happily ever after. But neither of them would be the people they'd become, stronger, struggling free of the shadows of their pasts.

"You and I would end up hating each other, Tony. You know that as well as I do."

"Do I?" he murmured. "Maybe I need convincing."

He palmed her cheek, his slender fingers drawing her close. He kissed her slowly and thoroughly. Willow closed her eyes and let him, willing herself to respond to the kiss, to him. Tony Salazar was every-thing a woman could ask for: successful, handsome, caring to a fault. It should have been easy to love him the way he wanted. But it wasn't his face that filled her mind, her heart.

"Excuse me."

The icy voice whipped through the room like an artic blast of air. Willow jumped away from Tony, flushing with guilt. "Brandt."

"You asked for the last of the invoices," he said, his features as harsh as his tone. He tossed a sheaf of papers on her desk. "Next time, close the damn door." He turned to leave.

"Stay, Mr. Hughes," Tony said. "Willow was just proving a point."

"Really." Brandt's tone indicated he really didn't give a damn. "And what point is that?"

"That I have an awful sense of timing." Tony pulled his keys out of his pocket. "At least I can still call her friend?"

Willow heard the questioning note in Tony's voice. Hurt welled in her, and overwhelming guilt. She had a feeling that when he walked out, she wouldn't see him for a long while. Added to everything else, the thought scared her, stole her voice. She could only nod, her eyes straying to Brandt's palpable disapproval.

"Take care of yourself, Willow." Tony gathered his briefcase and headed for the door, pausing to whisper something to Brandt that Willow couldn't catch. She clearly heard Brandt reply, "Anytime," in that tone of voice that said one of them would end up in a heap on the floor, and it wouldn't be Brandt.

"You said something about invoices?" she asked, hoping to distract him.

Tony left as Brandt turned to her. "You don't give a damn about the bills."

"It wasn't what you think. You know Antonio's my friend. My best friend."

He closed the door. "Mack's my best friend, but I sure as hell ain't swapping spit with him."

Willow wavered between bursting into laughter or tears. Instead, she took a deep breath. "What you saw was a way of saying goodbye, emotionally speaking. Hopefully now he'll be able to look for and fall in love with the right person."

He relaxed by degrees. "Are all your kiss-offs so damned literal?"

"Tony was the only one, the only serious one. Until you."

"So you told me." He moved closer. "Why me?"

"You know the answer to that, too."

"Because I'm convenient?" Sarcasm dripped from his tone. "Because I'm a special case and need special treatment?"

Intellectually she knew he was upset at catching her kissing Antonio, but that didn't make his words or his attitude easy to take.

Not today, not now. "You know good and well that I don't think of you like that!"

"Why else would you walk away from His Honor then?" He stalked forward. "The man was practically falling at your feet. Why the hell aren't you with him?

"Because he's not you!"

She clapped her hands over her mouth, but it was too late. Brandt stepped back, the same surprise she felt washing over his face. Just as quickly as her surprise came, it left, replaced by a calm realization. She loved him.

"He's not you," she said again, surer now as she stepped towards him. He stepped back, repeatedly, his eyes widening as his back came up hard against the door.

She stopped just a heartbeat away, staring up at him. "I wonder when it happened?"

"When what happened?"

"When I fell in love with you."

Shock ran across his face, widening his eyes. "No."

"Yes." It was the wrong time to say it, but there would never be a right time. "I love you, Brandt. That's why I can't be with Tony, why I'll never be what Tony wants. Because of you, because I love you."

"Y-you can't." He lifted his hands, as if trying to ward her off.

She rested her hands against his chest, willing him to understand and accept. "I love you, Brandt," she said again, her voice solemn. "I love your strength, your talent, and your body. I love the loyalty you have to my brother. I love the dedication you have to your work and the creativity you give life to with your hands. Your mind, your heart, your rare smiles—I love all of that. I love you."

"Don't say that." He closed his eyes. "Don't even think it."

"Why not?"

"Why not?" he repeated. "You know the answer to that. It's impossible."

"Don't, Brandt."

He wouldn't even look at her, causing a knot of cold uncertainty to form in the pit of her stomach. "Don't what?"

"Don't push me away." She latched onto his shoulders. "I can see it on your face. I know I've probably opened myself up for a whole world of hurt. It scares me to death, but it doesn't change how I feel about you. Nothing will change that."

"Willow." He stopped trying to loosen her grip, stopped trying to break away. "Think about this. You wanted to get over your hang-ups. I just happened to be in the right place at the right time. It could just as easily be Salazar standing here. It should be Salazar standing here, getting a second chance."

"Why? Why shouldn't it be you? Why can't it be you?"

"Because I can't do this! I can't be here with you, like this!"

His outburst caused her to step back as uncertainty froze into fear. She thought about the distance that had grown between them since she'd helped Deana. Even after they'd brought Zadie home, they had-n't been able to get past the discomfort. Why couldn't he be with her? Because of his past—or because of hers?

Her throat felt full of sawdust as she swallowed, found her voice. "Tell me one thing. If we were different people, would you be willing then? If we were other people and what happened to us had happened to other people, would you want to be with me then?"

Something painful swept across his face. "There's no point in asking that question, Willow," he said, his voice lifeless. "People are what they are. You can't change the past. You—it just wouldn't work."

He didn't want to be with her. Not because of his past. Because of hers.

Pain flared, so deep and consuming, it stole her breath. It had never occurred to her that Brandt wouldn't want her. She'd assumed that because he came to her bed so readily that he could one day love her, not just have sex with her. But he'd had time to think about every-thing she'd told him, her final confession.

Of course he wouldn't want her now, knowing she was damaged goods. Good for a short time, bad for a lifetime. How stupid of her to think he was different, just because he'd suffered a tragedy! And she'd thrown herself at him like some cheap—

No. He might reject her, but there was no way in hell that she'd let anyone make her feel dirty again.

Wrapping her emotions tight, she stepped back from him. "I know what I believe, Brandt, and what you think of me won't change that. I'm having some technical difficulties right now, but I'll try to have everything straightened out by tomorrow. We can settle everything then."

"I told you before, that's not necessary."

"I think it is. I'm sure you're eager to get back to Atlanta, now that you've done your part here. I don't want to keep you from where you really want to be."

He took a step towards her. "Willow, I—"

"Don't." She threw up a hand, shrinking away from him. Too much had hit her in quick succession. Her life was falling apart before her eyes and it was taking everything she had to keep it together, to keep from screaming and lashing out.

He dropped his hands, stillness creeping into his eyes. "I'm sorry, Wil."

"Yeah, me too." She took a deep breath, forcing her way into her PR persona. She'd need it to face the next couple of days. Maybe even the rest of her life.

"I wish you the best of luck, Brandt. If you need it, I'll be happy to be a reference for you. No one can deny the wonderful work you've done on the chapel."

She turned away, back to her salvaged desktop. She still had her work, however garbled it was on her system and in her head. She would work through her pain as she'd done the first time, as she'd done every time. She had no other choice.

She turned on her recorder, flipped it to voice activation. But once the door closed behind Brandt, her knees unhinged. She sank into her chair, putting her head in her hands. Everything she'd dreamed of, everything she'd hoped for, was going up in flames right before her eyes. Monica, Tony, and now Brandt. Now that Mack and Pattie knew what had happened to her, would they somehow leave her too?

"It's your own fault, you know."

Willow jerked her head up. Zee leaned against the closed office door, a slight smile on her face. "Now isn't a good time, Zee."

Monica's smile grew as she approached, reaching into her purse. "Oh, I think now is the perfect time," she said, extracting a small but mean-looking handgun. "I think it's a very good time indeed."

CHAPTER THIRTY-TWO

Willow instinctively lifted her hands as she rose slowly to her feet. "Zee, why are you pointing a gun at me?"

"Don't try your psycho-babble crap on me, you bitch," Zee spat. "I'm not crazy. Pissed, yes, but not crazy. I could have shot you while you were crying your eyes out, but it's so much better to see the look on your face right now. It's priceless."

Willow took a deep breath, trying to force away the fear. The longer she kept Monica talking, the longer she'd stay alive. Mack had to return for her computer, Pattie would return with lunch, and Brandt was still on the property somewhere, though he had no reason to return to her office now.

But she couldn't count on any of them; she had to rely on herself, her own abilities. Maybe she could talk Zee into giving her the gun.

"Zee, I'm sure we can talk about this without you having to point a gun at me. Why would you want to hurt me? Tell me what you think I've done to you."

An ugly expression crossed Zee's face. "You want to know what you did? You came back." The gun never wavered as Zee came closer. "It took years for people to stop talking about how you and Tony ran off together. Serena Bay became my town then. Ricky and I got married, and I got control of everything. Who knew Ricky would be so unbelievably weak? The captain of the football team couldn't do or be anything in the real world. Such a weak, pathetic man. He actually did me a favor, driving his car into the bay. Then Antonio came back, the heroic prodigal son, and I realized that I'd married the wrong brother."

Possessiveness crossed her features. "I wasn't about to give up everything I'd worked so hard for. I almost had Antonio wrapped around my finger until you decided to come back. He couldn't see anyone but you after that, and neither could the town."

"Zee." Willow licked her lips in a vain attempt to swallow her fear. "Tony and I, we don't have a relationship like that. You know that."

"Shut up." An expression Willow had never seen crossed Zee's face. Hatred. "Tony hasn't looked twice at me since you breezed back into Serena Bay like some big-time movie star. The town was talking about you again, talking about your plans for this old place. This place was supposed to set me for life once I sold it to developers, but no, the old bat of a sister had to give it to you. And Tony went along with it! I don't know if you screwed him into approving your plan or not, but I wasn't about to let that stop me. I just had to find the right way to convince you to leave."

Realization struck with lightning intensity. "You sabotaged my website."

Zee laughed. "You made it easy, Willow. You're way too trusting, like a cow going to slaughter. I almost feel guilty over how easy it was to convince you that I was your friend. I had a great time watching you drink my tea, knowing you hated every sip. Every sip literally making you sick, but you kept right on drinking it because you didn't want to hurt my feelings."

Cold settled into Willow's bones. On top of everything else, this betrayal was the worst. "You-you poisoned me?"

"Stop being so damn dramatic and wounded. I wasn't trying to kill you. Not then anyway. I just wanted to make you sick enough that you'd think Serena Bay wasn't good for your health. But you kept right on going, just like the damn Energizer bunny. Antonio was falling in love with you, and the mission was almost done. I realized then that the only way to get you to leave was to ruin you."

A tremble swept through Willow, threatening to shake her apart. She clenched her hands against a sudden burst of righteous anger. Her whole life was wrapped into the grounds of this mission. She'd given everything she had to make this work. There was no way she was going to let Zee ruin everything she'd built.

"I can't let you do this, Zee. I can't let you destroy Phoenix Haven."

Zee laughed again. "Do you really think you can stop me? You always were too arrogant for your own good."

"Think about this," Willow urged. "You know Mack won't believe that I killed myself."

"I know. That's why it's going to look like your carpenter shot you, then himself."

No. Willow clenched her fists. "You leave Brandt out of this."

"Why? He's the perfect fall guy. He already has a troubled past, and now he's upset that you won't be able to pay him. Or it could simply be a lover's quarrel. You know from experience how violent crimes of passion can be, don't you? As soon as I shoot you, he'll come running. He won't suspect a thing. Of course, I'll just happen to stop by after finding out about your website, and I'll find both your bodies. I'm going to be really broken up about it."

Willow tensed. She had to do something. She wasn't going to let Brandt get hurt. He might not want her, but she didn't want him dead. "Zee, you can't do this, you can't hurt someone like this."

"You don't know what I can do, if I'm pushed hard enough. Ricky found out soon enough. So did his mother." She smiled, her eyes hard. "And now you will too. You should have left when you had the chance."

Willow knew she wouldn't get another opportunity. She launched herself at her former friend just as Monica pulled the trigger.

Brandt stowed the last of his equipment into his truck, his movements slow. He'd finished, but there was a lot left undone.

Willow. Just thinking about her caused an ache deep inside, near the vicinity of his heart. He couldn't believe the pain and anger he'd felt when he saw her kissing Salazar. It had burned through him like acid, stripping away whatever little bits of goodness being with Willow had restored. All he'd wanted then was to punch Salazar in his smug face, until he'd realized it was pointless. Salazar was obviously the better choice.

But Salazar had left. He'd walked right by Brandt, saying, "If you hurt her, I'm coming after you." He'd been too angry to comprehend the meaning of the remark until Willow made her confession.

She loved him.

The simple realization shook him to his foundation. Somehow, she had fallen in love with him. Everything in him reached for her, reached for her goodness, the love that she offered. He didn't deserve it—he'd never deserve it—but he wanted it all the same.

He wanted to love her as much as she loved him, but the thought terrified him. He hadn't put his demons to rest. They waited just below the surface, ready to pounce at the perfect opportunity. How could he possibly be worth a damn to her when he was still broken inside? What if she didn't want him after he beat his demons? Worse still, what if Willow was only attracted to him *because* he was screwed up?

The thought had haunted him since the first night they'd spent together, sometimes lurking in the shadows but never gone. He didn't know what he could give her that she didn't already have. He didn't understand how she could choose him over the mayor, why she would want to fight for him when it took everything he had to fight for himself.

Maybe she was right. Maybe Serena Bay was his second chance. Maybe she was the reason he'd held on after Brady died, held on when all he'd wanted to do was surrender. He'd had to come here, put his heart and soul into restoring the chapel. He'd done it for penance, for absolution. He'd restored it for Willow and her dream, and he'd restored a bit of his soul in the process.

He'd regained enough of himself to know that he'd be little use to Willow as he was. Having her believe in him with no reservations gave him a strength, a hope that he'd thought all but gone. But he didn't want to come to her as something less than he should be. He didn't want to be half a person with her. He had to regain all of himself, make peace with the past before he could begin to look to the future.

Somehow he had to explain that to her. Somehow he had to find the words to explain why he had to go, to prove his intent to come back to her.

His cell phone rang. He glanced at the display. Mack. "Hey. Any news?"

"You could say that." Mack's voice was grim. "I'm on my way over. Is Salazar there?"

"He just left. You think he had something to do with what happened to Willow's files and that fake website?"

"Not him, his sister-in-law. We need him to verify it though. I've got people on the way to her place now."

"Wait." Brandt stepped back from his truck, looking at the parking lot. "You mean Monica Salazar, Willow's friend?"

"Yeah."

"And she drives a silver-blue Mercedes convertible, right?"

"Yeah...damn, she's there?"

"A car like hers is parked at the edge of the property line, under the trees." A sick feeling settled into Brandt's stomach. "I didn't think anything about it."

Mack cursed, and Brandt could hear sirens wailing. "Go in, get Willow out. I don't care what you have to do, you get my sister away from her."

"I will." Brandt headed for the doors of the chapel. A sharp crack had him crouching, reaching for a weapon that wasn't there. "God."

"What the hell was that?"

"Gunfire." Brandt could barely get the words out. He dropped the phone and ran, yanking open the front door, wrenching his shoulder in the process.

A second crack ripped through the quiet interior. Instinct and years of training had him scanning his surroundings, even though everything in him screamed with the need to get to Willow as soon as possible. Monica Zanteras would know he was onsite, would know he'd come running as soon as he heard the shots.

If she hurt Willow...

Willow was in there somewhere, and he had to find her. He had to save her. God had given him a chance, another chance to save a life, to make up for all the death, all the failure. He couldn't fail again. He'd promised Mack, he'd promised himself. He'd save her or he'd die trying.

He quickly searched his pockets, found a file. It was a poor match for a confrontation with a gun, but he'd taken out an enemy with less. Determination settled in him. He knew with a cold certainty that if Willow were hurt, only God could help whoever had hurt her.

He moved swiftly and silently down the corridor. Silence filled every empty space, as if all of Serena Bay held its breath waiting for his next move. He crouched against the wall next to Willow's door, slowly trying the knob. It turned. With a deep breath, he gathered himself, then flung the door open, rolling into the room, prepared to strike.

Willow leaned against her desk, shaking, arms wrapped around her waist. A semi-automatic lay at her feet. He was so relieved to see her standing that he almost stepped on her friend. Monica was lying face-down on the carpet in a blackish-red puddle. He checked her pulse, got a faint, thready thrum in response. She could rot in hell for all he cared.

"She tried to kill me," Willow said then, her voice horrifyingly normal as the acrid smell of gunpowder and blood rose around them. "All this time, she hated me, wanted me to leave. She was the one who put up that fake website and infected my computers. She wanted to ruin me."

A shudder rolled through her. "I couldn't let her do it. God help me, she was going to make it look like you hurt me, then yourself. I couldn't let her do that to you. I hit her and the gun went off and then she fell…"

Her eyes widened as she looked down at Monica's still form. Brandt stepped in front of her, blocking her view. His hands shook as he reached out, cupped her cheeks. "There were two shots, Wil, not one. Are you hurt?"

It took a moment for her to answer. "I think I pulled a muscle. My side hurts."

"Let me see." His heart in his throat, he knelt down in front of her and gently pried her hand away from the navy silk blouse. She gasped as his fingers touched the crimson wetness.

"That's blood," Willow said, as if explaining to Brandt what it was. "Am I bleeding?"

"Y-yes." Profusely, too. Blood bloomed across the navy silk like an angry rose. He could see the hole where the bullet had hit her, but he couldn't find an exit wound. The relief he'd felt at seeing Willow standing fragmented into a sudden and excruciating fear. The bullet was still inside her, lodged in her intestines, or liver, or womb—

"She shot me. She actually shot me." Willow's voice thinned with wonder as she looked down at him. "This is bad, isn't it?"

He looked up into her face, that kind, beautiful face, and wanted to lie. Whatever adrenaline rush had gotten her through her struggle with Monica was leaching away, leaving behind shock and growing pain. He saw the exact moment the pain registered, the widening of her eyes and the sudden tremor that shook her. "Yeah. It's bad."

"Oh God, it hurts." The blood was already soaking through the waistband of her pants, pouring out with each breath she took.

She leaned forward, the pain bending her double. He had to force her back upright. Wrapping his fingers around her arms, he said desperately, "You can't move, Wil. The bullet's still inside you. You could make it move, and it could hurt you more."

Gasping with the pain, her head teetered with a nod. "Y-you have to call Mack. And Pattie, and Tony. They need to know that I'm s-sorry. Brandt, I'm so sorry, I didn't mean to hurt any of you." She gasped again, pain thinning her voice as sweat broke out on her forehead. "I didn't mean to be a hypocrite, but I was so scared. Oh God, I don't want to die."

Her sudden tears tore at him as he grabbed the box of tissues off her desk to staunch her wound. "Ssh, Willow," he soothed, his fingers shaking as he pressed the wad of tissue against her stomach. "Don't talk like that. Mack is on the way, and so's an ambulance. I'm not going to let you die."

"Right." She gave him a jerky nod, a groan seeping from her. "I need you to know, I don't blame you for this, for anything. S-sorry I can't ch-change things. I would fix it for you. Take it all back. I-I would…"

Without another word, she slumped against him.

CHAPTER THIRTY-THREE

The nightmare wouldn't end.

Brandt sat in the hard plastic chair in the hard plastic waiting room, his head in his hands. The same images clogged his vision whether he opened or closed his eyes: Willow, looking at him with complete trust in her eyes before falling, an ugly, violent hole marring her beautiful skin, blood pouring from the wound like an angry flood.

He'd caught her as she fell, ripped off his shirt to try to staunch the blood, to try to keep her life from slipping through his fingers. He'd waited for what felt like hours, watching her blood soak through his t-shirt, talking to her, begging her to stay, demanding that she hold on.

He knew that no matter how long it seemed, the paramedics had arrived within minutes, Mack right behind them. He'd had to look at Willow's only living relative with the knowledge that he'd screwed up, that he'd failed his best friend and the best thing that had happened to him in eight years.

Deputies had arrived with the ambulance. Mack had ordered them to secure the crime scene, then climbed into the back of the ambulance with his sister. The deputies had asked questions and Brandt had answered them. He knew that, despite not being able to breathe, despite not being able to think of anything but the fact that Willow was hurt, that she'd needed him and he'd walked away. Her blood was literally on his hands.

Finally he'd answered all the questions he could, until his voice had given out. Then he'd watched paramedics wheeling Monica away, frantically trying to keep her alive while her blood drained away. For a moment the world spun, and he was standing in another church, staring at a tiny silver casket spattered with blood as someone took Sarah's body away.

Brandt looked down at his hands. He'd cleaned up before arriving at the hospital, although he didn't remember putting on a clean shirt and washing his hands. No matter what he did, he knew he'd always see Willow's blood staining his skin. Just as he'd always remember that the one time Willow needed him, really needed him, he'd left her.

Just like Brady, like Sarah.

"Stop."

Mack's strained voice had him lifting his head, staring at his friend for the first time since they'd arrived at the hospital. "Stop what?"

"Beating yourself up. She wouldn't want you to do that."

"I messed up, Mack!" He shot from the chair. "I walked away. You and I both know that if I'd have been there, things would have turned out differently."

"Maybe. Maybe you'd be the one getting operated on right now."

"That's the way it should be. It should be me in there. I would have taken the bullet for her, Mack. I swear to God I would have. I'd give my life for her."

"You think she'd want that?" Mack's voice hardened. "You think she'd trade your life for hers?"

"It would be worth it," Brandt said, meaning it. "She's worth it."

"You son of a bitch!"

Brandt turned, in time to receive the full force of Salazar's fist. He staggered slightly, more from surprise than pain. Just as the mayor got ready to throw another punch, Mack stepped between them, catching the other man in a half-nelson. "Tony, that's enough."

"You were supposed to protect her," Salazar seethed, straining against Mack's grip. "She loves you and you walked out on her! You let her get hurt! If she dies, I swear to God I'll kill you myself!"

"Careful, Mayor." Mack tightened his hold. "You don't want to go there. While you're tossing blame around, you might want to remember who actually hurt Willow."

"End this now, or I toss you out of my hospital."

All of them froze as the cool, feminine voice sliced through the tense room. A tall black woman strode into the room, her white coat fluttering about her. Her eyes were hard under the short cap of curls as she surveyed each of them. Mack straightened his tie. Salazar stared at the woman as if he'd been struck by lightning. Brandt took the opportunity to step away from them.

"Thank you." She eyed each of them in turn. "Now, who do I speak to regarding Ms. Zane's care?"

Mack stepped forward. "I'm Mackenzie Zane, the sheriff, and Willow's brother."

"Sheriff Zane." The woman's demeanor instantly changed, her features less harsh. "I'm Dr. Veronica Waters, and I'll be overseeing your sister's care. If you'll come this way?"

Brandt watched as she led Mack away. He lowered his head, clamping his hands over his ears in an effort to staunch the pounding press of blood against his eardrums. Vaguely he caught words. "...Bullet nicked...blood loss...intestines..."

He pressed his fists against his ears. *Don't say the words. Dear God, don't say the words.*

"Brandt?"

Against every desire not to, he lifted his head, stared into Mack's haggard expression. Blood pounded so hard in his ears that even though he could see Mack speaking, he couldn't hear the words.

Mack grabbed him by the shoulder. "Did you hear me? Willow pulled through. She made it!"

"The operation was successful," the doctor cautioned. "She's still critical, but if the next few hours go well and we've got all the internal bleeding under control, we'll upgrade her condition."

The operation was successful.

Brandt's shoulders heaved. Dimly he heard the doctor tell Antonio Salazar that Monica didn't survive the trip to the hospital, but Brandt didn't care. Willow was going to make it. She'd survived his stupidity and his failure.

The walls seemed to press in on him, mocking him for thinking, even for a heartbeat, that he deserved another chance. He surged to his feet, heading for the exit. Mack caught him by the forearm as the doctor talkedd to Tony Salazar. "Where are you going?"

"I don't—I can't—" He shook his head. "I have to go, Mack."

"Willow's coming out of surgery," Mack said, the lines around his mouth easing. "She'll want to talk to you. The doctor said she was asking for you."

"No." The farther away he was, the better it would be for all of them.

Mack's grip tightened. "Don't you break my sister's heart," he growled. "She believes in you. If you walk out on her now, it will rip her apart."

"It's too late for that," Brandt said, his voice strained with control. "We'd already said goodbye before—before she—"

"God." Mack released him. "Just, just don't do anything stupid until you talk to her, okay? You owe her that much."

"I know what I owe her," he said. He'd pay her back, by getting as far away from her as he could. It was the least he could do. The very least.

Without another word, he turned and left, knowing he was leaving his heart behind.

CHAPTER THIRTY-FOUR

Mack stalked down the hospital hallway, seething with anger. The damn vultures still haunted every entrance to the hospital, the sheriff's department, his apartment, and Willow's home. He'd returned to his place long enough to grab a couple of spare uniforms and jeans and had had to threaten to arrest a few reporters climbing up the side of the building to his balcony.

His every waking moment was spent protecting Willow's house and her privacy here at the hospital. He'd had to hire guards to physically patrol the house and the gate so that reporters wouldn't try to break in. And he'd arrested one posing as a nurse trying to sneak past the security guarding Willow's private room.

He really wanted to shoot somebody. If Monica weren't already cold, he'd shoot her himself.

At least the town was holding together, protecting its own. Sure, there were a few short-time residents who thought they knew all there was to know about the Zanes and the Salazars. The three people still alive who knew the complete history weren't going to talk, and Mack planned to keep it that way.

A tall, honey-skinned black woman with shoulder-length bronze hair stood as he approached. "Sheriff Zane? I'm Isis Montgomery."

"I know who you are." Everyone with a television knew Isis Montgomery, the Barbara Walters of the black community and just behind Oprah and now Willow on the celebrity-meter. Known for her love of basketball stars and the color red, it didn't surprise him to see her in a red silk blouse, though the hip-hugging jeans and spiked red leather boots were definitely not broadcast wear. "It didn't take you long to show up."

"I took the first flight east that I could get."

He sized her up. She was hot, but she wasn't getting soundbites from him. "You wasted your time. We're not giving any interviews."

"I'm not here for an interview, I'm here to see Willow," she replied in her famously modulated voice. "Your guards won't let me in to see her."

"No one gets in to see her," Mack replied, not bothering to keep the bite out of his voice. "Especially media."

"I'm not here as media," the media star said, digging through a purse even he could recognize as Prada. "I'm here as Willow's friend. Here."

She shoved a wallet into his hand. Mack looked down at a fold of photos. Younger versions of Isis and Willow, probably from college, sitting at an outdoor café table, sunglasses perched on their heads, laughing into the camera. The two again, glamorous and in Hollywood, grouped with some of Tinsel Town's most famous black celebrities.

"Willow and I have known each other since college," Isis Montgomery said, her voice low. "She's my best friend. Sometimes I think she's my only friend. I-I was supposed to spend Fourth of July here, but I couldn't make it, so I promised that I'd come out for Labor Day for sure, and now she's lying in a hospital bed."

She drew a shaky breath, tears spiking her lashes. "I just want to know that she's going to be all right. I'm still not leaving until I see her, but I have to know she's going to make it. Please."

Damn. He'd resisted her until she started crying. Even the surreptitious tears on this beautiful woman's face did him in.

"She's improving," he finally said, still cautious with the celebrity reporter. "When she wakes up, I'll ask her if she wants to see you." He handed the wallet back to her.

"Thank you," Isis said, gripping his hand between both of hers. "Thank you so much." She offered him a genuine, grateful smile.

Double-damn. That smile kicked him right in the groin. Even with her red-rimmed eyes, she had the kind of looks that could drop-kick a man stupid.

"You're welcome." He pulled away from her, though his hands wanted to keep touching that soft skin of hers. Instead, he focused on his sister's hospital door, blocking everything else out. He needed to keep his mind on Willow, not his raging hormones.

Dr. Waters looked up as he entered the room. The smile she gave him smoothed away his momentary panic of seeing her pull the sheet up around Willow's neck. "How is she?"

The doctor stepped away from the bed. "I'd hoped that she'd awaken by now, but that's hopefully just from the pain medication. I've modified her dosage, and I'll see how she responds over the next few hours. I tend to be more cautious than most, but I'll tell you that I'm cautiously optimistic."

Mack looked at the bed, the still form lying in it. "You're sure about that?"

"She's improving with every hour," Dr. Waters replied. "Every hour that passes lessens the chance of a lapse. All she needs now is time for her body to heal itself. I'd like to keep her for several days, just to make sure the surgery was completely successful. Of course, I'm sure you feel you can protect her better at home than here."

"You're right, no offense."

"None taken." She smiled, revealing a soft dimple in her right cheek. "I'd do the same thing if I were you. Now, why don't I give you some time with your sister? If you need anything, just page me."

Mack swallowed. "Thank you, Doctor. Thank you for saving my sister's life. She's all I've got."

She reached up, squeezed his shoulder in understanding, then left. He crossed the room, stepping through a botanical garden's worth of flowers to take the hard padded chair beside her bed. Feeling more exhausted than he had in years, he slumped into the seat.

With her braids in stark contrast to the white of the pillow, Willow looked all of fourteen. She'd been that age when he'd left for the marines. All too clearly he could remember her staring up at him with those big eyes shiny with tears, begging him not to go. If he'd only known what would happen, he'd never have left. He'd abandoned her, and her life had gone to hell because of it.

He scrubbed his hands over his face, mentally kicking himself in the ass. Brandt could blame himself all he wanted, but Willow was Mack's responsibility. He was her older brother; he was supposed to look out for her.

"You look as bad as I feel."

He opened his eyes, overjoyed with seeing her awake. "Yeah, well, you scared the shit out of me, not to mention a couple of years. Don't do it again."

"Believe me, I don't plan to." Her smile faded. "Monica?"

"DOA. Saved the taxpayers some money, and that's the best thing I can say right now."

She closed her eyes, and he hated himself for causing her pain, knowing that it was just the beginning. "Willow, we don't have to talk about this now. You should be resting, saving your strength to heal."

Her head moved against the pillow, and then she opened her eyes. "Water, please."

He lifted a plastic cup off the tray beside the bed, holding the straw for her to sip. Afterwards, her head fell back against the pillow, as if sipping water had taken too much energy.

"Brandt," she said. "You need to talk to him. He'll blame himself."

"I talked to him," Mack said, angry again. "Not that it did any good. He left."

"I thought he would," she said then. "He was getting ready to leave anyway."

Mack curled his hands in frustration. "But you guys were—I thought he—"

"I love him, Mack, but he doesn't feel the same. Things changed after he found out about my assault."

Surprise swept through Mack. "I know Brandt's changed a lot since we served together, but I didn't believe he'd hold that against you."

She stared up at him. "You wanted us to get together, didn't you? You planned it from the beginning."

"I didn't plan it, but I did hope for it," he said, unapologetic. "I thought the two of you would be good for each other. I didn't think he'd hurt you like this. Let me drag his sorry ass back here!"

"You can't. I don't want him to come back unless it's because he loves me and wants to be with me. But I can't think about that right now." Tears leaked from her eyes, infuriating him because he had no one to bring to justice on her behalf. "Right now, I have to deal with what Monica did to me."

"I've launched an investigation into how she managed to get her hands on records that shouldn't have existed. I thought I'd destroyed every copy."

Her eyes widened. "If you destroyed the old files, that means you knew."

"Yes, I knew," he said, his voice a lethal hiss. "I know what that bastard Garrick did to you, and what Dad did. Salazar told me, after I tracked him down in California."

"Tony," she murmured. "He didn't tell me you knew."

"Dad had told me you'd run away," Mack said, shaking with anger and anguish. "I couldn't get an emergency leave, and the private investigator I hired couldn't turn up anything because no one in town would talk to him. When I came back, I contacted old man Salazar, hoping he'd tell me where Tony went. Dad was dead, and no one wanted to answer any questions. Salazar's mother finally told me where he'd gone to school. When I called him, he cussed me out and hung up on me. So I flew out to California to convince him."

"It wasn't his fault," Willow said. "He thought—"

"I know what he thought. I know what you thought, that I'd turned my back on you. Damn our old man."

His hands shook as he clenched them into fists. "If the son of a bitch hadn't up and died, I'd have killed him myself."

"Mack."

Mack stared at her, knowing that he'd never be able to make up for what she'd suffered because he hadn't been there for her. "You know I wouldn't have left if I'd known what would happen, don't you? Tell me you'll forgive me for not being there like a brother should."

"There's nothing to forgive, Mack," she choked out. "You didn't know, and when you did, you came back for me. And I'm so very grateful to you for that."

He took a deep breath. "I'll be by you through this, Willow. No matter what happens. It's probably going to get ugly before it gets better, but I swear, I'll be beside you."

"I know." She stared up at him. "What about Tony? This isn't going to be good for him, either."

"He's not dealing with it well, but I think he'll be okay. He's good at handling the press. Speaking of press, Isis Montgomery is sitting outside your door."

"Isis is here? Already?"

"Yeah. She says she's here as your friend."

Caution shadowed her eyes. "She is. I'd invited her out for the holiday. She can stay at the house until I get home, but I'd feel better if you stayed there with her."

He shifted, uncomfortable with the thought of the reporter running around his sister's house. At least, that was the reason he gave himself. "Are you sure about this?"

"Yes. I need someone at the house. If not you, see if Pattie and her husband will move in for a few days. Boscoe and Zadie will need looking after until I get out of here."

"What about Brandt?"

She sighed tiredly. "I've done all I can for him. He's got to do the rest on his own. He's got to forgive himself."

"You're being extremely clinical about all this."

"Just because you don't see me crying doesn't mean my heart's not breaking," she whispered. "I couldn't banish his demons for him. Now I know that I wasn't supposed to. He's the kind of man who has to make his way himself, and I respect that. I'd like to think that I at least showed him the way, that I helped him that much. The rest is up to him. It's the only way this will work."

"And if he doesn't come back?"

Her eyes swam with pain and anguish. "Then it wasn't meant to be. I'll keep on keeping on. I had a life before Brandt Hughes, and I'll have a life after him. But with or without him, I will have a life."

CHAPTER THIRTY-FIVE

Three months later

Brandt stepped over the threshold of his parents' house and instantly began to salivate. The pungent smell of lemongrass, basil, and other spices made his throat tighten.

"Boy, I sure missed this," he said, entering the kitchen and scooping his mother into a giant hug.

"Is food the only thing you missed around here?" Loan Hughes asked, waving her spoon at him.

"Of course not," he said, giving her forehead a kiss before setting her back on her feet. "I missed you every day."

Loan paused, regarding him intently. He resisted the urge to shuffle his feet. Facing enemy fire was much more preferable than being interrogated by his mother. "What happened?" she asked bluntly.

He reached over her shoulder for a spring roll, not caring that it was still too hot to eat. "What makes you think something happened?"

She swatted half-heartedly at him, then handed him a napkin when he scalded his tongue. "After more than thirty years, you'd think you'd learn not to touch a hot spring roll," his mother said, but her eyes were serious. "You all but disappeared after those reporters showed up here digging up old memories."

"I thought it was for the best." He knew the reporters were just doing their jobs, but they didn't have to be so exuberant about it. But after dealing with his mother and father, they'd gotten scarce soon enough.

"Mom, really, there's nothing to talk about," he said, wanting to convince her, and maybe himself. "I did what everyone wanted, and saw a head doctor."

"And?" his mother prodded.

"And what?"

His mother turned, one hand waving the spoon, the other on her hip. "Are you going to make me beat it out of you?"

Loan Hughes stood five-three on a good day, but she sure could swing a mean spoon. He'd better placate her, and quick. "Did I ever tell you how beautiful you are when you're pissed?"

He leapt back as she swung the spoon at his head. "It's not nice to try to distract your mother. Sit, or you'll be wearing *pho*, not eating it."

The last thing he wanted was steaming hot soup dumped over his head. Not that his mother would waste her world-famous soup like that, but he wasn't taking any chances. He planted his ass in the nearest chair.

"Talk to me. What happened in Florida?"

"Nothing much. I restored a chapel, fell in love, saved her life, then broke her heart."

"My, you have been busy," his mother said dryly.

"Yeah, busy making an ass of myself."

"Don't swear," Loan said automatically. "Was this falling in love mutual?"

"Yeah," Brandt said. "Except that I never told her."

"You're right." His mother nodded sagely. "You made an ass of yourself."

"I miss her." His voice sounded stark with the truth of it. "I miss the smell of her skin, the way her eyes light up like black diamonds when she's excited. I miss hearing her laugh. But what I miss most is how she looked at me, as if I was someone worthy."

"If she thought you worthy, how can you think you're not?"

"Dammit Mom, what can I give her?" He tightened his hands on his knees. "Even with three months of intense therapy, I'm still screwed up. I was on the edge, so close to just-just giving up. Before I went down there, I almost—" He bit his lip and turned away, not wanting to burden his mother with what he'd almost said. What he'd almost done.

"But you didn't, did you? You still held on. I know how hard it is to do that, especially when it seems that everything has been taken away from you."

She settled a hand on his shoulder. When she spoke, her voice softened with memory. "When your father was evacuated out of Hanoi and I was left behind, I thought my world was over. I had some money that he'd given me, but no place to go. My family would not take me back because I had disgraced them by giving myself to an American—and a black one at that. Every day I thought, 'I will die this day. He will come back and find that I am dead.' But each day I found a reason to live, because I promised your father that I would wait for him. He'd given me a promise also, that he would come for me.

"And so I lived and waited, first alone, then with Carson Junior growing inside me. I waited for two years because I knew I could do nothing else, because I believed in the love your father had for me. And he came back for me, brought me here."

"Mom." He'd heard the story. All the children in the family knew how their parents had met. But he'd never heard his mother speak so starkly of the years she'd spent waiting for his father to find her.

"All I'm saying, son, is that when it comes to love, you have to have faith. Some of us have to have more faith than others. She knows about Sarah and Brady?"

He flinched, but not as violently as he usually would have. "Yes, I told her."

"What has she asked you for?"

"Nothing." He stared into the darkened backyard. "She didn't ask me to stay, she didn't ask me for forever. Hell, she didn't even ask me to call."

"Maybe she knew you had things to work out. Maybe she was afraid to ask you for something you weren't ready to give."

"Like I'm ready now?" he snorted. He leaned on the table, then confessed his greatest fear. "I don't want to be her project, Mom. If I can't be her partner, if I go back down there and all the crap starts up again and the nightmares come rushing back—"

He stopped, curling his hands into fists. "That's assuming she even wants me."

His mother covered his hands with her own, so small to be so strong. "It seems to be that this is the one woman who can help you heal. A woman who you say loves you and accepts you. I don't know if things will turn out right for you if you return to Florida. What I do know is that if you don't, you'll spend the rest of your life wondering, and regretting."

"You're right, Mom," he said. "I know you're right."

He rose, kissed her on the forehead. "You can't leave yet," she protested. "You haven't eaten!"

"I'll be back," he promised. "There's something I need to do first."

Brandt brushed stray debris from the small headstone, then placed the bouquet of flowers on the ground.

"I told you I was going to Florida, to restore a chapel," he said softly. "I put my heart and soul into it, I really did, because it needed it, so very much. I needed it."

He sat down in the grass. "What I didn't count on was meeting Willow. I didn't count on getting to know her, to discovering just how warm and beautiful she is inside and out. I didn't count on falling in love with her, but I did. And you know what? She fell in love with me."

He lifted his face to the sky. "She fell in love with me, and gave me the gift of the words. A gift I was too afraid to give her in return, thinking the words couldn't possibly be true, that she couldn't possibly love me. I was afraid, and because of that fear, I almost lost her."

He swallowed. "I might have lost her, but I have to know for sure. I have to go back and ask for another chance. If this is God's idea of giving me a second chance, I have to take it. I want to take it."

He pinched his eyes shut. "I'm going to always love you, Brady. I'm going to always miss you. You'll always be in my heart. Always."

Slowly, Brandt climbed to his feet. For a long time he stared down at the small headstone, then turned and left, carrying the memories but leaving the guilt behind.

CHAPTER THIRTY-SIX

Willow folded her arms across her chest, staring at the pounding dark water. She'd always loved this, standing at the edge of forever, feeling the wind wrap around her and the sea beating like a heart against the shore. It had made her feel connected, in tune with life, and that had comforted her.

Now all she felt was alone. One tiny speck of life staring up at the star-crowded sky.

Barks sounded above the rumbling bass of the ocean. She smiled, watching Boscoe and Zadie romp in the waves. Zadie was doing a lot better than Willow, barking and playing despite the loss of her leg. Willow almost wished her losses were as simple.

She'd lost a friend and a friendship in Zee. That loss still hurt, though not as deeply as the betrayal. Now, every memory of every moment spent with Monica would be forever tainted.

She'd lost the depth of her friendship with Tony, if not the entire friendship. She hadn't seen him face-to-face since she'd left the hospital. Guilt rode them both: him, because he hadn't realized Monica's obsession; her, because she couldn't give him what he wanted. The tear in their friendship had widened further, and Willow wondered if they'd ever be able to repair it.

She'd lost a part of herself as well, mentally and physically. A few inches of small intestines had been removed, necessitated by Zee's attempt on her life. A small scar on her right side reminded her of that terrible day, as if she needed physical reminders.

Her confidence and her judgment had taken a heavy blow that day. That she'd doubted Pattie for even a moment still ate at her. Her relationship with Pattie was back on track, but it had been a close thing. She'd feel guilt over that for a long time. She also knew that, at least for a little while, she'd look carefully at the people entering her life, wondering what their motives were.

It saddened her, but now she had no choice. Because she'd also lost her privacy. Her shooting had apparently occurred on a slow news day. Once the news stations in Miami had heard about it, the incident had made national headlines. When they'd discovered that Serena Bay's mayor was involved, however indirectly, the media became even more voracious.

Nothing like a good scandal to make everyone forget their own problems.

Crews had camped outside the hospital, then outside her front gate after she was released. They'd run jet skis onto her beach. She'd had to surrender and hire security to guard her house and Phoenix Haven after a tabloid cameraman had injured himself climbing atop the mission to get a shot into her yard. Now she only came down to the beach at night, and only when she was fairly certain no boats were close enough for a night scope or telephoto lens to plaster her image everywhere.

Life had definitely changed. Her publisher had gone back to press on her first two books about the Phoenix Principle. She'd delivered the rescued manuscript with a new introduction, and they were rushing it through production. She'd refused all requests for interviews, citing her need to recuperate, but she planned to give an official interview to Isis, once it didn't hurt so much.

It conflicted her, capitalizing on tragedy, even though the tragedy was hers. Hers and Antonio's, and even Brandt's in a way.

Brandt. She thought about him every day, and every day it hurt. He'd never returned the one call she'd tried to make to him, the day the story of his involvement with her broke.

Her heart thudded painfully. If he'd thought about coming back to her, having his private pain splashed across the front pages of tabloids had probably changed his mind.

He wasn't coming back anyway. He'd never said he loved her, had never promised her anything but that he'd finish the chapel. He'd done that, and he'd gone. If he hadn't stayed after saving her life, there was no other reason for him to come back.

He didn't want her.

Tears slid down her face, but she hurriedly wiped them away. After three months, she'd thought she'd cried herself out, but the grief would still strike her unawares. She'd fallen in love with him, and he hadn't loved her in return. She'd been real with him, true with him as she'd never been with anyone, and he'd rejected her. And her life had immediately crashed and burned.

So she had two choices: she could let herself burn out, or she could let the fire forge her into something better, something stronger.

She'd made her choice, and it really wasn't a choice at all. She'd go on, and she'd live her life. People were waiting for her to fail, waiting for her to be a coward and call her own philosophy a lie. She wasn't about to let that happen.

She wiped at her cheeks with determined fingers. This was the last time she'd cry over her losses. She'd lead her life and she'd be damned good at it. And if she never gave her heart to anyone ever again, it would be a small price to pay.

"Come on, guys," she called, clapping her hands. "It's time to go inside. Mommy's got a big day tomorrow."

The dogs ran ahead of her, barking joyously as they sped up the path towards the house. She followed slowly, her mind focusing on the next day and what amounted to her first public appearance since she'd left the hospital: the official grand opening of Phoenix Haven.

As she mounted the steps leading to her deck, Willow paused, frowning. Light glowed from the garden room. She didn't remember leaving a light on. Gripping the flashlight firmly, she stepped through the doorway.

"Oh, my God," she breathed.

The carving, gleaming in the incandescent light, stood at least two feet tall and as much wide. Wings outstretched in triumph, a phoenix rose majestically from leaping flames. Power and victory and joy radiated from the carving that seemed to be made from a single piece of golden-red wood. She'd never in her life seen anything more beautiful, more perfect.

Overcome, she put her face in her hands and started crying.

"That's not the reaction I was hoping to get."

Her heart in her throat, Willow whirled around. Brandt stood in the doorway, the dogs flanking him. He looked gorgeous and tired, and alive. The past three months had obviously been good to him.

She wrapped her arms about her middle. "What-what are you doing here?"

"Apologizing." He stepped into the room, instantly filling it. He touched one outstretched wing on the carving. "I didn't have the words, but I did have this in my head. I worked on it every night, wanting to get it perfect for you. As soon as I finished it, I packed it in the truck and drove down."

Her eyes kept going to the carving. Her fingers ached to touch it, but it would bring her close to Brandt, and that wouldn't do. "Why didn't you have it delivered?"

He let his hand drop. "I didn't want it damaged," he said, his voice low. "And I didn't want to take the chance that you'd refuse it when you realized it was from me."

She wouldn't have refused it, not after looking at it. She couldn't refuse it now. But how was she supposed to look at it and not think of him, yearn for him?

"You don't have anything to apologize for," she said, not looking at him.

"I have everything to apologize for," he cut in, his voice blunt. "Beginning with the way I left."

She nodded, remembering regaining consciousness to Mack's worried face and no Brandt. "That hurt worse than the bullet did. It's just as well, though," she added when he flinched. "The tabloids wouldn't have let you have a moment's rest. Were-were they bad up there?"

"Not after the first couple of days," he answered, his voice as careful as hers. "The family rallied together, which helped."

She nodded again, wondering why she was being so calm, wondering why she didn't ask the questions she desperately wanted answers to. "I worried about you," she said, looking at the phoenix. "I was so afraid that you would blame yourself for what happened."

"I did. I still do." His voice roughened. "I'd promised to protect you, Willow. You were my second chance, after losing Brady and failing Sarah. You were my last chance. When you got hurt, when I literally saw your blood on my hands, I believed it was proof."

"Proof of what?" she asked, trying to understand.

"That I didn't deserve another chance. That I didn't deserve you. What good is a man if he can't keep his family safe?"

Willow felt her heart clench. He wasn't really talking about her, he meant the family he'd had, then lost. The family she couldn't hope to replace. "So you left," she said, her voice brittle. "You just took off."

"I ran," he said simply, a matter of fact. "I already knew that I'd blown it with you. By the time I reached Atlanta, I knew that I couldn't come back here the same as I'd left. I had to try to fix things, fix myself."

She darted a quick glance at him, then just as quickly looked away. It still hurt too much. "I don't understand."

"I'm screwed up, Wil. We both know I have all kinds of crap weighing me down. When you told me you loved me, I couldn't believe you meant it, that I was somehow special to you. I couldn't believe I had anything to offer you, so it was easy to think that you just needed a project to work on."

"Brandt." She didn't think he could still hurt her, yet he had.

"I didn't believe it, Wil," he said earnestly. "But I was afraid of it. The only thing I could think of to do was to try to get right. I wanted to get right for you, and for myself, but I knew I couldn't do it here, with you. I had to do it on my own."

"So you left me." She said the words, and the words hurt. "Everything in my life was going to hell, and all I wanted was you. I didn't want a hero. I wanted the man who celebrated my kissing him by taking me out for ice cream. I wanted the man who ruined a tuxedo to care for a dog that wasn't even his. I wanted the man who helped me learn the beauty of intimacy. I wanted the man who made me feel free when he held me. I wanted you, Brandt. But you didn't want me."

"Didn't want you? How in the hell could you think I didn't want you?"

"You said so. That day, I asked you a question. I asked if we were different people, and if what had happened to us had happened to other people, would you want me. And you said—"

"I said the past is the past, and people can't change what they are."

His eyes widened. "God, you thought I meant you? That I didn't want you because of what happened to you?"

"You didn't, did you?" She clenched her hands into fists. "Things were fine until I told you about being assaulted. You held me while I cried that day, but you stopped reaching for me at night. Then you told me that you couldn't love me. I laid my heart out for yout. You saved my life that day, but you ripped my heart to pieces."

"Willow." Suddenly he was in front of her, hands on her shoulders. "My feelings for you have nothing to do with what happened to you. I'll admit that I didn't know what to do, and I should have talked to you about that. It just killed me to see you hurting and not know the right words to say or things to do."

"Brandt."

"I told you before that I'm not good with words," he said. "I'm trying to find the words now, to let you know that I love you."

She gasped. "It's the first time you've said the words," she whispered. "The first time."

"It won't be the last, I swear." He lowered himself to one knee, pulled out a small velvet box. "I love you, Willow Zane. Will you marry me?"

"You want to marry me?" she said, incredulous. "Why would you want to marry me?"

"Because you're the first thing I think of when I get up in the morning. You're the last thing on my mind when I go to sleep, and then you follow me into my dreams. You believed in me, and I thank God for that, because you gave me the strength to believe in myself. I love you, Willow. I think the word's too small to describe what I feel in my soul right now, but I don't know what other word to use."

He looked down at the ring. "I know I'm damaged," he said softly. "I know I've got a long way to go and I'm terrified of screwing this up, but if you'll marry me, I swear to God—oomph!"

Willow crashed into him, sending them both sprawling to the floor. "Shut up," she said, fierce tears streaming down her cheeks. "You talk too much. Just shut up and kiss me."

"Yes, ma'am." He laughed, freely and easily, before obeying her command.

Willow's heart overflowed with laughter, and love. She knew they both had a long way to go to complete their journey to happiness, but she knew without a doubt that they'd complete it together.

ABOUT THE AUTHOR

Seressia Glass has always been a voracious reader, cutting her teeth on comics, cereal boxes—anything at hand. So it came as no surprise to family and teachers that she began writing stories about some of her favorite characters and her own original short stories. Her greatest achievement: winning the "Living the Dream" essay contest for the inaugural Martin Luther King, Jr. holiday celebration in her hometown of Atlanta. Today, Seressia weaves the ideals in her winning essay into stories of diverse people realizing the universal dreams of love and acceptance.

A resident of Atlanta, Seressia works full time as an instructional designer for an international home improvement company. She is currently working on a sequel to *Through the Fire*.

Excerpt from

I'M GONNA MAKE YOU LOVE ME

BY

GWYNETH BOLTON

Release Date: March 2006

CHAPTER 1

Palmer Woods Historic District, Detroit

"It's just so archaic—a throwback to the dark ages or at least pre-enlightenment!"

Grimacing as he watched his wife brush her hair, Kyle thought about the best way to respond to her statement and decided humor was the way to go. "Well, I don't know, Karen. Seems like you could bump it up to at least the Victorian era. I don't think people were arranging marriages for their children in the dark ages."

Fixing the bow tie on his tuxedo, he gave her a smile as she paused brushing her hair to glare at him.

"It's not funny, Kyle. Really, Black folk just don't do this kind of thing. We don't pick spouses for our children."

Sighing because he thought they were through with this discussion, he tried to think of yet another way to get his wife to understand what she clearly did not wish to understand. Having long since made the deal with Jonathan Whitman that allowed him to regain control of Taylor Publishing, he was too far in to back out. Whitman made him an offer he couldn't refuse—a chance to save the Taylor legacy, business, and family name.

"You'd be surprised at what Black folk do, especially *our kind of people*. It's about control, breeding, and family. I've heard stories about mergers in my family that did not start out based on love, as we like to think about it." Untying his failed attempt at a bow, he tried again. "Believe it or not, those mergers were the very mergers that brought the family the most success. *Love* didn't get my parents anywhere."

Were it not for his father's gambling and bad habits, Kyle wouldn't have even considered the offer. In many ways, they were lucky the Taylor name still meant something. A scandal like the one his father had left would have annihilated a lesser family.

The overly indulgent lifestyle his own father had led almost ruined the family name and made Taylor Publishing vulnerable to a hostile takeover by Whitman Enterprises. Whitman offered a chance to earn it back, albeit at a high cost.

"Well my father is a Kansas City barbecue king, and although I grew up well-off and attended all the *right* schools, I was not among that elite group of *your kind of people*. So, forgive me if I don't understand this!" Karen put the brush down, crossed her arms over her chest, and narrowed her eyes on him. "Those two kids who you and Whitman hope will one day marry *cannot* even stand each other. They argue every time they are near one another!"

Kyle sighed. He knew the children didn't get along and hoped the childhood rivalry between his daughter and Whitman's son would eventually go away.

"You know," Karen's voice calmed to a whisper, "if your family arranged a marriage for you, or if you didn't have the guts to date and fall in love outside of your tight knit group of black elites, you and I would not be together now."

"Probably not. If my life had followed the path I started out on, if my father were half the man he should have been…" Stuttering slightly, he closed his eyes in search of the words that would make her understand.

"I have a chance to rebuild my family's legacy. To do all the things my father wouldn't or couldn't do."

"And it will only cost your daughter's future. Her right to choose who she wants to fall in love with? Don't you see it's crazy? And did I mention, Alicia *can't stand* Darren Whitman? The two of them are like oil and water!"

"What I see is that if I don't try this, my child won't have the lifestyle she deserves. I can't abide with that, Karen. I won't! She will have the world and will grow up in a world where the Taylor name still means something." Reaching out and touching her shoulder, he continued, "They are kids now. Most boys and girls don't like each other when they are young. She might grow to like him, even love him one day."

Karen lowered her gaze. By the way she clenched her teeth and clutched the brush in her hands, he could tell she was simmering. "I don't like it, Kyle."

"It will work… It has to work. When you think about it, what more could two parents wish for? Our daughter will marry one of the richest men in the world. Could it be so bad for our little girl to grow up and become Mrs. Darren Whitman?" Hearing his own voice, he realized that in addition to trying to convince his wife, he was trying to convince himself. Things had to work out.

Letting out a ragged breath, he continued, "Jonathan Whitman is letting me run my family's company. I'm making a lot more now than what I made when I was trying to work my way up the corporate ladder. Taylor Publishing is my legacy. The dinner party that we are hosting this evening is just the start of the big things to come. Think of the important people who will be here. I'll have a chance to build the company back to its original luster. I know I can do it. It's my birthright."

"I'll get to run it for now, and once they are married, part of the company will revert back to the Taylor family. Once there is an heir, another part of the company will revert to the Taylor family. Doing this will give Alicia and her future children the family's legacy."

Straightening his slouched shoulders, he shrugged and sighed. Things were truly out of his hands. "If Alicia grows up and decides she just cannot marry the young, rich man her daddy picked out for her, then we'll lose everything. Don't you see I had to try? I *have* to try."

When his wife finally turned her gaze back to him, he used his own expression to plead with her to understand. He hoped one last time that she did and that they would not have to rehash this discussion.

Alicia giggled as she eavesdropped on her cousin Kendrick and his friends, Darren and Troy. The three boys irritated her to no end, and she awoke each morning thinking of ways to ruin any idea of fun they might think up. The one thing an eight-year-old girl with braces and pigtails hated most was twelve-year-old boys who teased her and pushed her around at whim.

Each of the older boys annoyed her and Alicia could not decide which boy annoyed her most. Her cousin came to visit every summer because her father said Uncle Kelvin was a loser like the grandfather who died before she was born. Darren Whitman and Troy Singleton were just boys who came around whenever Kendrick was in town. Troy lived right across the street in a big red brick house, and Darren lived in a huge mansion in Bloomfield Hills.

The rich boy, Darren, was the one she decided she hated him most of all. Not only was he rich and a pain, he was also the meanest. He tugged her pigtails anytime she got within arms' reach and called her names like metal-mouth, brat, and antenna head. The nerve of him calling anyone names when he was so bony and his voice went all low and then high, sounding like tires screeching all the time.

The boys were planning to come inside out of the heat and watch a stupid karate movie on the VCR. Racing into the family room of their six-bedroom classic Tudor home in Palmer Woods, Alicia turned on the TV.

"Get out, metal-mouth; we want to watch a movie on the big screen!" Darren barged into the room followed by Kendrick and Troy.

"I'm watching it, so you can't." Gripping the remote control in her small hands, she gave the boys her best attempt at a threatening glare.

"Come on, Licia, you have a TV in your room. Let us watch our movie in here." Kendrick's request was just a little nicer than Darren's.

Letting out the kind of exasperated sigh she saw glamorous women give in the movies whenever someone was getting on their nerves, she replied, "What part of no, don't you understand? You have a TV in your room. I was here first. Get lost."

"I'm tired of this! Give me the remote and get out of here, brat!" Snatching the remote Darren yanked her left pigtail extra hard before walking away.

She let out a loud piercing scream, and her mother, Karen Taylor, came running from upstairs where she was supervising the help and getting ready for a big dinner party.

"What is it now? You children know I am busy getting things ready for Kyle's dinner party. I really don't have time for this." Karen placed her hands on her hips and gave each child a pointed stare.

No visible tears accompanied Alicia's sobbing. "I was here first watching something, and they came in bothering me. I was here first, and Darren hit me. He's mean and horrible! Mommy, they know the rules. But they don't care." Burying her face in her dainty hands, Alicia dramatically fell on to the sofa.

"Boys, was she here first?" Karen said in her no-nonsense tone.

Almost tempted to peek up from her production to watch, Alicia didn't want to risk having the tone turned on herself.

"Yes," the boys murmured in unison.

"Well, you know the rules. Go and watch TV in Kendrick's room until Alicia is finished."

The boys followed her mother out of the family room with Darren bringing up the rear. Lifting her head just in time to stick out her tongue at Darren, she relished the view of his face twisting up in anger.

The show that was playing, like every other show, was a re-run and didn't interest her. Her best friend Sonya was away at Jack and Jill camp for *two weeks*, and Alicia had no one to play with or talk to. Although Alicia was also a member of Jack and Jill, her father felt she was too young to go away for two weeks. So she amused herself day after day.

Deciding to go and spy on the boys again, she got there just in time to follow them out to a huge cluster of oak trees that extended just a few yards from the backyard of their home. The backyard was huge, and just behind it was what the kids felt was a mini-forest. It didn't have nearly as many trees as a forest, but for kids living in the city, it was just as good. Forbidden to go back there alone, Alicia reasoned she wouldn't *really* be alone. She would be with the boys, only they wouldn't know it.

Darren kicked the rocks with all the force his twelve-year-old feet could muster. Unaccustomed to not getting his way, he focused his anger on that metal-mouthed brat Alicia. He was almost tempted to call his driver and go home, but there was nothing to do there and no one else to play with.

He really loved spending time with Kendrick and Troy. They were like brothers. In fact, they'd made a blood brothers' pact in their secret spot earlier that summer. They were now headed to their secret spot to come up with ways to make sure the brat didn't ruin the rest of the summer. They stopped under the dark shade where oaks met so closely they almost made a circle.

"Well, she did it again. She messed up a perfect afternoon." Vocalizing what they all thought, Troy was the first to speak.

"Well, we could spend the rest of the summer at one of your houses." Bowing his head, Kendrick kicked a rock.

Irritated, Darren pointed out, "If we do that, she wins. No way is that little brat going to win. It's us against her! We can't let that metal-mouth win."

"It's like she always knows what we're going to do next, and she beats us to it," Troy complained.

A slight noise in the bushes drew Darren's attention. Motioning for the boys to be silent, he caught a glimpse of the yellow ribbon at the end of Alicia's long-curly pigtail as she darted behind a tree.

"That's it, brat! When we catch you, you're toast!" he yelled.

Alicia let out a high-pitched scream and took off running. The boys followed, but she was fast. They each took different directions, hoping to corner her. Gaining ground, Darren had her right in his sight. Glancing back at him, Alicia did not see the big rock in her path.

He watched as her foot hit a big rock, and she tumbled to the ground. He stopped in front of her and saw that she was holding her leg and crying. It wasn't the loud fake sobs that she had let out earlier, just streams of tears down her cheek. He sat down beside her and put his arm around her.

"It's going to be okay, Licia. Can you move your leg? Can you walk?" He had heard people on TV ask people who were hurt if they could move the injured body part.

Alicia moved her leg and continued to cry. The others came running up from different directions.

Throwing up his hands, Kendrick groaned. "Oh, man, this is guaranteed punishment for at least a week."

"She has hurt her leg. You two go get your aunt and uncle, and I'll stay here with her." Guilt-ridden, Darren wanted to make sure that Alicia was okay.

The other two boys ran back to the house, and he talked to Alicia while waiting. He could have sworn that he even made her smile—either that or she was grimacing from the pain.

Relief washed over him when he saw Mr. and Mrs. Taylor come running through the woods followed by Dr. Samuels. They were all dressed in fancy clothes, and he knew that he and the boys were going to be in big trouble for interrupting the dinner party.

He smiled down at Alicia. "See, I told you everything would be okay. Here's your mom and dad." He waited until the adults got there before removing his arm from her shoulder.

While examining her, Dr. Samuels asked if she could move her leg and Darren smiled.

Mr. Taylor picked Alicia up to carry her back to the house. The doctor had said she had a bad sprain, and she wouldn't be running around for a while. When Darren was on the verge of feeling sorry for her, Alicia lifted her head from Mr. Taylor's shoulder and stuck her tongue out at Darren. Furious that he had wasted his time being nice to the little metal-mouth brat, he kicked a rock.